MISAPPROPRIATED

MEANS

OTHER TITLES BY CHRISTINE CHIANTI:

SHORT STORIES

The Shocking Truth
One Night
New Kid in Town
Witless Protection
Unbalanced Conspiracy
Ever Green

NOVELLAS

Whole Once More
Manicure and Murder

NOVELS

DREAMS SERIES

Desert Dreams
Blue Ridge Dreams
Christmas Dreams

CARSON CAPERS

Silver Linings

SLEEPY HOLLOW HIGH

Fiendish Fall
Wicked Winter
Savage Spring

MISAPPROPRIATED MEANS

CHRISTINE CHIANTI

Golden Lark Publishing

CHRISTINE CHIANTI

MISAPPROPRIATED MEANS

An Organized Crime Taskforce Romantic Suspense

Misappropriated Means

Published by Golden Lark Publishing

Copyright © 2015 by Robin DeMarco Enterprises, Inc.

Cover art: Gray Sweater © Harris Shiffman | Dreamstime.com

Background art: Central Park Statue © Pierrette Guertin | Dreamstime.com

Cover design © 2015 by Golden Lark Publishing

Excerpt from Silver Linings Copyright © 2014 by Robin DeMarco Enterprises, Inc.

Golden Lark Publishing

P.O. Box 1602

Lockport, New York 14095-1602

www.goldenlarkpublishing.com

To my mom, Terry DeMarco, who taught me to be strong and that sometimes to reach our full potential we have to risk it all.

CHAPTER 1

"Hey, Sunshine, let's go. You got yourself a visitor today."

Bridgette Mahoney looked around at the empty rec room and at the solitary guard who stood in the door. "But I never get visitors," she stammered. "Who is it?"

The guard shrugged his shoulders, "Dunno. Some guy came in asked for you."

Fear curled in her stomach. Was it someone sent by Angelo Rodriguez, the leader of the Black Mambas? Were they here to kill her she wondered. Well, she was going to find out regardless. What ever was waiting for her in the visitation room had to beat sitting alone.

Keeping her thoughts to herself, she followed the guard to the visiting area since she'd never been to this room before. Never had a visitor, so why would she?

The door clanked open, and she was escorted in.

Blue tile lined the floor, and gray paint covered the walls and small tables sat scattered about the center of the room. In fact, if it weren't for the bars on the small high windows and the guards at the doors, Bridgette thought, this could almost pass as a cafeteria in a government building.

Her eyes spied the Coke machine that was positioned near the visitor's entrance. She longed for a Diet Coke, but they weren't allowed to have money in here. And since this was her first visitor ever, she didn't hold the odds high that she'd be having one today.

She sighed.

"Don't cross the yellow line," the guard said as he turned her towards a small table to the right.

She saw the dark haired figure there and scowled instinctively. How dare he?

She nearly turned back to the guard to request to be taken back. But he raised his eyes to look at her.

He looked nearly as miserable as she did.

His dark hair was cropped short, almost like a military cut. Dressed in a gray tee-shirt and blue jeans, he slouched at the table disguising his six-two frame. She knew that his ice blue eyes held secrets, and that his mind would be trying to ferret her secrets out.

He'd looked up at the sound of the heavy door. She stood there for a moment looking into his eyes, wondering what she should do.

She was tall, only a few inches shorter than he was and had moss green eyes that had long ago been happy. She liked her looks and was proud that her heritage showed through as well as it did. She tried to flip her unruly fire red hair in a casual way so that it would hide her face.

A thin smile tried to form on his mouth. He reached down beside him and lifted a can of Diet Coke and with a beckoning motion set it on the table.

She walked slowly towards him, trying to figure out what he was doing here. This was the man who was responsible for her being here right now.

No. She stopped herself. She was the one who had committed the crime. He was only doing his job when he arrested her.

"Agent Franchini," she said gently as she slid into the bench that was mounted to the floor. "I'm not sure I'm supposed to talk to you without my lawyer. But, what brings you here today?"

"Hi, Bridgette. I need to talk to you about..." his voice trailed off.

"I gathered that. But don't we normally have to go to the other room for that? Agent—"

"Dom. Let's start with this. Please call me Dom today."

Bridgette sat back startled. This was so unlike the stiff formal agent who had badgered her over the first two weeks of her incarceration. She looked at him again, and he truly looked perplexed, almost as if he were weighing options. "Okay, then, Dom. What's going on?"

"I think," he stammered again, "that I need to begin by telling you a story." When she shifted and gave him a strange look, he tried to smile. "I think it will help both of us."

Popping the top to his own Coke, he took a quick swallow and then began. "I was the middle child. I had two sisters, Elaine was older than me by three years, and Cindy is younger by two." He looked up into Bridgette's moss green eyes. There was confusion, hurt and strength there. He'd pushed open this door, now he had to follow through.

"When I was fourteen, Elaine was dating a guy by the name of Todd Kinyon. Todd seemed to be an okay guy, but unbeknownst to us he had a drug problem. His problem was that he was selling the stuff. Worse yet, he had stiffed his supplier.

"He and Elaine were stopped at red light in Cincinnati, when gang members opened fire on the car. Elaine was pronounced dead at the scene, and my life was thrown into chaos. I vowed at that moment that I would do whatever I could to protect others from what my family and I suffered. And I would make it my life's work to get the gangs and the drugs off of the streets."

There was sorrow in his eyes Bridgette noted. But a good actor could do that too, she knew. "Why are you telling me this?"

"Bridgette, I know that you don't trust me. And I can't condone what you did. But I can understand the reason that you hacked that system. I also know that you've been trying to tell Shawn Daniels something important, and that he keeps shutting you down. I also know that the D.A. wants to nail you to the wall so that he can ride the wave all the way to the governor's mansion.

"Right now, I'd like to get your side of things."

Tears began to form in her eyes. "Why? Why do you care?" she asked fighting back the sobs that were so close.

"Because I know how I felt when I lost Elaine. You? You've dealt with losing your entire family to them. I guess you could say, I empathize with you."

"Why now? Why not come in during the day with your partner?"

"Fair question," he admitted. "Officially I've been ordered to let this go. I can't do any of this on company time. But, when I found out about your history, and knowing that you kept trying to tell the attorneys things, it just didn't add up. So, I came on personal time. To try to be a friend."

Bridgette gnawed on her lip. This was it. This was the guy who'd slapped the cuffs on her and dragged her out of her apartment. This was the only person who'd paid attention when she was trying to share information that might get her a little leniency. She was doomed anyway, at least if she told him the truth someone would know.

Maybe she'd actually have one friend.

She sipped her prized diet coke and began the tale.

Dom leaned back in the wing chair in his living room and thought about what Bridgette had told him. If things checked out, he'd have no option other than to take matters into his own hands.

But how? That was the real sticking point.

Officially, he wasn't supposed to be involved with her case any longer. But if he didn't do something, she was going to be spending the next twenty years behind bars.

Oh, there was no doubt that she'd done what they were accusing her of, but now that he had the rest of the story, he could see that there were definitely extenuating circumstances.

If her story checked out.

He jolted back to reality when the phone rang.

"Hello?"

"Hey, Dom! Missed you today at the golf course." Brian Moran's voice boomed through the speaker.

"Hi, Brian. Something came up. Sorry."

There was a pause on the other side, "You okay, Dom? This is the first time in five years that you've missed a league game."

Dom weighed his options. The safe course was to keep everything to himself. But, if he let Brian in on what was going on, the Mahoney woman would have two people in her corner.

"Bri, listen, I've got myself into a real mess here. I'm stuck and I don't know where to take it."

"I'll grab Deke, a pizza and a six-pack and we'll be over in about thirty."

Before he could say anything else, the line went dead.

For the next twenty-eight minutes, he paced the room wondering how he was going to tell his two best work-buddies about his activities today.

They didn't knock; they just entered like they owned the place. Like the brothers he'd never had, Dom mused.

They'd met each other at Quantico several years before as they were going through one of their training rounds and had hit it off immediately.

"Okay, the cavalry is here," the blond headed Brian Moran, joked as he walked in balancing the pizza box on one hand.

Deke Kirkpatrick followed carrying a six-pack of Guinness. "I sure hope you blew off this dweeb today for someone who has long legs and a toned body."

Dom dropped paper plates onto the table. "You'll be happy to know that yes, a woman was involved today."

Deke smiled, "Involved or the star attraction?"

"You ditched a golf match for a woman? You could have at least brought her along. You know moral support, and all that stuff," Brian said, dropping a slice onto his plate.

Dom stopped, a slice of pizza dripping cheese in his hand. "There's no way I could have," he mumbled.

"What's that, Dom? You know that girls play golf too. What's holding you back? Afraid that I'll steal her out from under you?" Brian asked with a wag of his eyebrow.

The pizza dropped from Dom's hand, and he leaned his head forward covered his eyes with his palms.

"Dude, I was just joking about the girl, and," he paused. "Man, she's really got you tied up. Listen, why don't you call her now and—"

"I can't call her! She's in prison!"

"Dom," Deke said silencing Brian with a look. "Can you tell us about what's going on?"

Closing his eyes, Dom leaned back in the chair and took a deep breath. "You guys remember that case about a month ago? The sting that we were trying to put on the Mambas and the money that we'd arranged to use to buy the weapons and that whole fiasco?"

Deke nodded, while Brian answered verbally. "Yeah. That Moloney woman screwed everything up. Now the agency is breathing down our necks wanting the money back. The D.A. got a confession out of her and now she's cooling her heels in the slammer. Good riddance, I say."

Dom's eyes flashed open. "I thought that you were supposed to be the romantic one, Bri." He let out a long sigh. "Her name's Mahoney, but anyway, that's the case."

Deke leaned forward, his forearms resting on his thighs. "Dom, you know Meyers' took you off of that case, right? Said that your mind was getting conflicted over the memories of your sister. Jacobs got his confession, so all that's left is for them to tell her how long she's a guest of the state."

"Do you know anything about her past?" Dom asked. "Before you condemn her, I just want to ask you a question."

Both men looked at him.

"How far would you go if it was your family that had been killed by the gangs?"

"Dom, look, Deke and I agree that what happened to you with Elaine was rough. But you made your choice. She made a different one. You choose to work within the law, she broke it. She stole a million dollars from the taxpayers. She's got to pay. Why are you getting all worked up about this?"

"I went to see her today."

Deke's mouth hung open for a second. "You went to see her? At the prison? On your day off? What the heck are you trying to do, get yourself fired?"

Brian surged to his feet, and went over to the window. Standing with his hands on his hips, looking out over the small lake that cut through the valley. "Okay, tell us why you're disobeying the director's orders and visiting jailbirds on your day off."

Before Dom could say anything, Deke blurted out, "Did she happen to tell you where she hid the money?"

"I went to see her today, because the last time I was in interview with her, she kept trying to say something to both of the attorneys and neither would listen.

"She admits to hacking the computers and siphoning the million, but there was something else there. And Daniels wouldn't let her say a word."

"Listen, pal-of-mine, you're right.   There is more there. Under that red hair and green eyes is the mind of a manipulator," Brian snapped. Turning back towards the table he continued, "I understand that she's had a crappy hand dealt to her. How does that really concern you?"

Dom shifted in the chair, sipped his beer. "I guess I need to know that justice was done."

"It was. She's in a cell now. How much more justice do you want?" Deke asked, now perturbed. "Look, if she wanted to get back at the group who killed her family, or whatever, why not help law enforcement agencies instead of working to undermine us?"

"She tried." Dom stated simply. "That's why I went today. To listen to what she had to say, and try to connect a few dots that I've uncovered."

Brian hissed, "Great! You're working on this off the books, and you've dragged us into it."

"Brian, I didn't want to get you guys involved with this. Really. But her story just tears at me."

Deke sighed, "We're already in this far, Brian. Let's sit down and hear him out." Turning to Dom he said, "Tell us everything."

Dom took another swig from his beer and began. "After her family was gone, she put herself through school, worked and created a life for herself, eventually moving up into a position with Jokam and Hyde, the defense attorneys. While she was there, she uncovered and fed information to various agencies. The state police, county sheriff and, when it was prudent, even the FBI hoping to bring down the gang that she sees as responsible for killing her family. For some reason, nothing was ever done with anything that she delivered, and I don't know why.

"She found out about the weapons buy a few days before it went down, but based on past track records of what didn't happen with her intel, she decided to go vigilante. In her words today, she was afraid of what would happen if that group got that much clout—what they would be capable of doing."

Dom looked at his two friends. "She's never once said that she didn't do it, you know. She admits to taking the money, says she's sorry that she screwed up our investigation, but she's never apologized for taking the money from the Mambas."

Brian looked over at Deke, then to Dom. "It'd go a long way if she'd tell us where the money is now. It might help with her sentencing, if we can give the money back."

"That's not going to be possible," Dom said soberly. "She doesn't have it."

"She took it, but doesn't have it? We nailed her less than forty-eight hours after the theft. Where'd it go?" Deke demanded.

"To charity."

Deke and Brian looked at each other, and then to their friend. "What do you mean, 'to charity'?" Brian wanted to know.

"She set up the siphon so that the money went from the account we put it in, through a few dummy accounts and then into the donation box of a women and children's fund anonymously. She wasn't trying to steal the money for herself, she was trying to keep the gang from getting stronger, and helping the people that group preys on. She was doing it the only way that she knew how."

"Holy cow," Deke exhaled in a rush. "Can we prove any of this?"

"Does it matter if we can?" Brian challenged. "The D.A.'s already got a guilty plea out of this. She's going to have to pay for it."

"You'd think that her lawyer would try to use this to get her a better deal, wouldn't you?"

Dom shrugged. "That's why I went to see her today, Deke.

She'd been trying to tell both of them what happened, but they were only interested in her admission to taking the money."

"What can we do?" Brian asked.

"Well, about the only thing that I can think of right now is to corroborate her story. If it all checks out, I'll have to figure a way to get it to Judge Forsyth, because Daniels and Jacobs are too narrow minded."

"Not to rain on your parade, but what good's it going to do? They've already gotten the plea. They're not going to let her withdraw it. She's convicted, she'll do the time."

"Maybe. But it might also cut the sentence down. Either way, I can be her friend and be there to support her. At least she'll know that I tried.

Over the rest of the pizza and beer, they discussed what could be done to prove Bridgette's story.

"How is she doing?" Deke asked while Brian was taking a bathroom break.

Dom looked to his friend. There was sincerity in his eyes. "She seems to be holding up reasonably well. I don't think she has many friends."

"Inside or out." Both of them winced. "Sorry, that was uncalled for," Deke admitted.

"It's all right. I don't think she has many of either. I'd wondered why she hadn't made bail before the hearing. I don't think anyone was willing to stand for her."

Brian came back down the hall. "I was thinking," he said. "Jacobs asked me to take a look to see if I could figure out where the money went. If she made any of those reports via computer, there should be a record of it on hers and on the receiving one. I can try to poke around there over the next few days while I'm looking for Jacob's info. Nothing else major on the board, and I don't think I'd raise too much concern poking around."

"That's a great start," Dom said. "If you find anything, then perhaps I can try to sweet-talk Ashley into helping me dig out the file on her. I want to know why nothing was ever done."

"You know what, Dom?" Deke said. "Let me do that. She owes me a favor, and there is no interdepartmental record denying me any access to files."

"What does that leave me to do?"

Deke smiled, "Be her friend, Dom."

Chapter 2

Friday, Dom drummed his fingers nervously on his desk while he eyed the clock. He'd rearranged his work schedule so that he could leave at noon. No explanation had been given to the Director, other than he was interested in trying a different schedule.

Assistant Director Fredrick Meyers strolled into the room, leaned against the doorframe and sipped from his ever-present coffee cup.

Looking over to Dom, he sighed, "You ever going to explain to me what the heck is going on, Franchini?"

Dom glanced over at the director. "Perhaps. But not today. Besides, I've gotta run." He grabbed his suit coat and headed for the door.

"Dom, listen, I'm not sure what you're up to. But do yourself a favor and keep clear of that Mahoney case. Sentencing is coming up in a week, and then the whole thing will be behind us."

Dom swallowed nervously. A week, he thought to himself. They had less than a week to figure out how to get the information that they'd uncovered to the judge.

Of course, he rationalized, if he wasn't careful, he could very well be unemployed before the week was up.

Sliding into his Explorer, he cranked the tunes and tried to clear his mind for his visit.

Bridgette sat in the small rec room, angling herself towards the window pretending to read a book while in reality she watched the trickle of visitors coming into the prison lounge. Would he come today, she wondered. Dom had made no promises, but only said that he would look into the information that she had given him.

Sighing, she forced herself back into the book that she'd gotten out of the little library.

"Hey, Mahoney!" the squat guard snarled. "You got a visitor."

She nearly jumped to her feet with excitement.

Dom sat at the same table he'd been at a week earlier. Again his head jolted up at the sound of the heavy door.

She smiled when their eyes met. For the first time since she'd been brought here, she felt as though there was a chance things would be okay. And that would have to be enough, she decided.

He stood, held out his hand, "Hi, Bridgette."

"You came. I didn't think you'd come back, but you did. Thank you."

Before he sat, he pulled a can of Diet Coke out from his jacket pocket and placed it on the table.

"How're you doing?"

Small talk? Bridgette wondered for a moment, and then decided that it would be like almost having a real friend. "I guess I'm doing okay. Trying to get used to my new reality." She wiped a tear away, "Sorry. It's still kind of hitting me hard that I'm not going to be out for a while."

Dom smiled, "I'm working on making sure that it's sooner than later."

Bridgette looked at him, "What are you doing? Mr. Daniels says that if I accept the plea that's being worked out, I should be able to be out in about seven years."

Dom glanced at the nearest guard. Slowly he reached out and took Bridgette's hand. When no one yelled, he gave it a slight squeeze. "I took the information that you passed on to me last week, and I've been working with a few of my associates to try corroborate it all. Everything that we've found so far, says that you've been playing it straight with us.

"My sources are telling me that your sentencing is coming up next week. We're going to be picking up our pace and getting this information to the judge. I'm hoping that we'll be able to get some leniency for you."

She smiled, "Thank you."

"You're welcome. I've got a few questions for you. They may help us."

"I'll do what I can."

As the sun began to set the conversation turned from how and where she gained her computer experience to more personal matters. When the guards announced that visiting hours were over, they stood together.

"Thanks for coming to visit me, Dom. It makes things easier, even just the illusion of having a friend right now."

"It's no illusion, Bridgette. I am your friend. Let me give you my number, so you can call me."

Her face looked like she'd been zapped by a live wire. "You can't give me your number! I mean I do appreciate it, the offer, but you're a cop. Besides, they'll take anything that you give me before they take me back to my cell."

Dom pulled out his pen, and turned her hand over. On the back of her hand, he wrote his number. "I am your friend. I'll be there for you, however I can."

He pulled her in and gave her a tight hug.

She nearly purred. She did cry. It was the first hug she'd had since her mom had been killed nearly ten years before.

"You hang in there. Just remember that I'm doing everything that I can on this side to get you out of here."

Bridgette could only nod as the tears flowed thicker.

She watched him go. Her friend.

She had a friend now, and with that came the certainty that she'd be able to get through whatever came next.

Dom's phone rang at two-eighteen. "Franchini," he mumbled into the receiver.

"Um, hello. This is lieutenant Jameson at the Hillside Correctional Facility."

Dom's eye snapped open. "Bridgette?"

"Sir, there was an altercation between inmate Mahoney and two other women. Miss Mahoney was stabbed three times and is currently undergoing surgery at Mount Olive Hospital. We didn't know whom else to call. You've been her only visitor and she just listed this number as an emergency number today, so we thought you might be able to reach her family."

"She doesn't have anyone else right now. I'm on the way to the hospital now."

He hung up the phone and tried to rub the sleep and concern from his face. He had an hour long drive that he'd have to get through.

When the cell phone sounded moments later, he swore then laughed when he saw the number.

"Brian, I can't talk right now. I've got to—"

"You've got to shut up and get moving. Deke and I will be to your place in about ten. We got a call about Bridgette. She's been involved—"

"I got the call from the prison. I know the score, I'm trying to get ready to head out."

"From what we heard, she's going to pull through okay. Deke and I are about a block away and we'll take you in. And just giving you a heads up, Meyers knows about things."

"Crap. What does he know? Never mind, tell me on the way."

The ride in was much faster due to the flashing emergency lights. They arrived at the hospital in just over forty minutes.

Dom rushed to the information booth, "Bridgette Mahoney, please. She was brought in from Hillside."

The woman sitting at the desk appeared to be appalled that someone would want directions at this early hour. Giving him the eye, she tapped her screen. "It seems patient Mahoney may only be seen by family or police officers. Are you either of those?" she snapped.

Dom reached into his back pocket and pulled out his shield.

"Hmm, I guess FBI counts. She's in room two-seventeen."

He took the stairs two at a time and burst out the door into the hall and skidded to a stop. The hall was full of at least fifteen officers, but the faces that caught his attention were those of Assistant Director Meyers and D.A. Jacobs.

"You've burst through the door, Dom, let's go take care of the girl," Brian said as he grabbed Dom's arm and pulled him down the hall.

"Franchini, what the devil are you doing here? Aren't you in enough hot water about this woman?" Meyers demanded. "And you two? I know that I told you to get here, but I don't remember asking you to bring him with you."

"Sir, I'll explain everything in a few minutes. But I need to know. How is Bridgette doing?"

The director stared at him. "There's more than just a parallel between you and her. You've got feelings for her. God's sakes! What's gotten into you, boy?"

District Attorney Carmine Jacobs walked over. "I think you've got some explaining to do, Franchini. You were taken off of this case two weeks ago because you couldn't separate yourself. Now you're here? This had better be good, otherwise, maybe I'll need to consider filing charges against you for interfering with a criminal investigation."

"Shut your pie hole, Carmine. Franchini is my man. I'll take care of any disciplinary measures that need to be taken. Now why don't we—"

A doctor walked out of room 217. "Is there a Dominic Franchini here?"

"Right here," Dom yelled and started pushing his way to the front of the mob.

"Miss Mahoney has asked for you, several times."

Dom couldn't explain the feeling he had as he pushed open the door.

The room was dark, and silent except for the rhythmic beeping coming from the machines next to the bed. He crept over to the bedside. His throat closed as he looked at her laying there, blood still caked in her hair. His eyes burned, and he sniffled lightly.

"Dom?" her voice was weak and pained.

"I'm here, Bridgette," he said lightly, taking her hand.

"Thank you. I need a friend right now and…" her voice began to quake.

"Shhh. It's okay now. I'm here, and you're not alone. Try to sleep a little, okay?"

"Stay. Please."

He brushed his hand across her forehead, used his foot to catch and drag a chair over so he could sit. "Sleep now, I'll stand guard for you."

The sun was streaming in the window when he opened his eyes. It took him a minute to remember where he was and why he was here. His head snapped to the woman on the bed.

Handcuffs were attached to the bedrail, and she still held his hand, but now she rested comfortably.

A noise from the right brought his head around.

A nurse stood there. "Sorry to disturb you, but we need to clean up our patient and check her over. There's a pretty good food service downstairs for families. Perhaps you'd like to catch some breakfast. We'll take care of your wife while you're gone."

He choked, "She's not my wife, but she is special." He leaned down to whisper in Bridgette's ear. "I'll be back shortly."

Her eyes slit open, and she squeezed his hand. The handcuffs strained and rattled on the rail. She smiled, "I'm not going anywhere."

Giving in to impulse, he kissed her temple and then made his way to the door.

The moment he was in the hall, he leaned back on the wall, and ran his hand over his face. What was he doing? He might never know, but right now the best that he could come up with was he was keeping a promise.

"How is she?" Brian asked coming up the hall.

Dom turned his head and looked at his friend. "She's trying to make jokes, but I know that she's hurting. She's scared. Let's face it, right now her life sucks big time."

"It's better today than it was a few weeks ago. She's got you in her corner, and that's going to carry some weight."

"The question is will it be enough, and will it be helpful or not."

As they talked Dom noticed the nurse coming back out of the room. "She's all set."

"Thanks," Dom answered. He turned his head and watched the director, Deke, Shawn Daniels and D.A. Jacobs come around the corner. "Wonderful. The whole bloody gang's here."

"Franchini," the director began, "we're going to let Moran and Kirkpatrick go in and talk with the woman. Jacobs and Daniels will be there as well. That means that you and I are going to find a little room to have a chat."

Dom nodded and watched Daniels go in first. "I'm sorry, Sir. I guess you feel that I let you down. But to be honest with you, knowing what I do right now, I'd do it again. It's been the right thing to do."

The door opened up. "She's ready for us," Daniels told the assembled group. He hesitated, and then called out, "Dom? She'd like you to be there too."

Meyers shrugged, "Go be with her. If she finds you comforting right now, perhaps it'll help her. Jacobs may want to crucify you later, but we'll deal with that later."

Dom reentered the room. She was sitting up, her face was swollen from the bruising. The others had assembled in a semi-circle around her, so he headed for the edge of the group.

She looked at him, held out her hand a little and then dropped it back at her side.

"Miss Mahoney, do you know who attacked you?" Brian led off.

Jacobs snidely remarked under his breath, "Probably someone she stole from."

Dom's eyes bored in on Jacobs.

Jacobs tried to brush over the uncomfortable aura that he now felt. "You know, once a thief, always a thief. Probably just a guess, but somebody didn't like your service."

Bridgette began to sob and shook her head.

"Jacobs!" Daniels snarled. "That's pure conjecture. My client has not admitted to stealing anything from anyone in that prison. And that's who did this unless you'd like me to believe that one of the guards roughed her up."

"Don't tell me about how good your client is, counselor. She's admitted to taking the money from the sting. Has she returned it? No! Why? Because she's figuring that if she keeps quiet about its location, she can collect it after her sentence. Decent pay day."

"She doesn't have the money!" Dom nearly shouted.

The ensuing silence was deafening, and all eyes turned on him.

"Well, maybe since apparently you've gotten all chummy with the prisoner, she gave it to you for safe keeping?"

"Jacobs, you really need to pull that stick out of your butt. It's affecting your train of thought," Dom retorted. Taking a deep cleansing breath he followed instinct and walked to the bedside. Reaching over the rail, he gently took Bridgette's hand, shocking everyone in the room.

"Through everything, Bridgette has cooperated as best as she could. Every time she tried to tell you both something, you quieted her down and refused to listen. Now you're shocked because I know something that you don't."

"Do you know where the money is, Franchini? If so, you'd better turn it over before I add you as accessory after the fact."

"No!" Bridgette's voice was weak. "Dom is right. I've been trying to tell the two of you, but neither of you would take the time. It's almost as if you're more interested in getting me behind bars for your own promotion rather than finding out the full story."

"Bridgette," Daniels reminded her, "you're still under oath. Now where is the money?"

"I never took possession of it, but gave it to charity."

Jacobs smiled, "Now there's a likely story. Sounds good, too doesn't it? She didn't steal it for her own good. No! She's a modern day Robin Hood. Steals money and then gives it away. Nice try."

"Actually, Jacobs," Brian said taking a step closer to the bed. "When she gave that information to us, we began tracing the money. I can't tell you exactly where it is right now. We've only been able to reconstruct the first three hops. None of which we could have done without the information that she gave Dom."

"Bridgette, I told you not to talk to anyone without me present," Daniels scolded her.

"I came to see her one day during visiting hours. I knew that she'd been trying to tell you something, but you kept pushing her off. I'd been taken off the case by then, so I decided to try a direct friendly approach. It worked."

"It looks a little too friendly, if you ask me," Jacobs snarled.

Brian blew out a breath he didn't know that he'd been holding. "Maybe we could all just get back to the situation at hand. You know, the one that landed Bridgette here recovering form multiple stab wounds."

"I think in a very round about way, you may have been on to something, Carmine," Daniels said. "I think this is the result of the one theft she's committed. I'd be willing to bet that there's a few Mamba women in there."

Brian walked closer to the bed, "Bridgette, did you see who attacked you?"

"Yes. I don't know them. They're in the cell down the end. I only see them when we're out in the yard for rec time."

Brian looked to his partner, "Agent Kirkpatrick, why don't we see about getting some pictures from Hillside, and we'll see if we can identify our assailants."

Deke smiled, "It'd be my pleasure. I'll also see if there's a current roster of incarcerated Mambas. Maybe we can tie everything together."

The two agents patted Dom's shoulder as they walked to the door.

Jacobs said, "This act doesn't make you innocent in my book," before he stormed to the door.

Daniels said nothing, but smiled and hurried after the DA.

Dom still stood by her side, holding her hand. "We'll get you through this, Bridgette."

"I feel more confident knowing that I've got a friend to stand with me."

The door opened slightly and Brian's head poked in. "All clear?"

Dom nodded, and Brian and Deke came in.

"Bridgette, I'd like to introduce you to these two characters who've been helping out behind the scenes. Brian Moran and Deke Kirkpatrick."

"Pleasure to meet you, Bridgette," Deke said. "And for the record, everything that you passed to Dom here has checked out so far. Which means that we're in your corner now too."

Brian nodded in agreement. "I've been trying to follow that money, and even with the roadmap you gave us, it's been a challenge. It's a shame that you—"

Deke kicked Brian's shin.

Brian's face reddened. "Sorry. Errant thought. I did want to see if you recognized any one here?" He held out a series of photos.

"I recognize several of these faces, as they're in the cells near mine. But this one and this one," Bridgette said pointing, "are the two that attacked me."

"Well, Franchini, it looks like you're batting a thousand since both are known Mambas. By the way, the director wants you in conference room B in ten minutes."

"Will you come back?" Bridgette asked.

"They're going to have to kick me out," he said giving her hand a squeeze.

CHAPTER 3

Conference room B was set up as a small office Dom decided. Since he wasn't the one calling this meeting, he steered clear of the main desk. Instead, he paced around the small office, running his hands over the stubble on his face stopping only when he heard the door open.

"Franchini, pull up a chair. You want some coffee?" Assistant Director Fredrick Meyers said as he strode in holding out an extra cup.

Pulling up the nearest chair, he ungracefully flopped into it. "What's up, Sir?"

Meyer looked over at his agent. Franchini had always been able to keep a case from getting to him, but just one look at the man sitting there was enough to tell, even the most junior sleuth, that this case was cutting too close to the bone. "Dom, I'm worried about you," he said casually as he settled into the leather chair behind the desk. "It looks like you haven't gotten much sleep in the last week or so, and I can only attribute that to the Mahoney case. A case, which

I might remind you, you were removed from a few weeks ago."

Dom lifted his head from his hands and shrugged. "I keep thinking about Elaine, Sir. This case really brought things back to the forefront for me. I just keep thinking about Bridgette, and how her life seemed to be running parallel to my mine."

"Ah, damn it, Dom. You're not her. You've put your entire life into putting away criminals, not being one. I can see that you'd relate to her since her family was killed like your sister, but c'mon."

"Sir," Dom paused, measuring each tone and word. "I'm not saying that I can justify what she did. Far from it. But the reality is, she was a victim too. One that the system failed; not just once but a multiple number of times." For the first time since he entered, he looked Meyers in the eyes. "She lost everything when she was just a kid. Too old for the system, too young to be on her own but she fought.

"She went to school, and for several years, fed different agencies information on Angelo Rodriguez and the rest of the Black Mambas. But the slimes always find ways to slither through, so again the legal system fails her.

"She finds the intel that the Mambas are making a deal, selling weapons for a cool million. She instinctively knows that if they get that kind of money, her town is toast. She's between the proverbial rock and the hard place.

"She decides to do what she can. She passed the information along, but also made the decision to give up working within the law and just settles for getting retribution for what they took from her. She found a way to hit that group for nearly a million dollars. It was her first time, and she had the bad luck to bump into us. She took the money no doubt, but how much did she keep? None of it, she gave it all to charities that are involved in helping the victims of the gang; groups that didn't exist when she needed their help.

"Now we're going to send her away for twenty years because

she's the one who got caught?" He slumped back into the chair, "No, it doesn't sit well with me."

Meyers leaned back in his chair, "Dom, I'm sorry. There really isn't anything that I can do about this." Removing his glasses, he stared across the desk. He knew that the news he had wanted to share with Franchini was definitely not going to be welcome. "She got caught red handed by a team of agents, led by you, breaking several federal laws. D.A. Jacobs saw this as an easy win and a feather in his cap for his bid for governor. He pushed at her, and to be honest, she was honest too. She pled guilty to the charge. I talked with Jacobs and Daniels a little bit ago, while you were in with Moran and Kirkpatrick. They're planning to recommend to the Judge for six to nine. Sentencing was supposed to be this Monday."

Dom's head snapped up, "So what happens now?"

"They've postponed it. Once she's able to go back to Hillside, she'll be officially transferred there, and a new date will be set. The reality of it all is really a formality. She's already in a federal facility, she'll just find out for how long. Again, I'm sorry, Dom. I didn't realize how this had affected you."

Dom sat quiet for a minute, his hands folded as if in prayer and his eyes closed.

"The part that annoys me the most, is that I don't think her lawyer is doing her any good. They coerced her into pleading guilty."

"Dom, you said it yourself, she did it and we can't condone it."

"That may be true, but when she tried to give them the facts, both Daniels and Jacobs ignored her. They're only worried about their upcoming political careers. They see that they can use her as a scapegoat, a 'look what we've done about organized crime' thing. But in reality all they've done is further destroy a life that just needed one person to stand up and lend a hand."

"You broke several rules yourself, going to the prison to talk to her. Did it do anything?"

"It did. She gave me information that she had been trying to give to Daniels. Information that would weigh heavily for the judge to go lenient with her."

"Can any of it be substantiated?"

"Between Brian, Deke and myself, we've confirmed ninety percent."

"Only ninety? What about the other ten?"

"You'd have to ask Brian where it stands right now. She ran that money through so many different places, so fast that we'd have never have found it. She gave me the road map, and Brian is using that and still hasn't reached the end."

Meyers held up his hands to stop Dom. "Wait. You're telling me, that everything that she's given you is true. You're on the trail of the money, only because she sent you there, and you still have more to go?"

Dom smiled and nodded his head. "Yeah. She's scary smart on the computer end of things."

"So, you've documented that she sent tips in, and nothing was done about any of them?"

"Local law agencies acted on the first two tips she sent in. They reported back that in the first case the buyer, Manuel Hernandez, didn't show up. With the second tip, Casey Thornton from the Mambas didn't come. Because her tips didn't pan out, they marked her as unreliable.

"What nobody checked for were things that happened out of her control. She had no way to know that on the night of the first buy, that Hernandez was going to be pulled over at a routine traffic stop and taken into custody on an outstanding warrant. Just like she had no way to know that Thornton was going to be killed by a drive by shooting that afternoon.

"We've checked her tips, and back checked with our own data sources. She was right on every one of them. If people had acted appropriately on the information that she'd given us, we'd have shut that group down a long time ago."

Meyers shifted in his chair. "It doesn't seem fair, that we'd ignore her and then sacrifice her. Unfortunately, I don't think that there's anything that we can do."

"This is crap, Sir," he finally said. "Plain and simple, its just crap."

"Dom, I wish that there was something that could be done. She's smart, but there's no way out of this one."

"I'm not trying to get her exonerated. I just want her to have justice."

"Be careful on how far you push, Dom. I don't have to remind you of what Jacobs said when you showed up in the middle of the night, do I? If you push too hard against him, he just may drum up some trumped up charge to get you thrown off the force. Think before you act."

Dom straightened in his chair. "I seem to recall a certain commander who taught me that sometimes in this job we had to lay it all on the line to protect those that we serve. Maybe this is a skewed way of doing it, but if I don't fight for her, I'm not going to be able to look at myself in that mirror every morning." After a slight hesitation he added, "Sir."

"You know that I can't give you permission to do anything about this, right?"

Dom nodded. "Yeah, I know. But I've got to think of something that will let us all, her, me, you, live with what happens."

Meyers' eyes softened a bit. "Unless I'm mistaken, you've become a little soft towards her. Have you thought how you're going to handle it when she's imprisoned for years? How will it look if it becomes knowledge that one of our own is keeping company with a convicted felon?"

Dom slumped forward. "I've been trying to think it through,

Sir. Really, I have. I went to see her that first time to try to find what she'd been trying to tell the lawyers. She trusted me, gave me the information that she could and knew that I was going to follow up on it. She did that willingly.

"When I discovered that she'd done nothing less than tell the truth, yeah, I guess my heart softened a bit. I went back as her friend. One who was trying to help her through a very tough spot in her life. I don't think she's had many friends in her life, and sure as anything, the ones that she did have, left her high and dry when we arrested her.

"I'll find a way to do everything that I can to make it work. Maybe it'll mean that I spend my Friday afternoons visiting with her. Keeping her spirits up. Maybe I'll bend a few rules," he said with a smile. "I can always go up during the week, and use an interview room to talk with her."

Meyers simply grunted at that. "You're walking a tightrope right now. You'd better figure out a way to keep your balance."

"I just wish there was a way to side-step the dance that Jacobs and Daniels are setting her up for," Dom muttered.

"Yeah, it would make things easier for you. But again, I don't see how we can supersede the attorneys and their wishes."

Both men stared at the window of the small room in silence.

Dom's eyes flashed wide. "Yes there is, Director!"

Meyers sat upright, surprised at the reaction. "What are you thinking, Dom?"

"We've been fighting for years to get into the Mambas' computer systems. She's done that! What if we exchange her sentence for her cooperation? Get her on probation, and she works with us."

Meyers leaned back in his chair. "That's an interesting angle. And a good one. If she's as good as you say on the computer, we could really use her. How do you propose to change the minds of our two friends?"

Dom leaned forward, arms resting on his legs. "I'm not sure we have to."

Meyers' eyes shot up.

"Hold on a second, Sir," Dom held his hands up. "Let's consider this idea. We give each of them a copy of the data that we have, with a request for the sentencing. Now, unless we are mistaken, they're going to just blow over everything and go for the kill, and ensuring their political careers. But what if we also got that information to the judge in charge of Bridgette's case? She can ask questions, require follow up, and more importantly, she's the one who will hand down the actual sentence."

Meyers scratched his chin and thought. "I think we're on the right track. This is now your new assignment. Get that list compiled, back everything up and then put the balls in motion." He thought for a moment, "You can tell the rest of the three-amigos, but no one else. Especially not your new friend."

Dom sat in the visitor's chair in Bridgette's room. She slept as a result of the medications, so he used the time to make notes on the pad he'd acquired from Brian and let his mind wander trying to think of the best way to present the idea to everyone involved.

The door creaked open, instinctively, he closed the notebook and tucked it into his shirt pocket before he looked up.

"Hey, Deke. Brian. What's going on?"

Deke looked over at Bridgette, smiled and shook his head. "Got some stuff to talk with you about. Let's do it out here so we don't wake her."

They found an alcove in the hall, just down from Bridgette's room.

"What's up?" Dom wanted to know.

"First off, Brian and I went over to Hillside. With the identification that she made, we were able to begin the search there.

Found a pair of shivs. They're currently on the way over to the lab for blood and prints. But it'd be a good guess that we're going to be making her assailants' stay a bit longer.

"Secondly, we talked to Meyers. He told us to talk to you about your proposal to get her sentence commuted to working with us. What can we do to help?"

"I'm thankful that he talked to you about this, so you know that what we're doing is at least above board, but being done on the down-low. I think that the most important aspect is to document everything that we can. Once we have all of the proof, we can assemble the package and get Daniels and Jacobs to sign for it and see what happens."

Deke clapped him on the shoulder, "We'll do what we can. Now, the other problem is that you're beginning to smell and we need to head back to the office. Why don't we say good-bye to our friend and take you home for food, rest and a shower?"

Dom had thought about arguing, but realized that they were right. Leading them back into the room he whispered, "I don't want to wake her. She needs the rest."

Pulling out the notebook and his pen, he scrawled a note, and left it on the table by the bed.

He leaned down and whispered, "I'll be back soon. Get some rest."

With one last look, he turned and headed out the door.

By the time they'd pulled up to his apartment, he had a headache. He hadn't been able to think of much else than how to help Bridgette. Pulling himself up from the back seat of the SUV he said, "Thanks for the ride, guys. Catch you later."

"Dom," Brian called. When Dom turned back, he continued. "I know this is a mess. But try to get a little sleep. It'll help you focus, and that's what she needs right now."

"I might try to catch a nap, but it's going to have to be quick.

I'm heading back up as soon as I can. She doesn't deserve to be alone right now."

"Be safe," Brian said as Deke backed out.

As the hot water poured over him, Dom thought about a woman who was handcuffed to a bed in the bloody hospital. She'd lost so much.

He knew that her furnishings had been sold to pay legal costs, and to recoup some of the money that she'd—not exactly stole, he decided, but more re-routed.

He was back at the hospital just before dinner, and made arrangements for a plate to be brought up for him.

"I appreciate that you came back out tonight, Dom," Bridgette said. "You've had a long day, and that drive can't be exactly fun."

"The trip back here was better. I knew that you were recovering and out of danger."

She smiled. "It's nice to know that somebody cares for you." Her voice hitched. "It's not something that I've had a lot of since my folks were killed."

"No extended family?"

"No. Both of my parents were only children. My grandparents passed away when I was little. So, when I lost my mom, it was only me in the great big world."

He took her hand. "You've got people who care now. Friends who'll stand by you through thick and thin."

The nurse came in. "Miss Mahoney, there you go," she said placing the tray on the little table. "Mr. Franchini, this is what they sent up for you. Enjoy."

Bridgette looked at her tray and sighed.

"What's wrong?" Dom asked looking up.

She'd slid the tray over as far as she could and was attempting to cut the chicken breast they'd brought her with the plastic fork and knife while her right hand was still shackled to the bed.

"Let me get that for you'" Dom stated.

"Thanks," Bridgette sighed. "Wait! No! Dom, you can't undo the cuff. You could get in serious trouble for that."

He looked at her tenderly. "Bridgette, you've never asked for anything from me. I'm sitting here, with the key in my pocket, yet you don't ask. Why?"

"I don't want to get anyone in trouble. I've caused enough on my own as it is. I don't need to make things worse."

"I'll tell you what," he said thinking quick. "What if we move the cuff?"

"I'm not sure how that'll help with anything?"

"You don't want me to leave you uncuffed because you're worried about me getting in trouble. I don't like seeing you handicapped to the point of being able to use only one arm. So, let's compromise," he said as he released the cuff from her wrist.

"What are you doing?" she asked when he slid it down to the foot of the bed.

"Slide your foot over." When she did, he lightly attached the cuff. "There. Now we're both happy and able to enjoy our dinners. And nobody can get in trouble."

CHAPTER 4

"Your Honor!" Dom shouted as he raced down the hall, chasing after the Judge that had been assigned to hear Bridgette's case. She was also the woman who would decide what punishment Bridgette would get.

Judge Judith Forsyth had been a judge in the federal courts for the last ten years and an attorney for three decades prior. Hearing the call, she turned to look at the man now dodging pedestrians. "Agent Franchini. What can I do for you?"

"Ma'am, I'm wondering if we could possibly speak in your office?"

Forsyth thought for a moment. In all of the years she'd dealt with the FBI, she'd only met agents like Franchini a handful of times. Given the nature of the case that she had been given, and his proximity to it, and the rumors that she'd heard about how this particular agent was befriending the guilty party, she made an educated guess. "Dom, is this about the Mahoney case?"

"Yes, Ma'am."

"Then you know that you really need to follow protocol on this. If you skirt around Jacobs, he's going to put his sights on you."

"I know that, but there are times when doing the right thing means risking it all."

She studied him. His face was set and determined.

Sighing, she gave in. "All right, let's take this to my chambers," and led the way.

In her chambers, she dropped her purse and the leather briefcase on the antique oak desk. "Please, sit," she motioned as she hung up her coat.

Pouring a cup of coffee for herself at the credenza, she turned to Dom. "Would you care for a cup, Agent Franchini?"

"Please." He fidgeted in the chair not from physical discomfort, but from concern.

Taking her seat, Forsyth looked him in the eye. "Okay, Dom. You look as nervous as a virgin in a whorehouse. Now, what's going on?"

"Trying to sum it up in one-hundred words or less, I think that the DA and the PD on this case are more concerned about their future political lives than they are about finding justice." He pulled an envelope out of his inside pocket and handed it to her, "These documents contain information that was shared with both of them, but neither has requested follow up on it.

"What this shows is that Bridgette Mahoney tried to follow the letter of the law as a private citizen. She never broke the law until the night of the sting. And she only did it to benefit the city. The money that was taken was transferred via multiple hops to a charity that works to help women and children affected by gang violence."

Judge Forsyth looked at the paperwork and back to him. "You say that District Attorney and the Public Defender both have this information?"

"Yes, Ma'am. The last page of the packet includes the signatures of delivery."

Forsyth flipped to the back page. "Hmmm. Seems to me that you're playing a very dangerous game, Mr. Franchini.

"I received letters from both Mr. Jacobs and Mr. Daniels the other day, and they recommended that Miss Mahoney be sentenced to nine years in federal prison. She'd serve six with good behavior. From what you're showing me now, I take it that you don't agree with that."

Dom shook his head, "No. I can't justify that for her."

"So let me ask you, what punishment would you deem prudent for this type of offense?"

Dom smiled. His gamble had at least a glimmer of paying off. "I spoke privately with Assistant Director Fredrick Meyers about this. While we can't condone the offense, we can understand the reason that the offense occurred. When we started tracking down the moves that she'd made, we began to see the scope of her knowledge with computers. We feel that Miss Mahoney might be better served, and do more service for others, if she was placed on probation and assigned to work with our offices."

He let the idea hang there, waiting for her to make the next move.

She smiled at him. "Dom, I can't promise you anything other than I'll look at your documentation and think about what you've said."

She rose, indicating that the meeting was over. "I expect that I'll see you in court in three weeks."

"Is that when her sentencing has been rescheduled for?" he asked surprised.

"It is. You've given me plenty to think about between now and then."

"Thank you, and I'll see you in court." With a nod, he headed out the door.

Time flew by, and the days seemed to blend together on Dom. It had been six weeks since Bridgette had been stabbed. For the week that she was in the hospital recovering, he worked eight hours, then made the hour drive up to see her for the evenings.

After she'd been returned to Hillside, he'd spent nearly ten hours per day working so that he could free up Fridays to make the drive to Hillside and have the time to visit with her. He'd seen a real change in Bridgette these last few weeks. When she'd first been moved back to Hillside, she'd been pale and weak. But her strength returned and on his last visit, she was smiling like before.

Something else had happened as well. They'd truly become friends during those visits.

He no longer looked at going as an obligation to right a wrong, but as time spent helping someone he cared about.

They'd spent time talking about the possible outcomes of her sentencing hearing. She was fully aware of the recommendation made by the attorneys, and the probability of her sentence covering a significant amount of time. She'd never asked, and he'd never volunteered, but they both knew that he would visit her until her release.

It still bothered Dom that he hadn't been able to tell her what they were trying to do. But he supposed that it was better that she not get her hopes up, he thought, as he pulled into the parking area for the Federal Courts.

Following the marble corridors, he went through the security checkpoints and made his way towards the courtroom. Brian and Deke had both arranged their schedules to be able to be here, he realized, not just for duty, but because of him. And Bridgette, he thought.

These two guys had gone above and beyond their own cases to help find the proof that what she had said was true. They'd spent hours of their own time working on that, as well as scheduling in time to be at his house when she called so that they could have a quick conference.

He'd even discovered that Deke had gone out to see Bridgette twice after she'd been released from the hospital.

Yeah, these guys would stand tall with you.

Deke smiled as he came up, "Thought you weren't going to make it."

"No way." His smile faded, and he shoved his hands in his pockets. "It's kind of weird, you know. I've been here how many times before, either to testify or for some other procedure. But I'm nervous today."

Brian slapped Dom's back, "She's become more than a case to you. She's a friend. To all of us. I think we're scared that Justice is going to be skewed today. But," he looked around carefully. "Perhaps your little plan will work."

"I'm hoping that it will," Dom admitted. "But the reality is that the other two have much more clout that I do."

The large oak doors of the courtroom swung open. Participants and observers from the last case filed out.

"Stupid question," Brian began. "Where do we sit?"

Dom stopped and considered for a brief moment. Usually he was part of the prosecution and would sit on that side. But, and it was a big but, today he was actively rooting for the defense. No, he concluded, he was rooting for the defendant. His decision was made. "I'm sitting behind Bridgette."

As they walked into the room, he noticed Jacobs and Daniels conferring at the table on the right. Bridgette had not been brought in yet.

Dom slipped into a chair directly behind the one that the defendant was going to sit in. Brian and Deke took the chairs beside him.

"Uh-oh," Deke mumbled as he noticed the glare that the D.A. was sending them.

"Well if he gets his way, we won't have to work with him in the courts much longer," Brian said.

Dom nodded, "Yeah. But then he might have the clout at that point to make our lives miserable. Ah well."

The bailiff closed the heavy doors in the back and made his way through the little door just to the right of the Judge's bench. Dom knew that the defendant in a case was held in a holding cell downstairs, and would be brought up and into the court through that door.

A moment later, the door swung open and Bridgette shuffled in. Her feet bound with shackles, and her wrists handcuffed. Her head hung low and Dom could see her concern. As she neared the defendant's table, she raised her head slightly. When she saw the three agents sitting there, hope glimmered in her eyes.

Dom scanned the room. Other than the court officers and Bridgette, the only others in the room thus far were the three of them.

The door to the left of the bench opened, and Director Meyers exited from the chambers followed by Judge Forsyth.

"Ladies and gentlemen, we are here today for the sentencing of Bridgette Marie Mahoney, prisoner number 11325-3969. At the preliminary hearing, the plea entered at that time was guilty. Counselor is there any change in the plea?"

Daniels stood, "No, Your Honor."

"At this time, I'd like to give each of the counselors time to define their stand and recommendations. Mr. Jacobs, you first."

Jacobs stood, "Your Honor, the defendant pled guilty to charges of hacking into a federal bank, robbery, money laundering, and conspiracy to deceive. Although the defendant has no previous record, her crimes constitute offenses that could be construed as harmful to the general populous. However, it cannot be overlooked that once caught she did not try to deny her role in these crimes. Therefore, it is the recommendation of my office that she be sentenced to a minimum of nine years in a minimum-security federal facility."

"Thank you, Counselor," Forsyth said. "Mr. Daniels, any further statements?"

Daniels rose and tugged on the lapels of his suit coat.

"Your Honor, Miss Mahoney feels deeply sorry about the crimes that she committed. As Mr. Jacobs pointed out, she understands that she did wrong and pled guilty almost immediately. However, we do understand that a punishment must be doled out for the crimes that she did commit.

"Since she has no record, going back as far as her early teen-age years, she never had even a brush with the law, it is therefore the opinion of the Public Defender's office that Miss Mahoney be given a term of no more than nine years in a minimum-security prison."

He sat down, turned towards Jacob and gave a small wink.

"Easy, Dom," Deke whispered while his hands were physically restraining Dom's arms.

Judge Forsyth's voice cut through his anger.

"Miss Mahoney, please stand."

Dom looked forward at the scrape of the chair. She stood back straight, eyes fixed forward. The only tell-tale sign of her nervousness was her visibly shaking hands.

"Miss Mahoney, I'd like to ask you a few questions before we proceed to the final sentence. First, why did you do it that night? What made you commit a felony?"

Bridgette obviously wasn't prepared for this as her shoulders slumped. She wiped her eyes and then began in a trembling voice.

"Your Honor, I realize that there is no excuse for what I did. But I crossed the line out of concern. When I found out that the

Mambas were selling weapons, I just couldn't stand it. If that group got that much money, they would take over the town. And that was something that I couldn't live with. They had to be stopped."

Forsyth was leaning forward with a slight smile on her face. "Why did they have to be stopped?"

"For the past fifteen years or so, they had been taking over the city. There were drive-by shooting and car bombs all too frequently. Something had to be done to protect the law-abiding citizens. I'd tried to pass information to various law enforcement agencies in the past, but nothing ever happened. I-I-I guess that's why I did what I did. I realized that no one was going to help us. I couldn't let them have that money, so I took it."

She glanced quickly over her shoulder. "I took the money and messed up a federal sting operation that was underway. A sting that was trying to do the same thing that I was. I'm very sorry that my actions hurt others."

"Did the Black Mambas hurt anyone directly connected to you?"

Choking back tears, she nodded. "As you know, Rodriquez was directly responsible for a car bomb that inadvertently killed my father and sister. We sat through a lengthy trial, and then watched as he was acquitted before our eyes. Apparently a rookie mishandled some of the evidence, which gave possible doubt. The jury had to let him go."

She paused and sipped some water. "As he left the room, he made a gesture like a gun firing at my mother, who was already distraught from the case. She bolted from her seat and ran out of the courtroom, and out of the courthouse all together. She ran directly in front of a city bus. She died a few hours later at the hospital, and at the age of seventeen I was alone in the world. The Mambas had killed my entire family, either directly or indirectly."

"What changed for you?" The judge now wanted to know.

"I tried to do the right things, things that would have made my family proud of me. I ran a small on-line company that my mom and I had started just before Lisa and my dad were killed. That kept the wolf from the door. For the next few years, I worked full time, went to school full time and had little time for anything else. But I survived.

"But all that time, the Mambas' strength grew.

"After graduation, I was able to get a job working with a law firm in town. I did most of the computer research. It was while I was at the firm, that I started digging on the Mambas. Usually I would do this after hours or on my lunch break. If I found something of interest, I would pass it on to either the sheriff or the state police, occasionally if it was something really big, I'd pass it on to the FBI. I never used the local police, as it was one of their officers who got Rodriquez off. When this latest event presented itself, I knew I had to make a choice. After years of turning over information and having nothing come form it, I decided that I needed to take a different path."

Judge Forsyth nodded. "So, now you've again admitted to taking the money. Why did you refuse to pay it back when Mr. Jacobs made that first offer?"

"Your Honor, if I'd kept the money, that would have been stealing. I would have taken something that didn't belong to me so that it would profit me. I took the money, or more correctly, I arranged to have the money electronically transferred from that account to one that I thought deserved it. The Mambas have been abusing everyone, but the ones who feel it most are the women and children. I used a series of sites to separate the money and then move it from the Mambas account to the account of the Bayview Women and Children's Center, which helps the victims of gang violence."

"So, in other words, you used a criminal act to try and thwart a criminal group and help victims of violence, correct?"

Bridgette, sighed, hung her head, "Yes, Your Honor."

"Did you know that what you were doing was wrong?"

Bridgette's head seemed to hang even lower. "Yes, Your Honor. I knew that it was a felony to do it."

"But you did it anyway. Now I'm interested in why."

This time Bridgette's head came up high. "I thought about it long and hard. Sometimes you have to make a sacrifice to help the whole. There are things in life that are worth risking everything for. When I weighed my options, I was fully aware that I risked imprisonment. But I also knew that if I didn't do something, the Mambas were going to throw Bayview into anarchy. I am but a single person trying to protect as many as I can."

"You may take a seat. Mr. Jacobs, were you aware of this information?"

Jacobs squirmed in his chair. "I recently received a series of documentation that alluded to this. I have not confirmed it."

"Mr. Daniels, same question."

He reacted a bit better, and didn't visible squirm. "I too received the information, Your Honor."

"Yet, neither one of you requested more information on this? It appears to this court that your motives are questionable at best. I'm not sure if you're serving the public or yourselves. Between the two of you, you made this young woman out to be incorrigible. Yet by her own statement, she did things to try and help others

"I also wonder why it is, that you got her to plead guilty, and then surprisingly you both used the same length of time as one of your boundaries in your recommendation.

"And Mr. Daniels, I wonder why it is when the Public Defender has a client who has acted in this manner, for the reason she did, why you didn't play it up and try to get her exonerated because she acted under duress.

"Well, in any case, it's up to me to come to a conclusion and pass sentence. Normally, I would give my decision at this time, however under the circumstances, I am calling a ten-minute recess to think about this. Court adjourned," she brought done the gavel, stood and walked out.

CHAPTER 5

"What the hell do you think you're doing Franchini?" Jacobs asked the minute the chamber door was closed.

"I'm not sure what you're talking about, Mr. Jacobs." Dom turned to Brian and Deke, "You guys got any ideas?"

They both shook their heads.

"This conviction means a lot to me," Jacobs snarled.

"You've got your conviction. She's already pled. Today is about the sentencing," Deke threw in.

Dom glanced over and caught the shake of Bridgette's shoulder. Instinctively, he turned and laid his hand on her shoulder. "Mr. Jacobs, Mr. Daniels, I'm going to ask that you please refrain from any more unpleasantness regarding this issue. To you, this is a notch on your belt, but this is more. It's about somebody's life. And regardless of what happens in the next ten minutes, your lives most likely won't be impacted a great deal. Hers is going to be irrevocably changed. Let's try to remember that."

He turned to face Bridgette. Her face was now buried in her

hands as she sobbed uncontrollably.

There was no hesitation. Dom simply stepped over the barricade that separated the observers from the participants. Gently he lifted her from her seat, and cradled her in his arms giving her all the comfort he could.

"It's going to be okay, Bridgette. You're a survivor, you'll get through this, no matter what."

"It's a comfort to me to know that I've friends that are standing with me. Please, will you make me a promise? All three of you?" she looked up to where Brian and Deke were standing.

They laid their hands on her shoulders while Dom held her tight. "Anything you need," they said almost in unison.

"What ever happens in a few minutes, please don't forget me." Her voice hitched, "I've made it through the past few months because I knew there were people who were outside that cared enough about me to visit, or write. People who I could call. It kept the loneliness away. I'm going to need that. I'll understand if it can't be all the time, but please don't totally forget me."

"I'll be there for you, Bridgette. You've got my promise on that. We'll get—"

The doors to Judge Forsyth's chambers opened and she came back into the room.

Dom tried to climb over the partition unnoticed, but she noticed. "Having a little problem getting back to our seat, Mr. Franchini?"

"I'm sorry, Your Honor," he said as he twisted and folded himself until he was able to take his seat.

Judge Forsyth looked around the room, sighed, and looked towards Bridgette. "I've worked in one way or another in this system for over forty years," she began. "As a counselor, you do your best to help your case, or client, as it may be. But as a judge, you realize that your thoughts and decisions have life altering consequences for people you don't know.

"For the vast majority of the people who pass through my court, I sincerely hope that I won't see them again, and that the punishment that I'm duty bound to hand down was the right one for that person at that time.

"That's not to say that I try to be lenient with those that come through my doors. But that I give them what they need, not necessarily what they want. And, I think that over the past forty years I've learned a little about human nature and what is best for the people that come before me.

"So, it with these thoughts in mind, that I've made the following decision."

She glanced at the defendant's table, "Will the defendant please rise."

Bridgette pushed to her feet.

Dom leaned forward and gently placed his hand on her back, letting her know that he was there.

"Miss Mahoney, up until the night of March the twelfth, you showed great skill in making your life decisions. Unfortunately the choice that you made that night was not the best one. You made a bad decision, and did the wrong thing for the right reasons. You've shown this court that you understand that this was wrong, and you've shown remorse for the inadvertent blowing of the sting operation. However, in your statement, you also expressed that you understood that you would need to pay for your crime."

The judge looked over to the plaintiff's table and then back to Bridgette. "So it is my decision that perhaps the best way is to let you make a choice of which punishment you would prefer."

"Oh good grief," Jacobs stage whispered.

Judge Forsyth looked at him with daggers for eyes. "Another outburst like that, Mr. Jacobs, and I'll fine you for contempt."

Jacobs waved in a form of silent apology.

Forsyth focused again on Bridgette, who was now gnawing her

lip, trying not to cry. "The options that you have, Miss Mahoney are as follows. You may choose to accept a sentence of five years in the minimum security prison at Hillside, with the possibility of parole after three years." Now the Judge smiled slightly, amused at the contortions that Jacobs was making in his silent protest. "Or, you may take the following deal. Your time of incarceration will be time already served. You will be housed in a federally approved housing complex under house arrest for a period of one year and fitted with a GPS electronic bracelet. You will spend forty hours per week working with the FBI, in the Violent Crimes, Gangs and Drugs Division on the Organized Crime Taskforce as a computer analyst at their Washington D.C. office. This is being done to give you a chance to complete the work that you attempted to do on your own, but with proper guidance and authorization. After your shift is over, you will report directly home unless other arrangements have been approved. After your year of house arrest is over, you will be on probation for the next 5 years.

"Do you have any questions before I ask you for your decision?"

There were multiple gasps around the room. Bridgette was clutching her hands to her mouth, tears streaming down her cheeks. Jacobs had his palms pressed into his eye sockets and looked like he'd been punched.

Bridgette caught her breath, "Just for clarification, Your Honor, with the deal, I wouldn't go back to prison? I'd be allowed to have some freedom and work?"

"You would need to go back to Hillside to go through the final checkout today. Assistant Director Meyers has already secured a safe house where you'd be able to stay. You would pay rent, but it would serve your purpose. You'd still be under house arrest for the next year, which means that basically you're allowed to go to work and there is a given amount of time that is built in for running household errands. Your whereabouts will be monitored exactly. If you go somewhere you shouldn't be federal officers will come and arrest you and you will spend the rest of the time of your sentence behind bars. There are exceptions for emergencies, but all of that will be gone over with you when you are fitted with your bracelet.

Bridgette wiped the tears from her eyes, "Then I think, I'd really like to take the deal you've offered me, Your Honor."

Forsyth smile broadly, "Good girl. I think you've made a very wise choice. Normally, I say to people that I hope that I don't see them again in my court, but for you Miss Mahoney, I think that I will look forward to seeing you here—when you are testifying for the prosecution."

She smiled again, "Bailiff, please release Miss Mahoney, and secure transport for her back to Hillside." As soon as the cuffs were off, she tapped her gavel, "Court dismissed."

Bridgette turned to Dom, threw her arms around his neck and squeezed. "Thank you, thank you, thank you. I don't know how you managed to pull this off for me, but other than going to check out I don't have to go back there."

Dom rubbed her back. "You've been given a second chance. Enjoy it." He looked up and saw the guard from Hillside waiting at the door. "Looks like your ride is ready to go. Would you like me to pick you up?"

"That would be nice. It's an awfully long walk from there to D.C. and I really don't want to screw up this chance."

Dom looked at his watch. "Giving time for travel and paperwork, I'll plan to arrive around four. That should let us get you right in to the apartment with little trouble. We can also stop to pick up some groceries for you on the way in, okay?"

Tears were again streaming down her face, so she just nodded. She mouthed the words, "Thank you" again before the guard led her out through the back door.

Deke and Brian were standing there smiling. "You did it," Brian said.

"So it was you, Franchini? You're the one who may have just cost me my governorship. I will not forget this!"

"Jacobs," Director Meyers said, "all they did was follow up on the evidence. I'm the one who approached the Judge. That girl's got skills we need. She's still going to be serving time, but it'll be time better spent helping to make Bayview and other places safer.

Riding in the van back to Hillside, Bridgette stretched out in the back. There was no one else there, and she was free. Okay, she thought, not technically free, but her hands weren't secured nor were her feet shackled. And granted, she was riding in the locked cage of the transport, but still it was the best she'd felt in the past three months.

Her mind spiraled around everything that she wanted to try. She was going to be very diligent in what she did and make the most of this second chance.

She realized that she had not been exonerated, nor had she expected to be. She was forever going to be a convict. She'd served time, and had a record. But that didn't deter her. She would find a way to get through life. There were people who had helped her, so that now she had a job and other responsibilities. She would work hard to keep the promise that she made, to earn their respect.

The transport van pulled into the prison garage, and the guard opened the back door for her. "I've already called things in, so they're expecting you. We're going to start by going to your cell and letting you pack up all of your personal items. From there we'll be going through almost a reverse process that you went through when you were checked in."

They walked to her cell quietly. It didn't take long to gather the few things that she'd acquired during her time here.

Then it was on to the endless paper work.

Bridgette stepped into the prison lounge at three-fifty eight. She didn't see Dom yet, so she sat in one of the rough covered chairs. Unconsciously, she rubbed her hand over the bracelet that was now affixed to her right ankle. It felt awkward, but definitely better than the steel cuffs.

Glancing at the clock, she began to do the mental math. She had to be checked into the apartment by seven-thirty. It took at least an hour to get there, and she was going to need to do some basic shopping for groceries and clothes so she'd be prepared to go into the FBI tomorrow.

She was pondering what they would have her do when the door opened and Dom strolled in.

"All set?" he asked with a smile.

"Yeah. I still can't believe it. Thanks again, Dom, for everything that you did."

Dom hefted her bag into the back of his SUV and then held the door open for her. Moments later they were on the road heading towards D.C..

"Am I allowed to ask, how did you pull this off?" she asked. When he looked puzzled, she shrugged, "I overheard people talking about it. I'm just curious, that's all."

"I just pointed out that everything that you'd done was for others. And, the part that swayed the director, was the fact that you've got some serious computer skills and have already hacked into the Mambas websites."

For the remainder of the ride, they simply talked. About the weather, and what was currently in the news and dozens of other simplistic things. They stopped at a WalMart so she could pick up some bare essentials in clothing, and then the Giant for her grocery list.

Hauling the five bags up the flight of stairs, they arrived at her new apartment just before seven. Dom had seen to getting the key before he'd left to come pick her up, so he opened the door for her, and stepped aside.

She walked in, reached and fumbled for the light switch.

The apartment was small. The kitchen was hardly big enough for the gas stove, a refrigerator and small sink. White cupboards hung along the wall. A small breakfast bar and two stools divided the kitchen from the living room.

Again, small was the best adjective. But it was clean and neat. And it looked comfortable.

"Sorry it's not better accommodations," Dom said as he set the groceries on the breakfast bar.

She turned to look at him. "Don't be sorry. It's bigger than eight by eight. The walls aren't made of concrete, and look, no bars on the windows." She stopped and stared out the window.

In the evening light she could see a small pond and a family of ducks swimming. "I promised myself that once I was out I'd stop crying," she said wiping the errant tear from her eye. "I'm just so happy. I know that I'm not really free, but this is a big step up from Hillside."

Dom took her hand, squeezed it. "And there's no set hours for visiting. Now, seeing as it's after seven, and neither of us has eaten, is there anything that you'd like?"

She blushed, "It's strange, but I've missed a good pizza."

"We can handle that." Dom's cell rang. "Hello? Hey Deke, no we just got in. What? I don't know, we were just about to order a pizza." He moved the phone so he could talk to her. "Deke and Brian were wondering if you'd like them to come over for a bit. Deke said they'd grab the pizzas and some beer—"

Her face went from smile to frown in a heartbeat. "What did I say?" Dom asked.

"Them coming over with pizza is fine, but no alcohol. That's part of the, um, conditions. No drinking, drugs or anything along that line."

Dom crossed to her, "Then he'll bring some Cokes and Diet Cokes."

As she lay awake in her bed that night, she tried to turn off her brain. So much had happened in one day. The sentencing that she'd been worried about had turned out to give her a new chance on things, tomorrow she'd start a new job, she was already in her new apartment, and even though there were restrictions that were very precise, she had more freedom than she'd had over the last three months.

She had friends who'd brought her pizza and Diet Coke, along with a television set and a DVD player.

Things were going to be just fine.

CHAPTER 6

Bridgette woke up euphoric, despite feeling tired. It may not have been the best night's sleep she'd had, but the circumstances definitely helped.

After three months of having her schedule dictated by someone else, it was a pure pleasure to be able to wake when she wanted to, shower for as long as she'd like and have what she preferred for breakfast.

The fact that she could wear clothing that wasn't orange and a touch of makeup didn't suck either.

She watched the clock. Dom had given her a schedule of times for the commuter train that left the station a mere block from her apartment and would leave her with a short walk to the FBI center where she was going to be working.

She had plenty of time, but was too anxious to do anything. But staring at the clock only made things worse.

Giving up, she grabbed her purse, and made her way out. As soon as she exited from the front doors of the building, she stopped and inhaled deeply.

Freedom had it's own smell, and she'd never forget it.

The train ride into Washington was uneventful. She was crammed into a car with thirty or so other commuters, each encapsulated in their own world. The only noise was the swish of the train as it swayed side to side.

Bridgette strolled along the avenue, taking her time so she wouldn't be so early that she would give the night security guards an anxiety attack. She still found herself standing in front of the squat faded brick building with fifteen minutes to go.

Looking at the doors and then at a little bench that sat under the small group of trees that lined the sidewalk, she tried to figure the lesser of two evils. Being annoyingly early or fidgeting in public.

"Ms. Mahoney?" a voice asked from behind her.

Turning cautiously, she saw an older gentleman coming up the walk. He looked familiar, but she couldn't recall his name. "Yes," she answered as he neared.

"I'm Assistant Director Meyers. I'll be your new boss."

Recognition flashed on Bridgette's face. "That's right. I'm sorry I didn't place you at first. It was all kind of," she waved her hands trying to find the right words.

Meyers smiled warmly, "Not a problem. We only met briefly at Hillside and then at the hospital. I've got a file," he said tapping his briefcase, "that has your picture in it to help me with my memory." Nodding towards the building, he continued, "I see you're a bit early today. Little nervous?"

Bridgette let out a breath that she didn't know that she had been holding. "Yeah, I guess. I've been running on adrenaline for the past day, and right now I'm too amped up to sit still. I couldn't stay at the apartment any longer, and I arrived here quicker than I thought, so..." she stopped, sighed again. "Sorry, I'm rambling on here."

Meyers motioned with his left hand towards the building, "Shall we get started then?"

He held the door opened for her as she walked into the building. She took in the room, noting the high ceiling in the foyer, the elevators that were positioned in the center of the room and then her heart stopped.

Two lines of people were forming. The first, had people who all had ID cards and badges out. The other led to the walkway between the metal detectors.

Bridgette thought of the monitor that was strapped to her ankle. How would she explain that?

"Miss Mahoney? Are you alright?" Director Meyers asked.

"I'm just worried about, the, um, metal detectors and the monitor."

Director Meyers nodded, "You're right. The detectors would find that, and that would put you in an uncomfortable position." He looked around for a second, as if he was trying to find a particular person in the crowd. His eyes brightened. "Wait here, I'll be right back."

He returned a moment later with a tall, dark skinned woman. "MaryAnn, this is Bridgette Mahoney. She'll be working in my department starting today, as part of a special program. I'd appreciate it if we could do the intake scan privately."

MaryAnn rolled her eyes, "What kind of program?"

"That's classified, MaryAnn. Now we can either go into the back room there," he pointed to her office area, "or you can pass her through on my say-so. Which would you prefer?"

Since it was obvious he wasn't talking to her, Bridgette kept quiet. She knew which one she'd prefer, but the odds were that wasn't going to happen.

MaryAnn shook her head and waved her arm, "We're going to take it to the office. I let you skip her through security, it'll be my butt that ends up waving in the breeze because of it."

Bridgette followed MaryAnn to the little office. She felt some relief when Director Meyers walked beside her.

Inside the office, MaryAnn stepped to the side of the door, and closed it once everyone else was in the room. "Okay," she said looking at Meyers. "What's so special about this program that she can't go through the regular setup?"

Meyers sighed, "It's part of her release program. She's wearing—"

"Release program!" MaryAnn's voice had risen a full octave, while her eyes nearly bulged out of her head, and a vein was now evident, throbbing on the side of her neck. "Are you telling me that this little girl is an ex-con?"

Bridgette could feel her face flush and her head dropped. It was something that she knew she would have to get used to. "Yes, I am," she muttered, still looking at the floor.

MaryAnn's voice came back down to its normal register. "Frank, what the bloody hell is going on here? You said she was going to be working in your department. Last time I looked, we didn't, on principal, hire ex-cons. Now why do you want to get her in?"

"Look, MaryAnn, you're right. Normally we don't use people who have a record. But there is precedent here. What happens when some hacker breaks into our computer system? Often times we give them a deal, and they come to work for us. This is a similar situation.

"Miss Mahoney used a computer to get into a system that we were trying to run a sting on. A system, may I add, that we haven't yet gotten into ourselves. Before things got straightened out, she'd confessed that she'd done it. Jacobs was counting on her sentence to give him the boost he wanted to the Governor's mansion. Things came out, and we made a deal. She got a reduced sentence if she'd come work for us. But it means that she's got to wear an ankle monitor."

MaryAnn looked at Bridgette hard. "Why'd you confess?"

Bridgette's head came up, and she took a deep breath just as Meyers started to speak. MaryAnn turned, "Uh-uh. I asked her."

Bridgette looked her in the eye and said simply, "I'm honest. I tried to do what I thought was right. When I was arrested, I confessed. In reality the words that the Judge used were probably the best explanation of my situation. I did the wrong thing for the right reason."

A thin smile broke out on MaryAnn's face. "I may get to like you. Everybody makes mistakes. It takes a strong person to face up to them." She grabbed a wand from her desk, and after a quick swipe with the only alarm being on Bridgette's right ankle, she nodded. "Okay, you have a good day. Frank, you make sure that this girl has the proper ID so she can use the other line tomorrow."

By noon, Bridgette felt like her head was spinning in every direction. She'd filled out multiple forms, had her picture taken as well as being introduced to more people than she'd ever hope to remember, and given a five-minute tour of the department. The only downer of the day so far was when she'd been fingerprinted again. It just brought back too many bad memories.

She'd been given a U-shaped work area that contained five different computer systems and more monitors. She'd gladly gotten into starting to break back into the Mambas' accounts.

With her arrest, the Mambas had found out that their information was vulnerable, she guessed, so they'd spent the last three months trying to secure things. It'd slowed her down a bit, but she was already through the first layer, and she was concentrating on finding the algorithm for the next when a knock on the door surprised her.

Her head turned and she stared at the form in the door.

"You okay? You're looking at me like a deer in the headlights," Dom siad. "It's lunchtime. Brian, Deke and a few others are heading down to the cafeteria. Didn't know if you'd like to join us?"

She felt baffled and was definitely a bit scared.

"Is that a good idea? I mean, thanks for the offer, but what will everyone else say?"

"You're the new girl here. People will like you once they get to know you."

"Yeah," she said sourly. "They'll like me right up until they find out about where I spent the last three months."

"Bridgette, you've got a chance to remake yourself right now. I'm not going to share any of your past with people. Some already know. They worked on this side of the case. I'm sure that they'll link the name, the case and you. There's nothing you're going to do about that. If you stay locked up here, they'll make their own opinions about you. Since they're going to do that anyway, I'd say come down to lunch. Let them see the real you. Not the one on paper, nor the one that data points to, but the real Bridgette Mahoney. I know the people here. Some of them will likely surprise you and will put things behind and work to be your friend.

Bridgette hesitated for only a second. "Okay, I'll give it a try. Let me grab my purse."

The cafeteria was located in the basement of the building. But unlike most of the other motifs around, it wasn't institution gray. Bridgette appreciated the soft maroon color on the walls as she followed Dom through the line.

Seeing as she was still short of money, she opted to simply go with a cup of soup and a bottled water. Nothing fancy, but it would keep her going, or so she hoped, until she got home.

As they walked towards a table in the far corner, she could feel the eyes upon her. "Now I know how a goldfish feels," she muttered.

Dom smiled. "It's simple curiosity. You're the shiny new face here. Makes everybody want to see what you're about."

Trying to ignore the glances and the outright blatant stares,

Bridgette looked to the table and saw Brian and Deke sitting with three others. Deke was smiling, but shaking his head. Fear caused her stomach to churn. Now she just hoped that she'd be able to keep the soup down.

"Hey, guys. I dragged Bridgette down to join us for lunch," Dom said. Setting his tray down, he pulled out the last remaining chair and motioned for Bridgette to sit before he grabbed one from the adjacent table and slid in next to her. Pointing to the others at the table, he began the introductions. "That's Lucy, she's in communications. Her job is to keep things running smoothly during an op as well as assisting us with data collection. John is a grunt, like me, which means he tracks down the bad guys and then goes in to collect them. And lastly, this is Tammy who spends way too much of her time looking at financial records. Her specialty seems to be tracking money. Guys, this is Bridgette Mahoney. She's just joined the group working as a computer geek. She has some experience getting into some of the gang networks, so we're hoping that she'll be able to help expand our repertoire on that end of things."

"I'll say she's got some skill," Tammy drawled.

Bridgette felt her face flush, and her stomach contracted even more than it had before. "Maybe, I should've stayed upstairs."

"I take it you two have worked together before," John commented.

"Close enough," Tammy agreed. Now staring at Bridgette she continued, "We may have been on opposite sides, but I'll admit to admiring your work. And just letting you know how it is, I'll be keeping my eye on you."

Tammy crumpled the wrapper from her sandwich, tossed it back onto her empty tray and left.

Bridgette sat, staring at her cup of soup. What was there to say or do now? Tammy had all but made sure that everyone else here knew about her.

"Hey, Bridgette? Don't worry about Tammy," Lucy said with a smile. "She has a competitive streak a mile wide, and absolutely hates it when someone stymies her on a computer project. You, ah, did."

Bridgette looked up, her mouth forming a perfect 'oh' and her eyes wide.

"I remember her talking to Dom, there, about the grief you gave them when you screwed up the sting." Lucy continued.

"You-you," Bridgette's eyes tracked from Lucy to John and back again as she stammered. "You all know about that? And what happened?"

"Bridgette, Dom talks to these two characters," John said pointing at Brian and Deke. We had a pretty good play-by-play of the whole incident. At least up until about a month ago."

John looked over at Dom, "That's when he started getting a bit goofy in the head. Of course with him, that's not exactly unusual either. His two accomplices here kind of kept the rest of us filled in, so yeah, we know about what's been going on for the past three months."

"And you're okay with me sitting here for lunch?" Bridgette asked timidly.

"Honey, from what we heard, you were literally in the wrong place at the wrong time after our agency had dropped the ball too many times. Unfortunately, you got screwed in the process. But now? Now you're working with us. You do some of that voo-doo that you computer geeks are known for and get us the hard details, it'll go a long way to making you a real member of this team."

Bridgette sat on the small sofa in the main room of her apartment and thought about what Lucy had said at lunch as she looked out the window at the darkness. It seemed that many of the people that she had met today were willing to give her a chance to prove herself. It made her feel accomplished that she was going to be judged on what she could do to help people, not on what had happened in the past.

Her thoughts flickered to Tammy's reaction. She'd snapped a bit at Bridgette, but hadn't there been a backwards compliment there too?

If nothing else, just trying to find a way to prove to everyone that she would be a valuable asset to the team would be enough to push her to work harder than anyone else.

Rising, she strolled around the apartment, taking time to look out the windows at the night scenes that were taking place just outside her reach. A sigh escaped.

Laying her forehead on the glass pane, she closed her eyes. She may no longer be in a physical prison, there were no bars on the windows and she could open the door anytime that she wanted, but she was still a prisoner. She had the mobility to move about within her confinement, but not the freedom to leave whenever she wanted.

But, she thought, she did have time during the day to be out.

Her eyes opened slowly as a tear trickled down her cheek. She'd have to be content with that.

Heading for the bedroom, she grabbed a new paperback novel that she'd picked up at the train station on the way home from work.

Once in her nightgown, she crawled into bed and lost herself in the romance.

In her mind she traveled to a far off land, where the gallant knight, Sir Charles, dressed in battle-scarred armor fought to protect the fair maiden's honor. She cried when the enemy king kidnapped Robin. When the Sir Charles risked everything he had to ensure Robin's release, her heart longed for that kind of compassion.

She stopped, set her book aside and chuckled to herself. Hadn't Dom essentially done just that for her? Hadn't he risked his career to get her out of that jail cell?

And what had John said at lunch? Something about the way

Dom had gotten goofy in the head, wasn't it? "What did that mean?" she said aloud surprising herself.

Suddenly thirsty, she padded her way towards the bathroom for a glass of water. Flipping on the light, she stared at herself in the mirror while she filled the glass.

"He's a good friend," she confided to reflection. "But I can't think of anything else right now. He's got a life, and until I get things resolved, I don't."

She went back to bed, prepared for another fitful night's sleep. Lying back on the pillow, her thoughts of her personal knight played over in her head, dreaming of being the fair maiden of Dom's dreams.

CHAPTER 7

Bridgette woke the next morning to the patter of light rain. Crossing the room she went to the sliding doors. Flicking the lock she stepped out onto the small balcony and raised her face into the fresh cold water.

Freedom, she thought. She had missed the freedom of being able to stand in the rain while she had been incarcerated. To be honest with herself, she realized that she had missed the ability to go outside whenever the mood struck her. She owed Dom and Director Meyers that.

She stood lost in her moment for a brief few minutes before the cold water had soaked her nightgown. Shivering now, she stepped back into her apartment, headed for the bathroom and a hot shower.

Rinsing the conditioner from her hair, she began to think of what she wanted to do today. The best way that she could repay the favor that was done for her was to get the rest of the team into the Mambas' computer system.

Yesterday, she had been too tied up in getting her balance at her new job. Today, she decided, she was going to do that job. Somehow, she was going to find a way to get through the next level of the gang's security.

Entering the Hoover building, she joined the queue to go through security. This time she held her ID badge out to be quickly scanned and was passed through without a second glance. Five minutes later, she was booting up her computers when Tammy walked in.

"Getting an early start, Mahoney?"

Bridgette looked up and her smile quickly faded. "I want to get into this as soon as I can. I feel I owe people here who have given me a second chance. I just want to do my job."

Tammy sneered. "You've got skills, Mahoney. I've said that before. Just remember which side you're working for." She turned to walk away, hesitated and turned back. "One more thing. Stay out of my way."

Bridgette collapsed into her chair with a huff, and sat staring at her monitors. "What did I do to her that has her so uptight?" she asked herself quietly.

Shaking her head she needed to clear her mind, so she closed her eyes and said, "Ut tranquillitas et inspira" Latin for keep calm and breathe. It had been her mantra since she had dealt with the deaths of her family. Saying it everyday had helped her keep her head and focus on what she had to do. Even in prison, it had helped by keeping her sane. Now, she felt she needed that cool-headedness to break through the Mambas' walls and help her team. Maybe, she thought as she began to type, she'd find a way to get Tammy to at least tolerate her.

She jumped as someone placed a Starbucks to-go cup near her elbow. "What?" she asked spinning around.

"You've been over here tapping on keys for the past two hours. Thought you might like to come up for air and a quick break," Lucy said.

Bridgette looked at the small woman who stood smiling at her. Lucy was dressed conservatively in a simple blouse and skirt, but her eyes flashed with mischief. "Um, thanks," she said taking a sip.

"How are things going so far?" Lucy asked sipping her own coffee.

Bridgette tried to relax and leaned back in her chair and crossed her legs. "I guess things are going as well as I could have hoped for. I was able to get in today without any problems, and I'm doing work that I'm good at and thoroughly enjoy." Her eyes flickered across the room to where Tammy sat. "I'm hoping that somehow I'll be able to at least feel as though I'm not intruding here."

Lucy followed Bridgette's glance. "She'll get over you. Probably. As I said yesterday, she's got a real competitive streak, and she figures that you beat her with the work you did this past March."

"I wish there was a way to make it up to her," Bridgette said. "I don't like being on someone's hit-list. I mean, I understand that not everybody is going to be happy about the deal that I got. But it is what it is. Is it really that hard to accept it and let it go?"

Lucy laughed. "Honestly, I don't think this has anything to do with your deal. This is all about ego. For the past five years, she's been the best at getting in and around things. Now you show up. Someone who, as far as she's concerned, has beaten her at her own game. She's more worried about her standings as the computer queen down here." Lucy took another swig of her coffee. "So, what's going on between you and Dom?"

Bridgette, having just taken another sip, nearly spit it out in surprise. "What? What are you talking about?"

Lucy shrugged. "Dom seems, uh, very concerned about you. Some of the others think that you two have become an item. Any truth in that?"

Bridgette flushed. "No. He surprised me when he first came

to talk to me. Apparently he'd seen something during one of the interviews. When he came that day, he told me about his sister and then he listened to my story. He gave me something more important to me at that point in my life. He was my friend when I didn't have one. He, and Deke actually, came to visit me over the next few weeks. It's something that I will be forever grateful to them for. And as for making it anything else than that, I wouldn't want to risk that."

Lucy smiled and nodded before she looked at her watch. "Well, my break is almost up, so I'd better get back. See you at lunch," she said walking away with a wave.

Bridgette waved back, "Thanks for the coffee."

Turning back to her computers, she tried to focus her thoughts about where to go next in her attempt to break through the Mambas' first line of defense.

Dom sat at the lunch table nervously tapping his fingers on the table.

"Relax, man. Lucy said she'd be here," Brian said.

"I know, I know. It's just that I'm a little worried for her, you know. I don't want to constantly be checking up on her, but I want to make sure that everything is going well for her."

Brian smiled, and pointed at him with half a sandwich. "Does she know that you've got feelings for her?"

Dom's fingers stopped drumming. "I don't know what you're talking about," he managed to say with a straight face. That couldn't be it, could it? He'd never felt this way about anyone before, and truthfully, he really didn't know her that well.

He recovered quickly. "She's been through a lot over the past few months. Is it wrong to worry about a friend who's had to deal with that?" Dom asked.

Deke walked up to the table, "Hey pals-o-mine! I was thinking, what do you all say about after the golf game tonight, we head over to Clancy's and we can catch the game tonight? Red Sox are playing the Orioles."

"As much as I'd like that, I think my wife is going to have other ideas for me. I'm going to pass tonight." John said.

"Sounds like a great idea to me," Brian said. "Scope out some action, enjoy the game, grab a pizza while we're there. Doesn't get much better than that. What about you, Dom? You in?"

"Sure. Why not?" He saw Bridgette and Lucy walking towards the group. The weight that had been pressing on his chest suddenly let up, and he took the first bite of his sandwich.

"Hey guys," Lucy said as they approached. "Look who I dragged out of the dungeon."

"Here you go, Lucy," Brian said as he slid the chair between him and Deke out, leaving Bridgette the only open chair next to Dom.

Bridgette ate quietly, listening to the banter of the group at the table. It was nice that they were letting her sit here, but she still felt like an intruder. She looked around the table and realized that there was a face from yesterday that was missing. "Where's Tammy?" she blurted out.

Deke sighed. "She, uh, decided that she'd go somewhere else for lunch today."

Bridgette realized that there was more to what Deke had said and frowned. "That's not right. She's your friend. Why should she have to go somewhere else? I should have stayed upstairs and not interrupted the dynamics here."

Dom placed his hand over hers, and she felt her heart stutter.

"Bridge, no one forced Tammy to do anything. Honestly, I'm not sure that anyone could force her to do something that she doesn't want to do. Relax. You've got as much right to eat lunch with your friends as anybody else," Dom said giving her hand a little squeeze. "So, how's your day been?"

She swallowed the bite of sandwich to clear her mouth. "I guess it's okay. Tammy met me when I came in this morning for a bit of, er, I guess you'd call it a pep talk. But then I got right into things. I spent the morning—" She stopped and looked around the table. "I'm sorry. I'm not sure how much I can tell. Isn't there some kind of security measures that we have to abide by?"

Deke let out a low laugh. "Bridgette, everyone here is on the same team. We've all got security clearances. Relax. It's okay."

She gnawed on her bottom lip before glancing over to Dom.

"Deke's right, Bridge. We've all got clearance. And I think it's safe to say, that we're all interested in how things are going for you."

Bridgette sat motionless.

Lucy looked over at Bridgette and nodded before she held up a single finger. "Maybe we can try it this way. I know that from the, um, sting that went bad that you'd figured out how to get into the main sector of the Mambas' computers. Why did you even attempt that?"

Bridgette wasn't sure if she should be relieved that the question was something about her past or not, but she figured that it was a safer topic. "The firm that I used to work at spent a lot of time defending them. I'd chosen to work there since it would give me a way to legally poke in to various areas which meant I could get data that would theoretically help law enforcement officials close them down. The real idea of getting into their system came one day when Corina Sanchez came in. She was bragging to one of the staffers that the Mambas' system was more secure than our office computers were. When the staffer asked, Corina simply said that they used the computers to track every thing. The prostitution rings, drug shipments and payments, computer scams, the whole works.

"I realized then that if I could get into their system, I'd be able to play havoc with things, and possibly begin an internal war within the gang. I could hope that they would kill each other off until no one was left and then the city would be safe again." Bridgette sat quiet for a moment. "I know it wasn't the smartest idea, nor was it legal, but I'd run out of options. Every time I passed along information, nothing happened."

"How'd you get in?" John asked.

Bridgette smiled. "Getting through the first layer was relatively easy. I needed to find who they were using as a front."

"Wait," Brian said holding up his hands. "Why would they be using someone as a front?"

"Think about it, Brian. They're not going to want to put everything out under Mambas dot com. That would make your job way too easy, and they'd have been out of business years ago. These guys are smart. They operate like a regular business, just with questionable products. They need something that sounds innocuous. Something that everyone would just gloss over.

"I began working with legitimate sites that I knew were run by members of the gang. Getting a feel for the way they put things together, you know, the architecture of the site. This gave me, uh, a style, I guess you could call it, that I could focus on. Once I'd found a pretty clear pattern on their sites, I began searching for a hidden site. It took me a little while before I broke through, but I came across one that looked promising. It was a page that was about a little run down store in the neighborhood. What brought it to my attention were its physical location and the order of the page names. This one listed its Blog page first, then it had a Links page and then one called About. By following a few links I was able to find a hidden site which did have information about the basics of the Black Mambas."

"How did you know what links to follow? I mean almost every site has pages that are named like that." Brian asked.

Bridgette smiled wryly. "It was the order. Yes, many sites have similar page names, but that particular one had them in the right order. B-L-A. I realized that whatever links I followed would have to bring me to spelling out the rest of the name. This gave many possible wrong turns and provided them with a level of security. Once I found the site, I needed to find a way through their encryption software and break in. That was a bit more complicated, but still only required a matter of time as well as a bit of software that is available on line.

"After I was through the first time, I was able to set up a dummy account that let me in and out with no problem and gave me complete access to their membership rosters as well as their finances and internal messages." Her voice broke at the end. "This was right about the time that I learned about them selling a truckload of stolen weapons for a cool million. Um," she hesitated. "You know what happened next."

"Do you think they've changed their links since then?" Deke asked.

Bridgette nodded. "Once I'd finished filling out all of the paper work yesterday, Director Meyer told me that getting back into their system was to be my top priority. He said that I may get pulled to help somebody with a hot case, but otherwise I was to be working at getting back in. I started by trying the original sequence, but the first landing site has been taken down. I even took the time to track down the notes from my, er, case and see if I could use those to get in directly. No luck. That's what I spent the morning on. Working to see if I could find the first link."

Heads nodded around the table. "Having any luck?" Dom asked.

Bridgette popped the last bit of he sandwich in her mouth and chewed while she thought. "Maybe. I know the style I'm looking for. It's just taking a long time to run down the sites that might be possible. I don't know if they've just switched over from the one site to another that they already had or if they've created something brand new entirely."

Dom looked up. "Brian, what about the list of names that you collected from the sting?"

Brian's eyes went wide. "Well, yeah, I mean I have the list that we compiled in-house as well as the ones that we took into evidence. But what do you think you're going to be able to do with them?"

Dom swirled his soda can. "It may not be a quick fix, but if what Bridge says is right, it may give us a place to start. How about the way that they set up that first layer, do you think that they would have changed it?"

Bridgette opened her mouth and then closed it. She wasn't sure that this was a place for her to have an opinion or not.

"If it was me, and I knew that somebody had gotten through my security before, I'd change it in a heartbeat," Brian said. "That would be especially true if I knew that the person who had gotten through it before was working with my enemies now."

All eyes focused back onto Bridgette. "That's what I sort of figured as well. They may have changed how you get to the hidden section, but I don't think they'd change the mechanics of the process. There would be too much at stake for that drastic of a change. What I think is most likely, is that they've used a new front under an alias that is not part of their stomping grounds. Once we find that, we've got a foot in the door."

"Having any luck with that theory?" John asked.

"Maybe. I've isolated a few that are potentials. What I'm doing now is going through and testing each one. It's a bit time consuming. However, if you've got those lists, there is a distinct possibility that knowing their names and aliases will be enough to shrink my potential list down to real manageable numbers."

Brian smiled, "I'll get the lists and bring them to you after lunch. It'll probably be closer to one-thirty before I've got everything."

"That'll be perfect," Bridgette said.

"So," Deke asked the table. "I know that Tammy has been

saying that she's close to breaking through for the last year. Anyone here up for making a wager on who gets there first?"

Bridgette's head snapped towards Deke, but she remained silent, letting her thoughts run in her own head. So Tammy is also working on breaking into their system. I did it once; doing it the second time should be easier. All I need to do is figure out how to find that needle in this haystack, while keeping Tammy off of my back she thought.

CHAPTER 8

"Should have ordered an ark," Brian complained as he leapt from the Deke's car to race through the rain and into Clancy's.

"I think Brian's gone around the bend, Dom," Deke said.

"Hmmm. Sure looks like it. At least he's in. We can let him stand in line to wait for the table while we sit here and wait for the monsoon to let up a little."

Deke turned to look at his friend in the back seat. "True. Or, we could always take off and leave him here."

Dom peered out the window at the building that housed Clancy's. He knew that in the light the stone walls were a faint tan color, and that the building was twenty stories tall, housing business on the first five floors, with the remaining floors being taken by a small hotel chain. But he had always been attracted to the architecture of the building. Unlike so many others in the city, this one had character he thought.

He turned to Deke and shrugged. "We could, but what's the point? He's dry, has simple access to good food, fairly unlimited supply of beverages and he'd probably have no problem booking a room for the night. The only thing that leaving would do is to give him a good reason to get even with us."

Deke turned back to look out the window at the building as well. "Yeah. That's true, and in reality, he never just gets even. He's always been competitive enough that he needs to one up everyone." He glanced around, "I think it's about time to risk the rain. It doesn't seem to be letting up. Ready?"

Dom shrugged, "I guess so," he said opening the door.

They jogged to the double glass doors and stepped into Clancy's.

The first thing that Dom noticed as he stepped into the familiar venue was that it seemed too crowded to him. He shook his head trying to get things back into perspective for himself. Had they always had this many people hanging around the bar? He searched his memories but couldn't bring it totally into focus. "Big crowd tonight."

Brian stared at him with his eyebrows raised. Before answering he did a quick headcount. "There's less than thirty people here tonight. Normally when we stop in after golf they've got a couple hundred. We don't even have to wait for a table." He looked carefully at Dom. "You okay, buddy?"

"Yeah," Dom answered. "I dunno. Got too much on my mind recently, and I guess I'm not thinking too straight."

A young red-haired boy with a face full of freckles came over. "Are you ready to be seated now?" he asked Brian. When Brian nodded, he led them to a small corner table at the back of the restaurant section.

Dom hung his rain jacket on the booth's coat rack before he slid onto the bench that ran along the back wall. Deke followed him in while Brian took the seat across from him.

"Okay, Dom, what's going on?" Brian asked.

Dom shrugged. " I don't know. I just…I don't know."

When the freckled boy came back with their drinks, they quickly placed their order for pizza. Alone again, they turned the attention back to Dom.

"You said that there's been too much going on," Deke stated. "I get that. You've been slammed the past few weeks with everything that you were involved in with getting Bridgette out. But, she seems to have made it through the first two days at the office. From what I can see, she's at the minimum treading water. She's going to do fine. So what's the problem?"

Dom rested his elbows on the table and propped his head up with his hands. "I guess, I'm still worrying about her a bit, you know? I mean, she's not in prison any longer, but she's still got some people that aren't exactly happy with how things ended up. In the time since I started helping her, I haven't heard her talk about another friend at all."

Deke took a pull off his beer. "Dom, you've got to stop worrying about everybody. You went above and beyond the call of duty with her. You found evidence that gives her some version of her life back. At the office, you've helped to make sure that she's fitting in. What more can you do?" He looked up to see their server carrying the pizza over. "Now, why don't we sit back and enjoy this pizza before we watch the Orioles bury the Sox?"

As they ate the pizza, Brian and Deke talked shop for a few minutes about a few overlapping cases that they were wrapping up before the conversation turned to their golf league.

"You know, if we can actually beat Randall's team we have a decent shot at winning the overall title this year," Brian said.

Deke looked over the top of his glass. "Brian, you do realize that this is week three of a twenty week season, right?"

Brian laughed loudly. "Yeah, I know that. But think about it, Deke, for the past few years, we've pretty much been in second place because we take a few weeks to get up to speed. Usually, Randall and his group spend the winter months playing indoors and keeping things in shape. It's during those first few weeks that they tend to get a few points ahead of us and that's usually about the same number of points that they beat us by. But this year, we also spent some time at the dome, working on our game. It'd be a much fairer fight."

Deke shook his head. "I'll concede to your point there, but I think you're getting too hooked up in the idea of winning." He paused to look out the front window. "Of course today's rain date means we'll be playing our make-up with Randall in September.

"Too bad the golf match got rained out. I really wanted to beat him today," Brian lamented looking at the steady stream of water cascading down the glass walls of Clancy's.

"Hey, at least the match was called before we teed off, and we were able to get a table here. We've got a ball game coming on in a few minutes, good food and a steady supply of beer, " Deke said.

"Well, I think I'm still up for a little competition tonight," Brian added, nodding at a young blonde woman who had just walked in. "You guys want to see who is the first to score?"

"Son, I don't want to keep taking your money, but if you insist, I'll have no choice but to humiliate you."

Brian laughed. "Deke, you've barely had half a beer and you're already talking trash. There's no way I can lose to you. Now, him on the other hand," Brian pointed to where Dom was sitting staring into his beer. "I gotta keep an eye on him. It's always those quiet ones that'll upset the status quo, you know what I mean?"

Brian reached over and gave Dom's arm a light tap.

Dom didn't react at all. He just sat there swirling his beer, eyes focused on the bottom of the glass.

"Hey! Earth to Dom. You awake there, bud?" Brian said.

Dom's eyes flashed and it took him a second before he responded with, "W-what?"

Deke and Brian looked at each other. "You okay, Dom? It's like you're out in space or something," Deke said angling in his seat to look in Dom's direction.

Dom sighed, "I guess I've got a lot on my mind. Sorry."

"You said that before, Dom," Deke said. "Did you catch a new case that's got you baffled? You know that we'd be willing to bounce ideas around all night if you'd like."

Dom shrugged. "It's not work, or at least not exactly."

"Is there something going on between you and Bridgette that we don't know about?" Brian teased. When Dom's eyes shot an icy stare, Brian swallowed. "You want to talk about it?"

Dom peered over the edge of his glass at Brian. He took a long pull on his beer and shook his head. "The last time I checked, I was a guy, which means, no, I don't want to talk about it."

Brian just laughed. "Well that's a relief, cause neither do I! I know that she's had a real rough patch. But she's back on her feet, she'll figure it out from there." He looked around the room, his gaze pausing on the bar that sat at the center of the large room. "Now, how about we figure which of those fine looking women we're going to go after tonight?"

Deke stood and scanned the room. "Got some fine looking ladies to choose from. But there seems to be a particular brunette over by the bar, at the table near the wall. Looks like that's where I'll be working tonight."

Brian nodded. "Definitely not my type, but hey, you go for it. I'm still partial to the blonde. So, where do you see yourself going, Dom?"

Dom looked up at his two friends, shook his head before he downed the remainder of his beer. He rose and said, "Home."

As Brian and Deke looked on in shock, Dom grabbed his jacket and headed to the door and into the rain.

Once outside, Dom opted to walk instead of grabbing a cab. He pulled the hood of his jacket tight and shoved his hands into his pockets to stay as dry as possible. The rain was cold, and even with the layered waterproof jacket he felt it. It matched his mood almost perfectly. The only difference he could see between the two was that with a later sunset, the weather was several shades of gray lighter.

What was he doing? He didn't have the answer for that, and until he did, he needed to keep to himself, he decided. Brian and Deke were right, he'd gone out on a limb to help Bridgette and he'd managed to get what he considered a win for her. But was it? He stopped in the middle of a block hoping that the cold rain would wash away his restlessness.

Nothing seemed to fit. He'd been on his own for years. After Elaine had been killed, his parents had retreated slightly during their mourning. It was during this time that he had chosen his path. By the time things had been worked out, he was on his way to college. From that point on, he had relied on himself. Then he helped a woman who had blown his sting to pieces.

Suddenly the world didn't seem to fit right anymore. He found that he, a duly sworn officer of the law, had done more than just find justice. There was no more black and white. Now all he saw were shades of gray. What would happen if he acted on his feelings? How would she react? What would happen to his job? Would he put everything in jeopardy?

The phone in his pocket vibrated. He looked at it long enough to read Deke's name on the screen before he pressed the button to ignore the call. Deke and Brian were his best friends, but right now they couldn't help him with sorting out his thoughts.

Dropping the phone back into his pocket, he began walking again. He thought about the last two days in the cafeteria. He'd brought Bridgette down yesterday, hoping to help her break the ice with the people that worked in the group. And that had helped, as Lucy had apparently sought Bridgette out today. But, he remembered, Brian and Deke had maneuvered things so that he ended up next to

Bridgette. Had they seen something or was it just blind luck?

He wandered around aimlessly for better than two hours. Well, nearly aimlessly, he told himself. It didn't matter that every step he'd taken since walking out of Clancy's had been leading him to this corner. Standing just out of the circle of light from the street lamp, he looked down the street.

The squat four-story brick building stood bathed in light. Dom knew that there was a doorman who noted who entered and exited, and that it was located in one of the safer areas of DC. But none of that mattered to him right this minute.

His only focus was on the far corner of the third floor. Her lights were on. What would she think about him coming over tonight? What would he say?

He couldn't answer either question, but he turned and strolled towards the building.

Climbing the three stairs to the front door, he reached into his back pocket and pulled out a thin leather wallet. As an elderly doorman held the outer door, as he flashed his badge. "I'm heading for three-oh-one," he said.

"Yes, Sir," the doorman said. "I need to buzz you through, though." He limped over to the small desk that sat just inside the main lobby and reached down to a concealed button. "You have a good night, Sir," he said.

At the faint electronic buzz, followed by a soft click, he pulled the door open. "Thanks," Dom said as he stepped inside and bypassed the elevator heading for the stairs.

Dom climbed the stairs slowly, listening to the echo of his feet off of the concrete walls. He still wasn't sure what to say to Bridgette if he followed through with his thoughts. As he rounded the landing on the second floor he stopped. What if she doesn't want anything to do with me? He hadn't thought of that before. He was the one who had slapped the cuffs on her. If somebody had cuffed him and dragged him out of his house and then turned his whole world upside down, would he want anything to do with them?

He sat on one of the steps to ponder. The rain pattered out a steady staccato beat outside while his heart thudded out its own pattern. How could they make this work? Should they? Would she even care?

Standing, he started down the steps only to stop again three steps latter. He had to know. Bridgette was the first person he had ever felt any attraction to. He had to know if she felt anything or not. He remembered sitting with her at the hospital as she recovered. She'd trusted him and asked that he come back.

He smiled for the first time since leaving Clancy's.

This wasn't his decision. It was theirs.

They'd become friends while she had been incarcerated and he helped her out. What happened next would be up to the two of them. Friend's or something else, they'd figure it out. But right now he needed to talk to her to find out how she felt.

Turning again, he raced up the next two flights of stairs to the third floor and Bridgette.

CHAPTER 9

Bridgette was sitting on her little sofa with her feet pulled up underneath her. A cup of Chamomile tea was perched on her knee while she read a romantic thriller. The rain that pounded on her windows mirrored the setting of her book and she'd found herself totally absorbed.

She jumped at the knock on her door.

Cautiously, she set the book on the sofa and her tea on the floor. Walking slowly, she crossed the small room and leaned to peek through the Judas hole.

Her mind overloaded on what she saw. Dom? What was he doing here? She called out, "Just a minute," as she began unlocking the door.

Pulling it open she said, "Dom? What brings you here?" She studied his face. He looked absolutely…she wasn't sure. It was somewhere between excitement and despair, and that left a whole wide ocean of possibilities.

"Sorry to bother you, Bridge, but I was wondering if we…could talk?"

Okay. This was unexpected. "Sure come on in. Let me take your jacket," she offered stepping aside to let him through the door. As she hung his wet coat up, instincts from long ago kicked in. "Would you like something to drink? I've got tea, cocoa, soda and I might even have some coffee around here."

Dom paused, "Some tea might be nice."

She returned a moment later with a cup. "Come on in and sit. What's up?" she asked taking a seat herself.

"I'm not sure where to start. It's kind of confusing on one hand, and on the other it's quite easy." He looked up to her face. "I'm confused about you."

Me? Bridgette thought to herself. "Dom, what did I do that confused you? I'm sorry. I won't come down to lunch with everyone again if it's causing problems for you. I thought, I thought that we were friends."

"Bridgette," Dom finally smiled with the words. "We are friends. And no, you don't need to stay away at lunch. What's confusing me is that I feel, um, I guess the best way to say it is that I feel an attraction to you. Something that I've never experienced before."

His phone vibrated loud enough that they both looked to his jacket hanging by the door. "Maybe you should get that?" she asked.

He got up with a sigh, retrieved the phone and checked the number. "They don't let up. I'll have to call them soon, I guess." Seeing the expression on her face, he answered her unasked question. "Brian and Deke. They've each called a couple of times."

"Is everything okay?"

Dom flopped back into the chair. "I kind of walked out on them a while ago."

"Why would you leave your friends?"

"Because I couldn't get you off of my mind."

She stared at him. "Dom? I don't think I understand."

He took a deep breath. "When I first came to Hillside to meet you, formally, we were on opposite sides. It was only through the disregard of the attorneys that I ended up doing more research on you. Found out about your family and all. That's what led me to go back on a visiting day.

"As I spent time with you, getting to know you and seeing what had transpired to make you…" he fumbled for the right word. "I guess the best term would be that you misappropriated funds. I found myself caring for you. I think we became real friends, ones who have real feelings for each other. When we got the judge to put you into this program, I was so happy. I couldn't tell anybody what I really thought, how happy I truly was. All I could think about was that you were out."

Her eyes misted. "I'm a convict. That's something that I can't change, neither can you. I stole money. That's what I did, Dom. There's no nice way to put it. I took money that wasn't mine. While I may have given it to a worthy cause, what I did was to steal the money. I deserved what I got. But, I'm not sure that I deserve a friend like you."

Dom crossed over to her, took her hands and lightly squeezed. "That's nonsense, about you not deserving to have a friend who looks after you. Fine, you may have misappropriated means to get the Mambas, but you only did it after every legal step you took had backfired. I may wish you'd done it a different way, but the truth of the matter is, I'm sort of glad you didn't. If you had, we most likely would have never met. And I'd never would have started to have feelings for you." He lifted her chin, "You're the most amazing woman I've ever had the opportunity to know, Bridgette."

A single tear trickled down her cheek. "I've n-never mattered to anyone other than my f-f-family." Now the tears began to flow.

Instinct drove Dom to take the seat next to her on the sofa. He wrapped his arms around her, pulling her into his shoulder. "It's okay, Bridgette. You've always mattered. It's that other people haven't ever told you."

He rubbed her back in a way that she found comforting, and she wondered if what he said had been true or if those that had been around her for all those years had continually taken her for granted.

Her sobs slowly began to quiet. Her arms came around him and she held tight. "Thank you," she said softly.

"Are you okay?" he asked, moving her slightly so he could see her face better.

She didn't let go, but moved her face out of his shoulder. "Sorry about getting your shirt wet. I didn't mean to go to pieces on you," she said. She rubbed her eyes, wiping the last of the tears away. "After my folks were killed, I haven't had much physical contact. No aunts or uncles or cousins to give me hugs and comfort. You're the first one in over a decade to do that naturally. I can't explain how it makes me feel."

Dom couldn't fathom what it would be like to have lived through everything that she had over the last ten years, and never have had someone there to give her physical comfort. It also gave him another point to worry about. If there hadn't been a hug in ten years that also pretty much meant that she had had no experience with dating or other relationships. He was going to have to watch his step.

He shifted slightly and pulled her so she was leaning into his side. "I don't know what we do next, Bridgette. I'm finding that I'm attracted to you, in a more-than-a-friend way. I don't want to push you into something, and even more important, I don't want to jeopardize our friendship. You've become important in so many ways."

He was surprised when she tightened her arm that was wrapped around his waist pulling him in tighter.

"I don't know what to say or do either," she said before taking a deep steadying breath. "To be honest, Dom, you're the first real friend that I've had in years. I mean there were always people at work or school, but those relationships only existed within the confines of those jobs. I'm scared. You've done so much for me over these last few months. I can't afford to lose my friend, but I'm having certain feelings too."

Well, that made sense, Dom thought. "What kinds of feelings?"

She blushed. "You make my insides turn to jelly and there's a strange heat every time you touch me."

Dom smiled. "Seems like we have something in common. Now the question is what do we do about it?"

"I've got two minds about it," she said. "The one part says to not change anything, to take the safer path. The other side, the wild side, wants to see where this goes."

"Well, I showed up at your door after work hours, so I guess that gives you an idea of where I'm falling. But I don't want to hurt you. You've been through—"

"I don't want you to think of me as fragile, Dom. If we try to develop any kind of meaningful relationship, of course we'll hurt each other. We won't mean to, but if two people care for each other, they're bound to eventually do something that temporarily upsets everything. I think what's more important is what we would do after. Could we promise each other right now that if we decided to try taking things to a different level, that no matter what, we'd try to still be friends?"

"I'd like to believe that," he said running his free hand through his hair. Could he do it? Was he really ready to risk it all? "I'm willing to give it my best shot."

"That's all anyone can ask for, isn't it? To do your best." She snuggled in closer, laying her head on his chest with her arms secured around him. He gently rubbed her back. "I've never had a boyfriend before," she said. "It's nice."

His phone buzzed again so he twisted slightly and was able to reach the pocket of his coat. He removed the phone from his pocket and sighed. "I'd better take this before they decided to track the GPS in the phone and send in the S.W.A.T. team."

"Brian?" she guessed.

"Actually the caller I.D. says Deke, but if I know those guys, they're together," he said pressing the answer button. "Franchini."

"Hey Dom, you okay?" Deke asked.

Dom smiled as he heard Brian's voice in the background. "Yeah, man. I'm…I'm good right now. Sorry about bailing on you guys earlier."

"It's okay. Why don't I bring Yutz-oid here and we'll meet at your place and talk this out?"

"You guys want to head to my place, sure. I'm not there now, and probably won't be for the next, oh," he glanced at the clock on the wall. "I'm going to guess three hours or so."

There was silence on the phone for thirty seconds. "Dom, if you're not home, then where are you?" Deke asked cautiously. "You didn't get picked up for doing something stupid where we need to bail you out, did you?"

Dom laughed. "No, Deke, I don't need bail money, but thanks for asking." He paused to look at Bridgette. "I needed to get my head straightened out so I stopped by a very special friend's place."

"Dom, we, ah, called most of your hangouts. Brian and I are at my place, so where did you go?"

Dom sighed this time. It wasn't that he was nervous about letting Deke and Brian know about him and Bridgette. It was more a case of wanting to enjoy his time with her tonight. And he wanted to keep her off of everyone else's radar for a while longer. She was still the new-kid right now, and everybody noticed her. Given her past, she was already getting side-long glances. If they went public, it very likely would get much more intense.

"Listen, Deke. I don't want to get into that right now. I'm okay, I just needed to talk a few things out."

He could hear a muffled conversation between Deke and Brian, so he took advantage of the lull in his part of the conversation and leaned down to kiss the top of Bridgette's head. Her lips curved into a sensuous smile and her eyes danced with excitement.

Deke's voice came over the phone, almost a whisper this time. "Dom? Are you with Bridgette right now?"

He gulped. "What? Why would you assume that?" His voice betrayed him when it cracked mid-sentence.

"Uh-huh. That's what I thought," Deke said. "I'll keep Brian off your back, but tomorrow you're going to be answering questions, buddy."

"Right," Dom answered before the line went dead.

Well, how am I going to handle that? How could he tell his friends the truth and still keep Bridgette out of the line of fire?

"You're thinking too hard, Dom," she said.

Dom glanced down. She was still curled into his chest, her eyes were closed and the biggest smile he'd every seen stretched across her narrow face.

"Trying to figure out what I'm going to say to Deke and Brian tomorrow. They're going to press for details, and I don't want to throw you into a deeper pool than you're already in."

"You don't have to be so worried about me. I'm a good swimmer. I'll manage."

Dom continued to rub her back. "It's not that I don't think you can manage, I'd just like to be able to protect you from what some others are going to say."

She sat so she could see him. "Are you worried about what they're going to say about you?"

"No! It's not that, Bridgette. I'd be willing to try singing about my feelings for you during rush hour. It's just that I know that you're trying to find your footing within the department. This is just one more event that is going to put you under the microscope."

Bridgette sat quiet for a minute. "Tell your friends the truth, and don't skirt around the issue. If anyone asks me, I'll take the same path. I don't want to ever lie or deceive anyone again. I want to explore my feeling for you, to be with you and be honest with you. That was something I learned from my time in...inside."

"I'm sorry?" he said.

"So many of the women who were incarcerated with me, told stories of betrayals and lies. That was what put us where we were, Dom. I did the same thing. I let myself do something that wasn't honest and above board, just that one time, and it totally upended my life."

Her voice faded as she became thoughtful, and Dom guessed that she was reflecting on her choices that day.

"It's something that one day, you'll be able to look at and laugh about," he said trying to ease the tension.

"Maybe," she agreed. "But even so, I will always remember what happened when I wasn't as honest as I was supposed to be."

They sat quietly on the couch for a few minutes. "Do you want to do something tonight?"

She barked out a laugh. "Sure we could go bowling or dancing or maybe to a movie. Oh, wait," she deadpanned. "Dom, I'm under house arrest, remember? I can't leave the house. I'm sorry."

He pulled her tight again. "I didn't forget. What I was wondering was if you'd like to watch a DVD and maybe have dinner delivered."

Her eyes sparkled as she understood. "Yeah, that'd be nice. I don't have a big collection of DVDs yet, but I do have a few. They're all...you know, chick-flicks though."

"That's fine. Whatcha got?"

She stood and walked to the small table where her borrowed TV sat. Picking up three cases she splayed them out. "We've got our choice of *Letters to Juliet, Dear John*, or *Bend it Like Beckham*."

Dom frowned. "I haven't seen any of them. How about the Juliet one? I seem to recall something about that one."

"That works. Now what should we do about food?" she asked.

"I've got several places on speed dial, " he said holding up his phone. "What would you like? We've got our choices of Italian, Chinese, subs, or the ever popular pizza."

"I've really missed good Italian. Is that okay?"

Dom smiled, pressed the button on his phone. "No problem."

After the video was over, Dom stood and stretched before he gathered the takeout tray. "Thanks for the evening, Bridge."

"I should be thanking you," she said. "After all, you're the one who came over and initiated things."

He walked across the kitchen and with surprising speed scooped her up into his arms. "I'm happy about this. For the first time in weeks, I finally feel that I'm starting to get things on the right track."

He gently placed his lips over hers. She could feel the center of her core begin to heat up. Her heart began to race and thud like a drum. The kiss deepened.

She craved him. Wanted to be with him.

He pushed her back slowly. "Bridgette?" he said gasping. "I think that I'd better go. Before this goes too far."

She blushed immediately. "I'm sorry," her hands quickly covering her mouth. "I've never reacted like that before. I don't know what got into me."

"I can't blame you. I was right there with you. I'm going to say this upfront—it's never been like this before. So much more intense than anything I've experienced."

Bridgette smiled wryly. "Well, as I don't have much to compare this to, I can't say if it's more or not, but wow. Intense fits."

"I'll, ah, see you at work tomorrow, okay?" he asked brushing his fingers over her cheek.

"Yeah. Maybe we can grab a coke or something during a break?" she offered.

"Works for me." He leaned down kissed her once more before grabbing his coat and heading out the door.

She stood in the window watching for him to leave. When he exited at street level, he turned and blew her a kiss. She waved and backed away from the window before collapsing on the couch.

How had she ever gotten so lucky? A few months ago, heck, she thought, just a few days ago, she'd been facing decades alone in prison. Now she was half of a couple.

She may not be totally free, but she had freedoms that she hadn't expected to have. Her little apartment, her new job, and for the first time in her life, there was a man in it too.

Humming to herself, she started turning out the lights and got ready for bed. She had no delusions of sleeping, she was much too keyed up to even hope for a full eight hours. Dressed in her nightgown, she picked up the book she'd been reading when Dom had first arrived. Only this time as she read the words, her mind painted the scenes with her and Dom in the major roles.

CHAPTER 10

Bridgette had decided that time must have stopped the next morning while she was working on getting through the Mambas' new security

Glancing at the computer's clock for the fifth time in nearly as many minutes, she sighed. She was supposed to have a break coming up in ten minutes. Would Dom come to her workstation or was she supposed to go meet him? It was kind of fun thinking about things like that.

Tammy stopped at her desk, and then scoffed, "Do you still think you'll be able to break through their security?"

Bridgette made herself take a deep breath and count to ten before she replied. "It would make no sense for me to continue to work at it if I didn't think I'd get through. It's like any code, once you know where to start looking, the solution is usually fairly easy. Now, is there something that I can help you with, Tammy?"

The other woman sneered at her. "I still don't like the fact that they're trusting you to do things. It'd be more preferable if they'd left you in that cell to rot for the next twenty years."

Bridgette closed her eyes and listened to the sounds of Tammy's retreating footsteps. In her mind she kept repeating, "No one can make you feel inferior without your consent." It was a quote by Eleanor Roosevelt and over the years it had become one of her favorites.

"You okay?" Dom's voice asked.

Opening her eyes, she did a quick scan of the room to locate Tammy before she shook her head.

"Come on," he said gently taking her arm. "I'll buy you a cup of coffee and you can vent for a few minutes."

She grabbed her purse and followed him to the door. "How did you know I needed rescuing at that exact time," she asked when they were alone in the elevator.

"Lucy called. She said that things were being said and that it might be good to get you out for a few minutes. She was going to pull you out herself, but she's got a meeting in five with the director, so she couldn't get away."

They made their way to the little kiosk where she opted for a hot chocolate instead of the coffee. "I'm not sure what I did to her that has her so upset?" she confided after they'd found seats.

"Bridge, I can't say for certain but a few things jump out at me. First you figured out how to break through the Mambas' security from the outside faster than she's been able to do it with all of the toys here. Then, you were able to out maneuver her with those same skills a few months ago on the, uh, sting. I don't think that endeared you to her very much. And finally, I think she's still got some crazy idea that I should be dating her."

Bridgette choked on her chocolate. "What? Did you actually date her?"

Dom shook his head. "No. She expressed interest, but I had no interest. She kept trying to weasel me into doing something with her. I probably made her irate with how I was able to keep from doing anything with her."

Bridgette looked out the window. "Any suggestions on how to handle her?"

Dom shrugged, "Best advice that I can give you is to focus on what you're doing and don't let her drag you into a confrontation."

Bridgette grinned. "Wonderful. I'm supposed to find a way to work with a bully. Well it's not like I haven't done that before." She glanced at the wall clock, "I guess I'd better get back. Thanks for the cocoa and the break."

He rose with her, put his arm around her and gave her a quick kiss. "Go get 'em, Bridge."

Walking back to her cubicle, she started thinking about what Tammy was trying to do. By constantly belittling her, Tammy was trying to increase her own status. Would that happen outside of a work environment? Wasn't the gang a type of work environment?

She detoured and found Brian at his desk.

"Hey, pretty lady," Brian said.

"Where?" she asked turning to look around her. When he laughed she grinned. "You got a moment for a quick question?"

"Sure. What's up?"

She dropped her voice to minimize the number of people who could hear. "I know that when I first got into the Mambas' systems, Alex Caldwell was the number two guy. He would have been in charge of their security. Did anything change while I was...away?"

Brian looked confused for a moment. "I thought that maybe you'd heard. Caldwell was stabbed to death by his girlfriend. Ah," he rummaged through a notebook on his desk. "Here we go. He was found in Baskin's Park with forty-eight stab wounds back in late March. All wounds were consistent to a knife that was found on his girlfriend, one Justine Kildare. She took a plea deal. What are you thinking?"

Bridgette stared at a spot on the wall while she put her thoughts in order. "If he was killed in late March, then that would be what, a week or so after the, uh, sting that I screwed up? He was punished for the breach in security."

Brian leaned back in his chair. "I could work with that."

"From a different perspective. What if someone here had done something and was removed from their position? Who would take over?"

"I guess that would depend. I mean, if it's an agent their cases are just going to be divided among the other agents. But...if it's a managerial position, then it probably goes to the next in line. You're thinking that Caldwell was replaced, which would change the security measures?"

"Not exactly. But when they replaced Caldwell, his replacement would probably adapt the measures to meet his personality. If I know who took over, I should be able to tailor my search patterns a bit more."

Brian looked at his notes again. "Well, this is only a guess, and it's based on the best information that we have at this time. But if the boys and girls in the analysis department are correct, then the person who took over after Caldwell was, uh, disposed of would most likely have been Terrance Martin."

Bridgette nodded. "I don't know him well, but my last employer represented him in a few cases. Do you have an updated dossier on him?"

"No. We've been a bit short on manpower here over the past few months, so it hasn't happened yet."

Bridgette blew out a long breath. "Well, at least I have an idea who I'm playing against. Thanks for the help, Brian. I'll let you get back to work."

Riding the elevator back to her floor, Bridgette ran over the data that she could remember. Terrance Martin complained that Caldwell was too lax on the method that had been chosen to protect the gang's valuable data. She remembered that every time that she'd seen Martin while he was waiting for one of the partners, he was constantly doing cipher puzzles.

"Have a nice break? You know they're supposed to only be ten minutes," Tammy called out as she walked by.

"I needed to do a bit of research that pertains to the Mambas' case. Gave me a fresh perspective," Bridgette said as evenly as she could while walking by.

Back at her desk, she began calling up the sites that she knew had been Mamba sites. Bringing the first one up, she looked closely at the page. Nothing jumped to her attention. Methodically, she worked her way through the links. Nothing.

"Okay, what am I missing?" she asked in a voice so low that no one would hear her. "Come on! What are you hiding?"

She scrolled her mouse around the page and then stopped. Going back to the top of the page, she looked at the web address that was displayed in the browser tab. Inspiration struck. This time she checked the address of each link. There it was, the something that was off. "Now, what's the extra letter after the extension for?"

Her stomach tightened. She was sure that she was on to something, but how could she prove it?

Grabbing a pen and paper, she noted the floating characters down. None of the letters appeared in the gang name. She kept checking several of the known sites. A few sites shared links. That was what she had noticed the last time, she thought.

After an hour of going site to site, checking each link that was on the page, or embedded in the text, she sat back and rubbed her eyes. Leaning back in her chair, she studied the list of characters.

She thought back to the last time Martin had been in the law office. He'd been working on some kind of clock cipher. She lined each link up, and looked for a pattern. There were no words that she could see immediately. Taking the first few columns she found the letters GRTNE, NZMQY, QZTFA staring back at her. "Wait," she said to herself as she looked at the second group. "The first and third are only off by one letter. If I go with a cipher where an M is an A, and assume that they are constant..." she quickly began transcribing the letters. BLACK.

She reached for the phone and called Dom. "I think I may have something here. How far do you want me to take this before I show you?"

"I'm getting ready for a department briefing right now. How about right after lunch?"

"That'll work," she said. "I'll keep plugging away here. Um, could you do me a favor? Would you stop and get me for lunch?"

"Is this relationship humor?" he asked. "You want me to walk you to lunch?"

She chewed on her lip. "Not exactly. I just know me. When I get into a project, I tend to lose track of time."

Dom laughed. "I won't let you starve."

"Thanks," she said before the line went dead.

Dom stepped into the computer lab just before noon. Glancing around the room, he noticed that almost everyone in this department was getting ready for lunch. Only one station had the operator hunched over and tapping at keys oblivious to the movements around her.

She apparently hadn't been kidding about getting totally absorbed into a project. He walked over to her desk slowly, making sure that he made enough noise that she should hear him before he got there. She never looked up.

"Ah, Bridgette?"

Her head never turned, though her lips moved as if she was mouthing the words to something. What ever it was, it was much too low for him to hear.

He reached out and gently tapped her shoulder while calling her name.

Her scream stopped everyone in the room.

Bridgette panted trying to catch her breath and noticed the entire group looking at her.

Dom was too engrossed in the way her blush made her eyes more potent.

"Bridge? You okay?" he tried.

Her eyes focused on him. "I'm-I'm sorry. I got caught up, and didn't hear you."

Dom smiled. "Kinda gathered that from the way you screamed when I touched you. Good lungs by the way." He glanced down at the papers she had strewn around her workspace and the site that was currently on the screen. "Having any luck?"

She smiled. "I think so. Check this out," she said pointing to her notes. "It appears that they've added a new level of security onto what they already had. It appears to be a simple Caesar Cipher."

"Ah, you want to refresh my memory on what that is? It's been a few years since I did any training on code cracking."

"It's pretty simple." She took a fresh piece of paper and wrote the alphabet on it in order. "This part is straight forward, but we begin with every letter that we want to use. I had to make a few assumptions on this. First that they were going to use English and secondly that they'd keep all of the letters in order. Now we decide what value we want to skew this by. Let's say we want to use six."

She used the tip of her pen and counted over six letters. Below the F she wrote the letter A. "All that's left is to write the series the same way again, but this time we start here," she said pointing at the new A.

"So you're saying that the Mambas put everything into this Caesar code?" Dom asked.

"No. What they did was to modify one of the parts that they had used before. Instead of using a labeled page from several different home pages, they added floating characters into the URLs of several pages. Unless you were looking for them, the URLs, they'd probably go unnoticed. To the casual observer, they only appear as a slash with a random letter following. I'll also give them credit that they added enough on so that it wouldn't be obvious what they were doing. It took several tries before I figured out what they had done."

"What do you mean?" Dom asked.

"Let's grab lunch, and then I'll walk you through the whole thing."

Dom waited for her to grab her purse before he led her down to the cafeteria.

"Hey, Dom. Bridgette," Deke said as they pulled out chairs at the table.

"I told you, Deke, I'm not playing twenty questions with you today. We'll talk later."

Brian raised his eyebrows. "I guess I must really be out of the loop on this one." He turned to Deke, "You're going to explain it to me, right?"

Everyone laughed. "In time, Bri," Deke agreed.

Dom looked around the table. His team was here, he thought, so why not talk a little shop? "I'd like to ask everyone to meet right after lunch. The conference room up on seven is open. Bridgette has made some progress, and I think we all need to see what she's got. You two," he pointed at Brain and Deke, "can take the first layers of what she's peeled for us and begin some background work. John and Lucy, I'd like you guys there as well. The more eyes and minds that we put on this, the better off we are."

Lucy nodded. "Do you think we should pull in Tammy?"

"It might be a good idea," Dom said after a moment of thought. "I don't want her to get her nose too far out of joint, but I think we've made more progress in the last seventy-two hours than in the past few years." He paused, pulled out his phone. "Excuse me for a minute. I think Meyers should be in on this too," he said before stepping away and pressing a number.

After lunch, Bridgette carried her paperwork up to the conference room. Lucy walked in as she was setting up.

"You look nervous, Bridgette. Relax."

Bridgette took a deep breath. "I don't know why I'd be nervous. I haven't been here a week yet, and I just found out I'm running a meeting for the Assistant Director, several people on the team along with the woman who just yesterday told me she thought I should still be in a cell. Right, nothing to worry about."

Lucy walked over, draped her arm around her. "Listen, Hon, at this point you've got a few choices. You can either curl up and try to hide, or you can go for it and show everybody why you're here. I've got faith in you."

"Thanks," Bridgette managed to say despite the sudden lump in her throat.

The rest of the team trickled in over the next five minutes. Bridgette didn't notice when Assistant Director Meyers came in, but when she looked up from the computer screen, he was there.

Dom gave a few opening remarks, and explained what she had told him before lunch, and then turned it over to her. "Bridgette, I think I've covered the preliminaries. Why don't you take it from here?

"Dom gave you the basic procedure that I was able to use to begin getting through the first couple of layers. From my…past experience with dealing with this group, I know that there are several more layers in place."

Meyers asked, "Then you haven't gotten all the way through yet?"

She shook her head. "Not yet. I've gotten to a secure log in page however."

Brain was dumbfounded. "A secure log-in page? You mean that they have a network like we do?"

"Absolutely. Just because they tend to run on the wrong side of the law doesn't mean that they don't use the same technology as other big businesses. They just hide the page so that you need to go through a series of smaller steps to get to the hidden page."

A few muttered conversations went around the table. Bridgette just kept her focus on what she was doing. She looked at Dom, who appeared to be lost in his own thought.

Dom raised his voice over the others. "Bridgette, if they're running this off of a hidden page, wouldn't it be better to e-mail the link to specific people? I guess I'm not following the whole plan."

She smiled to herself. This was at least familiar territory. "In some ways, yes it would be better. But an e-mail list can be either an asset or a liability. If one member gets arrested and someone goes through his computer, there's a high probability that if a link exists, that it's going to be compromised. With the method that they have now, they can have a launch point and let people click their way through."

Dom leaned back in his chair. "But wouldn't that make it easier for someone to accidentally find their site?"

"Not necessarily. From the lead page," she said pointing to the main screen. "Everything here appears on the up-and-up. Even if I click on the follow through, nothing seems out of place," which she demonstrated. "The thing is, from the first page, the link that we needed to follow was in the menu. The second link was buried in the small text by the copyright. That link takes us to," she clicked again. "A hidden page on it's own. From here on, it alternates between being a menu item to something hidden. I'd also guess that they've got a logic sequence built in somewhere that if the computer doesn't come through a specified channel, the user is redirected somewhere else."

Dom nodded, "So what you're saying is that while it may be possible for someone to accidentally land on their log-in page, the odds are definitely not in favor of it."

"Essentially the odds are zero. You have to know where to start, what to look for or you're not going to end up here," Bridgette said.

Dom smiled broadly. "Impressive. Third day here and you've already broken through their security."

"She got lucky," Tammy quickly snapped. "Let's face it, she's already proven she could commit a felony once. How hard is it to repeat it?"

"Agent Cipone," Director Meyers said calmly addressing Tammy. "That is totally uncalled for." He looked around the table, at the face of each member. "We all know the circumstances that have led Miss Mahoney here. I know how she feels about what happened with our sting last March, and I know that she wants to set things right. I'm the one who brought her here, hoping that she could do exactly what she's just showed us. She is a member of this team, and she will be given the consideration and respect that goes with it. Am I clear?"

Bridgette held her breath. She had known that Dom had gone out on a thin limb to help her, and that he'd brought Deke and Brian along. She didn't realize that she had that much support from the brass. If nothing else, she was going to remember his speech and use it to push her forward whenever she needed that extra motivation.

"Miss Mahoney," the director said bringing her from her own thought. "You said you were able to get to a secure log-in page. Can you get through that on your own or will you need help?"

"To be honest, Sir, I can probably get through it on my own, but it's not my area of expertise. I know what I did the last time, but I have to go on the assumption that they've made changes there as well. Having someone who is a bit more versed on secure systems might be helpful."

"Agent Cipone, you will be working with Miss Mahoney."

Bridgette glanced at Tammy who was staring open mouthed at the Assistant Director.

Meyers continued, "I think with the two of you working together, I've got the two best geeks on it, and we should be through in a few days. Once we get through, we'll be monitoring every move they make and we can start to figure out the plan to take them down. Okay people, let's get to it. Mahoney? You did good, kid. Keep it up."

CHAPTER 11

Bridgette was still hunched over her keyboards while Tammy sat with her arms folded and a stern look on her face. "Tammy, I still think the password is going to be something like an acronym," she said.

"Why? What makes you such an expert on this? If you were so good, why did you tell the Director that you'd like the help?"

Bridgette sighed. "I've done this exactly once. It's not like I have a ton of experience breaking through secure pages. However, I did get through this one once before. This gang used one of the partners in my old office, so I've actually had run-ins with several of them. I'd never say that I know them, but I've been able to observe them. With that knowledge I can make a fair hypothesis on how they're going to react in a give situation. Like everybody else, they always go for their default position. It's where they feel most comfortable."

"Well I think that you're being unreasonable," Tammy said. "I've been doing this kind of work for nearly ten years—and I've always done it on the legal side of things. I think we should just let the computer at it. We've got programs that will do this automatically."

"I know we do. However if we just apply the brute-force method to this, we may be waiting a long time. Getting through this is of the essence."

"Why do you think we'd be waiting a long time?" Tammy demanded.

Bridgette stopped typing and pinched the bridge of her nose. "Look, I did some basic research before I tried breaking their codes the last time. I know that the higher the bit count on the password, the better the strength. If we assume that they require a password with at least eight characters, and that they'd allow for all normal characters to be used as well as have everything case sensitive, we are looking for a password that has a strength of approximately fifty-two. If that password has ten characters, that strength is up around sixty-five. From what I understand, utilizing the brute-force method, we can crack a code with a strength of around fifty-six in about a day, but something that has a strength of sixty-four will take around four years. Personally, I don't want to sit here for four years.

"What I'm doing is setting up a list of words that are of importance to the Mambas. The computer will try variations of these first. When I did this the last time...I didn't, um, have the access to the computer program. I had to use my knowledge of the gang members. It took me nearly three weeks to crack it, but it was still a variation of one of the words from my list."

Tammy got up and paced around the lab. "I really think that this is stupid. Why do you need to show off? Do you really think that if you break through this in record time that they're going to keep you on here? You'd be delusional. You. Are. A. Convict," clapping her hands on each word to emphasize it. "You can't be trusted. The only reason that I'm even here is because Meyers said I needed to be. And now, you're going totally off the reservation. Making up your own little dictionary based on what you know. I'm beginning to think that you're not really sorry about what you did. I wonder if you're actually a member of their gang, and you're trying to throw me off of their track while you keep helping them."

Dom walked into the lab at the end of her rant.

"Look, Tammy, you can believe anything that you want. But I'm just trying to help everybody out here. You're right on one point. I am a convict. I made one mistake, and I'm going to pay for it for the rest of my life. That fact is always going to follow me. But what I can do is use what I have to try to make things right. That's all I'm trying to do right now.

"I really don't see them making sweeping changes in their security. They got stung, they found out that I got through. They increased their layers, but the overall package didn't change much. It was the same steps that I had to go through before. That's another reason why I think that their password on this site is going to be a word off of this list. A tiger doesn't change his stripes. Neither will they."

Dom tapped on the door. "I agree with Bridgette on this, Tammy. The Director and I have had a long talk about this, and that was one of the main reasons that we asked the judge to have Bridgette help us. She is the only person that we know of that has working knowledge of their computer network. Once she gets us in, she can help us find their weak point and take them down."

"Well, whatever. It's after five. I'm leaving," Tammy said as she grabbed her things and stomped out the door.

Dom crossed to Bridgette, wrapped her in his arms and kissed her. "It'll be all right."

"Oh good grief!" Tammy's voice came from behind them. "I forgot my sweater, and this is what I find? No wonder you're always sticking up for her, Franchini. Does the Director know that you two are an item? Maybe if I tell him, he'll revoke her parole and send her back to where she belongs," she said throwing her sweater over her shoulder and marching for the door.

Bridgette and Dom stood behind the main desk, stunned.

"I think we may have opened Pandora's box," Bridgette said.

"I was hoping that we could avoid the attention for a while. But," Dom said pulling her closer. "I know you, I more than like you and I'm going to stand with you. No matter what happens."

"I like hearing that," she said resting her cheek on his chest. The problems that were threatening them would be there later. But for now, she wanted to enjoy feeling wanted.

Dom stopped off by his house long enough to change clothes and grab a bag of groceries that he'd set aside before he left for work. His phone rang just as he was opening the door. Setting the bag on the small table by the door, he pulled out the phone.

"Yes, Brian."

"Hey, Dom. Listen Deke and I were thinking that maybe we'd get together for a couple of drinks. So, anyway, I'll be over in about twenty to pick you up."

"Thanks for the invite, Bri, but I'm not going to be here. I'm heading out right now. Thanks for the invite and all."

"Huh? You sure you can't make it? You feeling all right?"

Maybe Deke hadn't said anything to Brian last night. That'd be nice, Dom thought. Of course with Tammy catching him and Bridgette in an embrace, he was sure that it was going to be all over the office tomorrow.

"Yeah, Bri. Positive I can't make it. Thanks anyway."

"'Kay. Catch you later," Brian said and the line went dead.

Less than thirty minutes later, Dom was standing in Bridgette's tiny kitchen playing chef. He'd brought along two quarts of his mom's homemade spaghetti sauce which he now had heating. The sausages were browning nicely, and the water for his rigatoni was just beginning to boil.

"Smells good," Bridgette said coming back from the bedroom. "It's been a long time since I've had a good home-cooked meal." She stopped and looked at the two wine glasses sitting on the table. "Um, Dom," she said, her voice shaky. "Don't you remember one of the conditions of my house arrest is no alcohol?"

Dom looked at the glasses and smiled. He grabbed the bottle from the counter. "Sure I remembered, that's why we're having sparkling grape juice tonight," he said offering her the bottle.

Now she smiled. "That's thoughtful. Is there anything that I can do to help?"

"Nope. It's just going to be a few minutes before—"

The knock on the door startled both of them. Bridgette eyed the door warily before she crossed and peered through the Judas hole. Turning back to Dom, her eyes were wide. "It's Brain and Deke."

"So much for Deke keeping things to himself," Dom muttered.

Bridgette released the lock and opened the door. "Hi, guys. What's up?"

Deke pushed past her looking worried and carrying a laptop. Brian followed. "We need to talk," he said

Dom stopped stirring the sauce and studied his friends' faces. "Something's up. What's going on?"

Deke opened the laptop and set it on the small counter. "We've got a few things that you need to be aware of," he stated. "First, I think you should know that we got a message from Tammy. She basically states that you two were involved with each other prior to the sentencing. She made sure that that particular message went to Meyers, Jacobs and Daniels. She's hoping that they'll rescind the house arrest and re-sentence.

"Next is the fact that she claims to have caught you both in a compromising position today at the office. And lastly, it appears our friends in the Mambas are aware that Bridgette is no longer inside, and have now put a price on her head."

Dom recovered first. "Can you run that last part by me again?"

"We don't know how, but somehow the conditions of Bridgette's sentence became known to the gang leaders. Pete Telebrue is a city cop. He's one of the guys I play hockey with over at the ice rink. He made a bust this afternoon, and the perp wanted to trade. He told Pete Bridgette's name, said that she was working for the FBI and that the bosses had said that there was a hundred grand for whoever silenced her."

Bridgette gasped.

Dom set down the spoon and crossed to her. Gently rubbing her arms, he pulled her in. "We'll get through this. Don't worry."

"D-don't w-worry?" she said. "I'm not worried, I'm scared! Why? How? Oh," she sucked in another breath, placing her arm across her stomach as if trying to hold her self together. "What am I going to do, Dom? I can't run and hide. I'm trapped here."

"We'll figure this out," Dom told her. "How much does the Director know?" he asked Deke.

Deke shrugged. "I was with Bri at Carmello's when the message came from Tammy. We were just discussing that when Pete called. We figured that getting this message to you was a tad more important than touching base with Meyers."

Dom looked at Bridgette. She was still pale from the triple shock. Which one to deal with first?

"Listen guys, dinner's ready here. Why don't we eat and we can toss things around as we go?"

"We, ah, don't want to cut into your time, Dom," Brian said with a silly grin on his face.

Bridgette's breathing was almost back to normal Dom noted when she stood. "Please, join us. I'm sure that there's enough," she offered.

Dom served the pasta and sausage right from the stove, and

they crowded around the small circular table in the kitchen.

"Okay," Brian said between forkfuls. "Let's get the record straight here. What's the story with you two?"

"Don't you have any tact?" Deke asked, shaking his head.

"I'd say that I'm not being nosy, but I am. However, I think we need to know where they are as well so we can know what to do about the threat," Brian answered.

Dom tilted his head. He could see Brian's question. On one hand the price on Bridgette's head was the biggest dilemma, but depending on what happened with the message from Tammy, they could both be suspended while things were investigated. It was a mess.

"I think," Dom said. "I'm going to call Meyers. I want to talk to him about this upfront. No hiding anything. We're going to nip Tammy's outburst in the bud before it can cause too much more damage. She's got something against Bridge, and that's coloring this. Maybe we can get one of us assigned to work with her, Bridgette, until the threat against her is eliminated."

"We've got to do something," Deke agreed. Looking to Bridgette he asked, "Do you own a gun?"

Bridgette stared at him wide eyed, like a deer in headlights. She swallowed a piece of sausage noisily. "I'm not allowed to own any firearms. I, um, kind of lost that right when I pled. I'm sorry," she said when Deke's face fell.

"Not your fault," Deke assured her. "I knew that, and forgot. My apologies."

"It's okay," she said.

After dinner, Bridgette washed the dishes and Brian dried while Dom talked to Director Meyers, pacing like a large cat. "Yes, Sir. We're all at Bridgette's apartment now. Yes, Sir. Thank you."

"I don't want to know, do I?" Deke said from the couch where he'd been working on his laptop.

Dom sighed. "Meyers wants to talk to all of us. He said he'd be here in about forty-five minutes."

"That just makes for a wonderful evening," Brian said shaking his head. "How'd he sound?"

This time Dom laughed. "He said he wasn't surprised at all about Bridgette and I getting together. He's worried about the rest of it though."

"Oh blast!" Bridgette said from the kitchen causing the three men to turn.

"What happened?" Dom said rushing to her.

"I just realized that I'm going to have people over. It'd be nice to be able to offer them a cup of coffee if they wanted it, but I don't have any. It's on my list of things to pick up when I get to go shopping Saturday. But I don't have much in the house right now."

Brian looked over at Deke and then back to Bridgette. "We'll go," he offered. "You guys supplied the meal, Deke and I'll pick up coffee and dessert. Be back in thirty, okay?"

With a quick nod, they sped out the door, leaving Bridgette and Dom alone.

Dom pulled her into his arms, and kissed her, and was pleased when she joined in the fun too.

"Okay, start from the beginning," the Director said. He was sitting at one end of the couch while Bridgette sat at the other with Dom sitting beside her in a chair from the kitchen.

"Bridgette and I both felt something. Last night, I ended up coming over here around seven and we talked. We decided that we were both adults and free to pursue a relationship. We did hope that we could keep this out of the office for a little while, but we both knew that it wouldn't be long before it got out. Today, around five, I went to the computer lab to pick Bridgette up and discuss our dinner plans, and overheard a conversation between Tammy and her. They were disagreeing on the best way to proceed with getting through the security for the Mambas. Tammy left, so we were alone and I kissed Bridge. Tammy walked back in during our embrace," Dom said. "That's all that happened on that front."

"You forgot the part where Tammy said she was going to try to get me put back in prison," Bridgette added.

"As for the two of you having a personal relationship, that's between you. Either of you goes AWOL for a little after lunch nookie and we'll be having a slightly different discussion. Am I clear?" When both had nodded, Meyers continued. "Now the part that is more concerning to me right now is how did the Mambas know about the deal that was struck?"

"I may have a string to pull there," Deke volunteered from his position at the table. "I talked to my friend Pete who first told me about things. After he called me, he did a little digging. Seems his bust today was a low level drug dealer who is related to a few key people, mainly the Martins and the Caldwells."

"Wait a minute," Brian interrupted. "You're saying that the guy who your pal busted today was related to Alex Caldwell and Terrance Martin?"

Deke simply nodded, but it was Meyers who voiced the question. "Those names sound familiar. Why?"

"Alex Caldwell was the head of the Mambas' security. At least until a smart red-head broke through and caused a bit of mayhem," Brian said with a glance at Bridgette. "Caldwell, was, uh, tossed out of the gang—permanently. His girlfriend is awaiting final sentencing for his murder. The Mambas needed a new security officer, and the likely choice was Terrance Martin. Bridgette stopped by this morning and asked me about the likely candidates, and I told her."

"By knowing it was Terry that I was playing against, I was able to figure out how to get through the first few layers," she acknowledged.

"Which brings us to the meeting after lunch," Captain Meyers noted with a nod.

"But it still doesn't tell us how they found out about Bridgette's deal," Dom said.

"I was getting there," Deke said. "Anyway, Pete's perp was scheduled to appear in court the same day of Bridgette's sentencing, coincidently in the same court room. He'd been arrested by a federal cop for transporting stolen weapons somewhere in Virginia two days prior. He claims he was standing by the door and he heard the ruling by the judge. Since his cousins were already mad at him for getting busted with stolen merchandise that week, he told them what he'd heard."

"What'd he get out of it?" Brian asked.

Deke smiled. "Well, he's not dead. At least not yet. And they let him try smuggling some dope up this way, which is when Pete got him."

Meyers chuckled. "That knucklehead should've quit before. At this rate he's going to be a three time loser in one week."

"Pete thinks that his arrests may be the least of his problems. If the calculations are correct, the weapons bust cost the Mambas nearly a million, and the drugs were closer to two."

Brian whistled. "This guy had better think about turning state's evidence, then heading for the witness protection program. If he chalked up three million in losses in one week, you can be pretty sure that they're going to be going after him soon."

"I'd agree," Dom said. "But knowing all that, what do we do for Bridgette?"

The agents looked at each other, shaking their heads.

Bridgette gnawed on her lip and then stopped suddenly. "May I ask a question?"

"Sure. Go ahead," Director Meyers answered.

"Thank you. If the Mambas are going to try and kill me, would I be correct that they'd have a very hard time getting to me at the office?"

"A hard time? Yes. Impossible? No. If they've got someone working inside our office, they may utilize that person to make the attack," Meyers conceded. "But the reality is that they'd be more likely to go after you on your commute. Easier to get to you if they don't need to pass through a metal detector."

"Captain, who knows about this threat? I mean outside of us," Dom said waving his hand around the room.

"This is it. What are you thinking Franchini?"

"One of us," Dom said pointing to Brian, Deke and himself, "will pick Bridgette up and take her home each day. We do it randomly, so no pattern can be established. That offers her the best protection for her commute. During the day, assign Brian to work with her. Outside of the computer lab, he's the best on the computers. Something tells me that they'll be into the Mambas' files tomorrow. Brian knows what we're looking for. That will alleviate the tension between Tammy and Bridgette, and keeps someone that we can all trust with her throughout the day."

Meyers thought about it for a brief moment. "That should work. I'll also speak with Tammy about her behavior. Both about your relationship and her interactions with coworkers." He stood to leave. "Until tomorrow, then. You can decide who is on driving detail in the morning." As he was sliding on his jacket, he turned to Bridgette. "Try and relax, Miss Mahoney. We protect our own. We'll get you through this, unscathed." He turned and let himself out.

Bridgette turned back to see the three agents playing rock-paper-scissors to decide who was driving in the morning. Her new life was nothing like her old one had been. But it was nice to know she had friends to count on.

CHAPTER 12

Bridgette walked into the small room at the back of the office and for the second time found herself surprised this morning. She hadn't been surprised when she checked on the progress of the password cracking. The program had struck gold on the third word on her list. Well, she thought, it was a variation of that word, but it was a logical one. Nor had she been surprised when Director Meyers had come into the computer lab a few minutes after nine that morning and had told her that she was to report here at ten-thirty to begin working with Brian. What did surprise her was how Tammy had looked when she came back in from her meeting with the Director. She didn't say anything, but she looked miserable. The second surprise turned out to be the room she and Brian were going to be working in.

The computer lab she'd been in for the past week was large and open. This room looked like a storage closet that somebody had crammed a mid-sized table into. The table was pushed up against the back wall and centered in the room. Bridgette looked at the space between the table and the side walls and wondered if either she or Brian would fit. There appeared to be enough room between the table and the door that someone could open it from inside, but only if they stepped out of the way. Two computers sat at the far end of the table, leaving just enough room on the surface for a few folders to be laid opened. Brian came in a few minutes later. "Sorry I'm late, but…" he had stopped so fast that the coffee in his cup sloshed over the rim. "Do you think they could have found a smaller room?"

"Glad I'm on the petite side of things," Bridgette said with a smile.

"Well, this is going to be interesting. Ready to get to work?" He asked squeezing into his chair.

Bridgette craned her neck an hour later to see Brian's computer screen. "What are you looking for?"

"Something isn't quite right here," he said pointing at the screen. "I can understand that the group wants to appear to be transparent to, um, new distributors, but I still think there's another layer here. Did you…" he hesitated.

"Brian. Just ask. Did I what?"

He huffed out a breath. "Sorry. It's still kinda weird, you know. Having been involved in, ah, busting you for messing up the sting and all, and then to be sitting here working with you, drawing on your knowledge to try get further in. I'm afraid that I'm going to say something that's going to permanently lodge my foot in my mouth."

Bridgette smiled. "Brian, listen, I can fully understand the confusion. When I came in the first day, I stared at those metal detectors and wondered how long it was going to take for someone to throw me back in a cell. But, you've yet to ask your question. Go ahead, ask. We're both aware of the past. Let's work on the present."

Brian nodded. "When you were getting ready to relieve them of the gun funds, how far in did you go?"

Bridgette sat back in her chair. "About this far. On the old site, there was a link to view their financials. I followed that, and then had to figure out how to get into their bank accounts. From there it was easy."

Brian flopped back in his chair. "Wait. You're telling me that they had a link so that anyone could see their financials? What in heaven's name were they thinking?"

"I guess I can see this from your viewpoint. Here's an illegal group putting up how they're doing so that anyone can see it. But I saw it differently. I saw this as a recruiting page. Almost a prospectus, if you catch me."

"A prospectus? Really? How?"

Bridgette pursed her lips trying to come up with the right words. "Okay, let me try it this way. When an investor wants to invest with a company, the company sends them a listing of what assets they have, along with any debts and what the current cashflow is, right?"

She waited until he nodded before she went on. "This web site is essentially the same thing. They have a listing of what," she used her fingers to make air-quotes, "'enterprises' they're involved in. They show their monthly reports to prove they've got the cash they're claiming. If you look at this from the point of view of either a want-to be member who was sent to the page by a member or as the leader of a rival gang who's looking to do business with this group, this is really a sales tool for them."

Brain looked shocked. "Holy conundrums, Batman. Maybe this is why we've always been unable to get into these gangs' tech. We only see it from our perspective. One that makes us wonder why they'd be so stupid to put this out there like this. We've been overlooking the obvious."

He went back to scanning the page on the screen. "So, what do you think the probability is of them having that same material available here now is?"

Bridgette crossed her legs, tugged at her pant leg to cover her electronic bracelet, and started to gently rock in her chair. "They didn't change much else. I was able to figure out the basic way in because it was essentially the same yesterday as it was several months ago. If I was a gambler, I'd bet that if we poke around enough here we'd find a way to tap into everything that was here before."

Brian snorted. "Well, you were sure dead on about the password stuff. I still can't believe that Tammy was so ticked at you this morning. I wasn't sure if she'd just taken a bite of a lemon or if she had major constipation."

"Well, there's no question that she really doesn't like me," Bridgette said. "The only hope I have right now, is that Director Meyers talked to her. Maybe that will be enough to get her to let things go."

"You really haven't figured her out, huh?" Brian asked looking up from his keyboard. "She was upset before because after your, uh, demonstration during the botched sting, you showed her up. Then the Director pulled some strings and you end up working here. Just rubs a little salt in her open wound. Within a week, you've succeeded in doing what she's been unable to do for the last three years." Brian took a breath and wiggled his eyebrows, "But the part that she sees as the biggest insult is that you got Dom. She's been after him since she started working here. And here you come along, and poof. Dom's off the market."

Bridgette stared at him with her mouth hanging open. Slowly her hands covered her mouth. "Oh, God. What have I done? I've got to fix this." She stood up quickly, her head swiveling from side to side. "I…I'm going to have to break things off with him. I can't get caught in the middle of this!"

"Bridgette. Relax and sit down," Brian said remembering what they'd taught him at Quantico about talking a person down using a calming voice. "I need you to relax now and take a seat."

She looked at him, her eyes were wild and tears stained her cheeks. Slowly she nodded and slumped back into the chair.

Brian let out the breath that he'd been holding in a whoosh. "Just because Tammy has been going after Dom for the last few years, doesn't mean that Dom shares her interest. In fact more than once, he's told her right out that he's not interested. He is however interested in you. He's not only said it out loud, but he's shown you with his actions too, hasn't he?"

Bridgette could feel the rhythm of her heart regaining it's steady tempo and her lungs no longer felt like they were empty. She thought about what Dom had done. In every case, he'd been the one to make the first move. He'd come to see her while she'd been incarcerated. He was the one to bring up his feelings. He'd been the one who'd kissed her. He had come to her apartment two days before, professing his feelings.

She smiled. "You're right. He has said it and shown it to me, yet it took you to make me see it. Thank you, Brian for getting me through that little panic attack and helping me see this better. It may not help the situation between Tammy and I, but at least I can see it from her perspective somewhat. Eventually, we might even be able to be in the same room and not snip at each other."

"Maybe," he said. "Now that we got the dilemma between you and Tammy at least identified, are you ready to see if we can find some hidden tabs?"

"Yep," she replied leaning over her keyboard.

"Keep pacing like that, you're going to wear a rut into the floor," Deke commented as Dom once again turned around and began to cross the room.

"I can't seem to help it," Dom said. "I feel as though we're missing something. What did we overlook?"

Deke's attention turned back to the open file that sat on the table in the small conference room. "I'm not sure that we've actually missed anything. I think it may be just the opposite, there's nothing for us to see just yet."

Dom glanced over with a puzzled expression.

"Okay, Dom, let me try it this way. Remember as a kid, the closer you got to Christmas the more you anticipated it? I guess I see this whole scenario in a similar way. For the first time that we know of, OCT has gained access into one of the largest gangs in the Northeast. We just don't know what kind of good stuff we're going to find when we start opening all of those packages."

Dom stopped pacing so his back was towards Deke. "I can see your analogy. But to follow along with it, don't you remember that one gift that you got every year from your Great-Aunt Hilda? You know the one that you opened it, smiled at her while you mumbled thanks, and then hid it on the floor in the back of your closet so that it would never see the light of day? That's how this is feeling for me.

"We may have found a way into their systems, but from the intel that Pete brought us, Bridgette's in a heap of trouble. How did we miss that step? How were they able to get someone that close and then report to the bosses?"

Deke pushed up from the table. Shoving his hands into his pockets, he sauntered over to where Dom still stood with his eyes closed, and placed his hand on Dom's shoulder. "You can't hold on so tight, man. We've been given a heads-up on this one. Bridgette and Brian are making progress inside the Mambas' on-line stuff. We'll hear about anything that potentially threatens her."

"I hope so," Dom said. "Okay, let's run the list of—"

"Let's go gentlemen!" Director Meyers said sticking his head through the door. "We've got an officer involved shooting at the federal court building. You two take it. It's related to what was discussed last night."

Deke maneuvered the SUV as close as the traffic would allow. Dom kept his trained eyes on the surroundings. The street in front of the courthouse was blocked by law enforcement vehicles of every shape and size, and the buildings were an eerie color from the flashing lights. But nothing disguised the amount of damage caused by the attack.

"What the heck were these guys using?" Dom asked as he stepped out of the vehicle.

Deke could only shake his head. "Meyers said it was a shooting. This looks like the aftermath of a small bomb going off."

Dom stopped and crouched, pointing to a bullet hole in a brick next to a shattered window. "Is it my imagination, or does that appear to be the result of a fifty-caliber?"

"I'd like to disagree with you, simply because I don't want to believe that it is, but I'd say your assessment is right. Who the heck uses a fifty to shoot up the courthouse?"

Dom stood and started towards the primary scene. "Are we sure that the courthouse was the target?"

"What? You can't be seriously thinking that somebody would try to do an assassination using something that size do you?"

"If I was the leader of a group, someone who didn't mind what collateral damage occurred and I wanted to send a strong enough message? Who knows?"

Deke frowned. "Well there's some joyful thoughts, huh? Let's hope that that particular hole was caused by something that happened many years ago."

Dom smirked at his friend's comment. Sure, they could pretend that it happened a long time ago, and hope that the impact marks, like the brass cartridges that littered the street, had just been missed by professionals everywhere for all those years. "Yeah. Right. Keep thinking it, pal, and maybe it'll even come true one day."

They flashed their badges towards the perimeter guard, ducked under the yellow crime scene tape and walked to where the temporary command center had been set.

"May I help you?" a frazzled looking woman who was tapping at a computer keyboard asked.

"This is Agent Kirkpatrick and I'm Agent Franchini. Director Meyers asked us to come down and lend a hand. Being that this is a federal court, we need to be involved, but right now we have no problem leaving the local force in charge. Can you tell us the current status?"

The woman stopped typing. "I'm Officer Mary Beth Hall. I was the first responder to the scene. Last report was that the officer who was hit was in serious condition. It was a through and through in the shoulder. Medics who treated at the scene said it looks worse than it probably is, and that barring any unforeseen problems Pete should make a full recovery. He was escorting—"

"Wait!" Deke snapped. "You said Pete?"

"Yes, sir," Hall said looking confused. "Detective Pete Telebrue was escorting Travis Allen from his arraignment. Just as they cleared the building, all hell broke loose. It sounded like automatic cannon fire." She shook her head as if trying to make the memory erase from her mind. "It was bad. Real bad. Detective Telebrue was hit once, Allen was hit three separate times and there were at least another dozen civilians who were either shot or injured from flying debris."

Dom looked to Deke who hadn't moved since hearing his friend's name. "Deke? You gonna be okay on this?"

"Good God. Pete?" Deke said. He closed his eyes, pinched the bridge of his nose and took three deep cleansing breaths. When he opened his eyes again, they were steady, but Dom noticed the intensity.

"I'll make it, Dom," Deke said. "I'm going to have to make a few calls; get his condition and call his wife Cheryl. But I'll be okay."

Hall shot a glance to Dom. "Whoever did this wasn't worried about leaving evidence. They left shell casings for three city blocks."

"How long after it happened did you get on the scene?" Dom asked.

"I was already here. I was escorting another prisoner in. I passed Detective Telebrue on the steps to the lobby only seconds before the first shot. I pushed my charge down kept him covered until the shooting stopped. I pushed him into the first floor holding room, handcuffed him to the wall and went back out. Total elapsed time, less than a minute from the time the shooting stopped. I'd already called it in before I had him in holding, so it was only matter of minutes before we had the whole gang here."

"Who is in charge of the investigation?" Deke asked.

"Well, that's a good question. Normally, this would be assigned to a detective, but right now the big-wigs are having a meeting in there. There are representatives from the local unit, Secret Service and I think even from Homeland Security, and now you're here from the FBI. Nobody really knows where this falls, and it seems like they're all trying to be the alpha."

"Well that just makes this perfect. Everyone is too concerned about getting the glory for running the investigation, and they're all too busy to work it," Dom said. "What do you think, Deke? Shall we grab the camera and take a walk and document everything we can. Maybe while they're in there seeing who can pee farthest we can get going on a few leads."

"Let's get cracking," Deke said. "Could you run back and grab the gear? I want to make a few calls."

It had taken nearly an hour to get clearance to walk the scene and take the photos that they needed. Now three hours later, they were standing directly across from the doors of the courthouse. "Is it me, or is the damage really localized there?" Deke asked pointing to a spot on the concrete stairs that was now pot marked with hundreds of small craters.

"I don't think that whoever did this was trying to hit the

courthouse. The target was specific," Dom answered. "I can't believe with all this that we don't have more dead. I think the bigger question is who were they after specifically?"

Deke stared over at the chipped stairs and the blood stains that were still too visible. "I'm thinking that it would have to be one of the people who was hit. They sat here, evidenced by the amount of casings here, until they were pretty much set. Yes, they kept firing as they fled the scene, but they stayed here until the job was done."

They turned to walk back to their SUV. "Do we have a list of the deceased yet?" Dom asked.

"Well, Allen didn't make it to surgery. Died enroute. Two other civilians died. One on the table, the other from complications."

Deke slid into the driver's seat and they pulled away while Dom processed the information. Only three casualties from this? Amazing. "I think we may need to get a good look at the surveillance videos," he finally said. "Something doesn't make sense. There had to be nearly a hundred casings there. A lot of shots for the relatively small number of hits. It's almost as if they fired enough warning shots to get most of the people down and then focused on their target."

"Dom, the reality is that we have a pretty good idea who's behind this. Travis Allen was the Mamba gang member who got busted twice in the last week for various things."

"Yeah, I was thinking about that," Dom admitted. "If they're using that kind of fire power to bring someone down, it scares the life out of me that they're after Bridgette. How do I keep her safe?"

CHAPTER 13

"I can't believe that it's been two days since that shooting, and all of the government agencies are still fighting over who has jurisdiction," Bridgette said as she and Dom made their way through a throng of people who were all inside the Old Post Office for lunch.

Dom held her hand as he led her to the far back corner of the complex. "It seems that since this place is a government town, everything is a political hot-potato. I think what it is, is that each of the so-called leaders of these organizations want the publicity for their own careers. Of course, all that's happened is we've given the perpetrators a forty-eight hour head start to get rid of the incriminating evidence."

"Where are we going?" she asked as they started climbing stairs to the second level.

"Well, I thought it'd be nice for the two of us to get away. You know, a little time alone? Thought I could take you out to lunch. My first thought had been to have a picnic, but with the current situation, and the fact that we haven't made much progress on the, uh, threat on you, I figured it'd be better to stay indoors and out of sight as much as possible. This just seemed to be the best idea."

They came to a small table nestled into a corner by a small window that overlooked a bright flower garden.

A small woman dressed in a maroon uniform with an overenthusiastic smile came over. "Welcome, welcome, welcome. My name is Jane, and I'll be your server today." The lunch specials were reviewed and selected and Jane hustled back to the kitchen.

Dom reached across the table and took Bridgette's hands. "This is something that I've been looking forward to for awhile. Taking you out on a date. Seems we kind of jumped into the whole relationship thing without really getting out together first."

Bridgette bit her lip. "My, um, circumstances don't really allow it. I'm allowed a little bit of leeway for travel and unforeseen events, but I'm pretty much home bound for the next year." She sighed. "I really wish that we could go out, and be a normal couple. But…" her voice trailed off.

Dom stroked her cheek. "It doesn't matter to me, Honey. I'm just happy that we're able to spend time together."

"But don't you wish that it was different? Shouldn't you be able to take your date to dinner and then go to a club to dance? I feel terrible that you're not hanging out with your friends after work like you used to. Brian said that you guys used to get together at one of the sports bars to watch the Orioles play. If you're with me, that can't happen."

"Hey," Dom said lifting her chin. "I'm where I want to be. I'm not going to be sad or upset that things happened the way that they did. If just one thing had changed, would we have ever met? Would I have gotten to know you the person? I'm not sure about that. But I do know that right now, this is where I need to be. I can be very content to go to your apartment and, I dunno, watch videos or have dinner in. We can be creative about what we do."

"This means a lot to me, Dom. It really does. I can't say that I have much experience with dating. Before my folks...I went out a few times. After my mom died, I was too tangled up with just trying to survive for the first few years. I didn't make time to do it. After I started working at the law firm, I thought that I'd figure it out, but I didn't fit socially, plus I had my own agenda that I kept working on. Trying to figure out a way to break the Mambas.

"I'd go out with a guy maybe once a year or so, but nothing that ever inspired me. We'd go see a movie or something and that'd be it. It never went any further," she said while swirling the ice in her glass. "I guess I'd never found what I was looking for. Then I screwed up your sting, and the rest is history."

Dom reached across the table for her hand. "You can't change the past, and you don't know the future. What we have is a present. It's a gift that we should enjoy."

"Enjoy your lunch?" Brian asked when Bridgette squeezed back into her chair.

"It was very enjoyable, yes. Thank you for asking. Have we made any more progress?"

Brian leaned back in his chair and folded his hands behind his head. "I'm not sure that I'd call it progress," he stated. "By following what you'd outlined before, and what we'd started this morning, I was able to find, um, I'm not really sure what to call it. It would be the equivalent of Facebook for gangbangers. Can you believe it? These guys have their own social media chat rooms and messaging sites."

Bridgette sipped her Diet Coke. "Unfortunately, I can believe it. From what I recall of the ones that came through our office, they were incredibly egotistical. But you'd think that they'd draw the line on their openness."

Brian sighed deeply. "There doesn't appear to be any limit

to what they'll put out there. There is one thing that you need to be aware of. Actually two, but I think that the one is a little more concerning at this time." He pulled two sheets of paper from under his computer and slid them across the small table.

Bridgette looked at them, reread them and then bit her lip. "Seems like they really want to make sure that I'm, uh, no longer a threat to them, huh?"

"Looks that way." Brian changed his position so that he was now leaning on his forearms perched on the table. "Bridgette, you know that we're doing everything that we can to protect you. I mean, I'd love to tell you not to worry about this, but the reality is that you've got to be ready for anything. Keep vigilant about your surroundings." He paused to think. "You've never been through agent training. I'll work with Deke and we'll come up with a scaled down version to help you through this."

"I'm not sure what's worse. When I was in prison, I never knew when the attack was going to come. I was fairly certain that it was, and they did a pretty good number on me," she said while her hand rubbed subconsciously over the scars from the attack. "But at least then, I had an idea of where to look. With what they put in this message, I've got no clue at all. It's almost as if everyone is out to get me."

Brian nodded. "I get the picture. That's why I think we need to give you some basic training. I, uh, also took the liberty to send copies of this to Lucy, Dom, Deke and Director Meyers. We're going to be meeting about this today at four."

Bridgette frowned, "Well I guess it is better to have a team looking out for me." She flipped through the pages again and looked back to Brian. "You said that there were two things. What's the second?"

"Well, that's part two of our four o-clock meeting. I'm not really sure what it is, but it's got a few of our well known names setting up some kind of meet. No idea of why, but we have the time and place. Now all we need to do is figure out how to get ourselves there," he said.

"Why don't I start looking at that file? It's less threatening to me than this other stuff is, at least on a personal level. Maybe I'll have something worthwhile to contribute this afternoon."

Bridgette slid into the empty chair between Brian and Dom with less than a minute to spare. "You've got a smile that reminds me of the cat who got the canary," Dom said.

Before she could answer, Assistant Director Meyers stepped to the head of the table. "Okay, people let's get down to work. We've made some decent progress on our assault against the Mambas. In the last week, we've found ways into what they consider their most secure electronic areas. I'm going to have Agent Moran and Miss Mahoney bring us up to speed on that in just a moment.

"Before I do, however, I want to update you on another matter. Forty-eight hours ago, an attack was launched at the courthouse, which resulted in several deaths and multiple injuries. The brass has finally finished dancing, and we've been cleared to begin working the case. Agents Franchinni and Kirkpatrick, you will be working this case as leads. Everything that you compile goes directly to me, and you may use the rest of our little group here to bounce ideas off of, or for drone work. Questions?"

Deke raised his hand. "Sir? Just wondering, if we're the leads, who are we working with at the other agencies?"

Meyers leaned back in the chair. "Right now, you guys report to me. I have to oversee everything that you're doing. From there, I report to DHS and Secret Service." Meyers consulted the notes that he'd brought in. "It seems that we were able to get a video of the shooting from the Metro Police. It will be available for the two of you to view when you're ready. Now then, let's have the report from..." he looked up from his notes and saw Bridgette whispering something to Dom.

"Miss Mahoney? Something that you'd like to share with the rest of us?"

Bridgette blushed, but nodded. "Sir, with all due respect, from what I've heard around the office, the one victim of the shooting who sustained the most injuries was a known member of the Mambas. While Brian and I have been working on data from the Bandit's site, no one has come right out and claimed responsibility for the shoot nor has there been any direct messaging about it that would indicate that it was an order from higher up. But I'm wondering if there is a connection. If my understanding is correct, isn't the victim the one who Deke's friend arrested recently? If it is the same person, he's personally cost the Mambas a ton of money in the last few days."

Meyers nodded as he thought through what she was saying.

"Director," Deke spoke up. "For what it's worth, I'd agree with Bridgette. My suspicion is that the Mambas weren't happy about what Allen had cost them recently. This is a gang that in the past has shown a very short fuse. They're quick to anger and explosive once they start moving."

"If you and Franchini think it will be helpful, we can run the video now for everybody, before we get to the main part of the report," Meyers said. When everyone nodded, he inserted a DVD into the player and pressed the play button.

The scene on the wall screen was split into four segments. One was focused on the court house, one on the intersection near the courthouse, and the other two were from one block north and one block south.

Bridgette watched as a gray Hummer came into view on the screen depicting the block north of the courthouse. At first glance, the vehicle didn't stand out since it wasn't speeding, and showed no outward signs of causing problems. Then, about half a block before the courthouse, a figure emerged from the sunroof. He kept his head down as he affixed the legs of the bipod to the roof and secured a large automatic rifle to it. His head came up as he prepared himself for the shooting, and Bridgette gasped.

"That's Manny Thomas," she whispered. "His older brother, Hector, used to run with Angelo Rodriguez. If I remember correctly, Hector is like Angelo's second in command. Manny was, I'm not sure what it's called, but he was the heavy hitter."

Meyers paused the video. "Miss Mahoney, are you saying you can identify the shooter?"

Bridgette stared at the screen, into the eyes of Manuel Thomas. "Yes, Sir."

"How well do you know him?" Deke asked.

Bridgette let out a long sigh. "Fairly well, I'm afraid. I went all through school with him. We were never close or anything. By the time we were in fifth grade, Manny had started tagging along with Hector. Of course, Hector wasn't big in the Mambas yet. That happened while Manny and I were in high school. We were in tenth grade, and Manny came into English class just covered in bruises. He was bragging about how his brother had gotten promoted, and he'd gotten beaten in early. He was thrilled."

She felt a hand squeeze her knee. Not in a hard you-need-to-stop way, but in a more I'm–here-for-you-if-you-want-to-talk way. She placed her hand over Dom's and squeezed back as a sign of thanks.

"I didn't run with that group, but I sort of knew who the leaders were. I didn't have much contact with any of them over the next few years, until I was working in the attorney's office. That was the next time that I saw Manny. One of the partner's was going to be representing him in a wrongful death suit. Some how, he'd managed to get out of the murder trial, but I'm not sure how."

Meyers looked around the table. "Thoughts?" he asked the

table at large.

Several conversations erupted around the table. Bridgette just stared at the picture on screen. There was something that she should have recognized, she was sure of it. The nagging feeling that she was missing a key point was relentlessly echoing in her head. She flipped through a few of the pages of notes that she had printed off.

She paused on one, looking at the time stamp of the message. It had been sent the day of the shooting, only minutes after Allen had been gunned down. Unfortunately, there was nothing that she could interpret from the message. There were no spaces between the letters and their random pattern was unreadable to her, which was why she and Brian had opted to bring it along to the meeting. Maybe someone here could crack the code.

Her mind kept coming up with questions, and unfortunately she didn't have the answers. If Manny wanted to let Hector know that he'd accomplished the goal of getting rid of their leak, would he have taken the time to compose an email? Wouldn't it have been easier to have stopped somewhere and use a phone? If they'd coded the message, wouldn't it—shouldn't it—have been an easy one?

Bridgette closed her eyes and forced herself to concentrate. The word BLACKMAMBA kept forcing its way through. How, she wondered, was that the key? She thought back to the first time that she had attempted to break through the security of the Mamba site. She had done copious amounts of research to figure out how they worked. She pulled in a deep steadying breath and forced her mind to quiet down, and ignore the conversations that were around her.

Another word popped into her mind. Vignere. To most, this word meant nothing, but to her a relatively old form of cipher began to form.

Tearing a sheet of paper off of her notepad, she began by writing out the alphabet on the first two lines. On the third line, she shifted everything over by one letter and repeated it, and then repeated it several more times.

The first five letters of the unknown message were BWLGX. If she was right whoever had sent this had used a Vignere cipher with BLACKMAMBA being the keyword. Using the matrix she had just come up with, she went to row B, the first letter in the keyword, and looked to find the first letter of the message. The B was in the A column, so she wrote it at the bottom of the paper. The second letter of the keyword was W, so she found it in the second row, looked up to the first row and found the corresponding letter to be an L. She repeated the same steps for the other letters. When she was done, she looked at the bottom of her sheet: ALLEN.

"Gotcha you smug bastard!" she nearly shouted.

The room was eerily silent. "May I ask what exactly you got?" Director Meyers asked.

"Sir, when Brian and I got into their system, we found that they had, for lack of a better term, a message board. Several of the messages were in plain English, but they didn't tell us much. Seeing the video with Thomas executing Allen made me think that I was missing something." Her stomach was fluttering as if it were filled with butterflies, but she pressed on. "I think that they're using a Vignere cipher with the keyword being blackmamba. When I tried it out briefly on a message that was time stamped less than ten minutes after the shooting, the first few letters spells out the victim's name."

Brian reached over and grabbed her papers. After a brief look he said, "At a quick glance, I'd concur, Sir. I'd recommend that we run this through the computer ASAP. Now that we have an idea of what they're using, we might have enough to start pulling them in."

"Moran, set that up to run overnight. We'll reconvene at ten tomorrow to see if we have any results. Mahoney? Good work."

Bridgette leaned back in her chair and placed her hand on her still jittery stomach as she watched the others file out of the room.

"Nice work, Bridge," Dom said. "Can I buy you dinner tonight?

We can celebrate a little."

"Dinner would be nice," Bridgette replied. "But—"

"I know the rules," Dom interjected. "I'll pick up whatever you'd like and be over around seven, okay?"

Bridgette smiled. "That works. And I think I'm in the mood for some red meat. A bloody steak sounds good."

CHAPTER 14

Bridgette shut down her computer and glanced around the small room. Brian had strewn his personal belongings across more than half of the flat surfaces in the room, while she had meticulously kept the few items she had on or in the small file cabinet. "You realize, Brian," she said when he walked in. "That although we may work together, I'm not cleaning up after you in here, right?"

Brian looked at the covered table. "I'd like to plead insanity." When she just gave him a glare, he raised his hands. "Okay, okay, I got the message. I'll clean this up now." He started grabbing the papers and cramming them into a stack. "By the way, I dropped off the encrypted messages with Tammy. She's going to run them through the encryption program for us."

Bridgette looked wary. "You didn't tell her that I'm the one who figured it out did you? If she knows about that, she'll sit on it forever."

Brian flashed her a smile. "No worries. I didn't say exactly how we came up with it, but that during our meeting about the data from the Mambas, we figured it out. She promised me that it will be ready in the morning."

"Okay. At least I hope it's okay. If she's doing this for you, she'll probably have it ready on time," Bridgette said, sneaking a quick glance at her watch. "Well, I'm going to run up and talk to Lucy before I leave. See you."

Brian waved at her as she headed out the door.

Walking through the hallways was an interesting endeavor. She may have only been here a week, but it was obvious that there were definite dichotomies that lived and thrived in the FBI in the forms of how they treated each other. Some people that she encountered smiled and greeted her with a wave or a nod, while the opposite end of the spectrum was populated with people who turned around at the first sight of her.

It's high school all over again, she thought as she made her way to Lucy's cubicle.

"Hey, Bridgette!" Lucy called from behind her.

Bridgette spun to see her friend jogging up the hall. "I was just coming to see you. What's new?"

Lucy shook her head, "It's the same old same old. We're trying to keep up with the request for the various investigations. Everybody wants what they want yesterday, if you know what I mean. How about things at your end? Have you had any luck getting into the files you were trying to break?"

Bridgette grinned, "I guess you could say that we're making progress. Brian and I were able to get through a few levels and into their message boards. I think we may have found the code to breaking their encrypted messages. We'll know more tomorrow."

Lucy raised an eyebrow. "How can you even think of going home if you're getting close to something like that?"

"Easy. I think I figured out the keyword that was used. Right now the computers are chewing on it. If I'm right, when I come in tomorrow, then all of those encrypted messages that Brian and I pulled will be readable. Not much that I can do." Bridgette sighed. "Of course, just because things here are running smoothly doesn't mean that everything is."

Lucy sank into her chair, and in a practiced motion pulled two cans of Coke from the small refrigerator under her desk. "So if things here are okay, what's eating you?"

"Not sure. I guess I'm nervous. Dom's coming over for dinner tonight."

Lucy stared at her friend. "So? You've had him over for dinner before, right? What makes this any different?"

"It's been a weird week. First off, Dom and I have started seeing each other. Romantically. So, after I figured things out today, he wants to celebrate. There hasn't been any one to share the ups and downs in my life for more than a decade. So the whole thing throws me off. Secondly, I'm not cooking tonight. He says he's going to take care of things. So now I'm worried that he's going to mess up my kitchen, that I'm not going to have the right pans or whatever. It almost sounded like he was thinking of getting take out, but I'm not positive. And then what in heaven's name do I wear? Should I dress fancy? He said this is a celebration, but I'm kinda stuck at home."

Lucy surprised Bridgette by laughing. "Whoa, hold on," Lucy finally managed between guffaws. "Do you always make things harder than they have to be?" When Bridgette only glared back Lucy shrugged and continued. "Look, let's take your concerns one at a time, okay? As far as you and Dom seeing each other, I think that that's wonderful. He's looked happier than I can remember these past few days. You're worried about the ups and downs, well think of it like this, riding a roller coaster is a bunch of fun and it's all ups and downs with the occasional loop thrown in for good measure. Getting scared once and a while is a good thing, and it can be fun too. And, like riding that coaster, riding with someone else makes it even better. Enjoy this.

"Don't worry too much about the food tonight. If Dom says that he's got it covered, then he does. You said that he wants to celebrate your breakthrough with you. If it was me, I'd probably go a little dressier than business casual, but you could always ask him what he'd like. Of course, he's a guy, so you're going to have to be ready to determine how far you're ready to go—"

"What? How far I'm ready to go? What are you talking about, Lucy?"

"Sex. Guys only think about one thing, honey. They want to know if we're going to put out."

Bridgette closed her eyes and fought back the bile that was rising in her throat. She'd never even thought about sex. With losing her parents so young, she'd been thrown into the deep of the pool and had spent all of her energy trying to figure out how to survive. Her dating experiences hadn't gone much beyond a single date if even that far. Would Dom really expect her to do that? "Oh, God, I don't think I can go through with this tonight. I'm…I'm going to call him," she stammered trying to pull out her phone, but her fingers wouldn't cooperate.

Lucy touched her arm gently. "Bridgette? Relax. I don't think Dom's going to force you to do anything that you don't want to. Come on now breathe. Breathe, Bridgette, you've got to breathe."

Dom tugged at the collar of his shirt. It seemed ridiculous to be nervous about going over to Bridgette's for dinner. But he was.

He'd never been someone that would have been termed vain, but there he was, studying his reflection in the mirror on the back of the bedroom door. "I'm freaking myself out," he mumbled.

The alarm that he'd set on his phone sounded reminding him that it was time to get out of the house and pick up the flowers that he'd ordered from the florist.

Rain pelted the windshield of the car as the wipers kept time with the song on the radio. He heard neither. Instead his mind was focused on the woman who had over the past few weeks had claimed his heart.

Dashing into Wanda's Flowers, he went to the back of the shop. The woman who worked the counter didn't look up from the bouquet that she was currently arranging. "Good to see you again, Dom," she said with a drawl that hinted at a life further south.

"Wanda," Dom answered, reaching over the counter to give her a one armed hug. She may have been old enough to be his grandmother, but she was one of the first friends that he'd made when he had first moved to Washington. He had been a young agent, fresh out of Quantico and looking for a place to rent. Wanda owned the building that housed her florist shop on the ground floor and had five apartments above. He had planned only to stay there for a year or so, but had stayed until he had bought his house in Alexandria a few months ago.

"Long time, no see. How are things going, Sweetie?"

Dom shrugged a little. "They're going. Some days are better than others, but we keep muddling through them. How are things here?"

Wanda glared over the top of the thin glasses she wore. "Business is okay, I guess. I haven't had any more problems with those thugs that you and your friends ran off last year. Of course, I think that they're still trying to intimidate some of my customers. Thankfully we're doing all right with the on-line sales and deliveries."

"Well, I'm glad that those bums are leaving you alone for the most part. We'll keep our eyes open and see if we can get them off of the streets all together."

Wanda looked at him carefully. "So, you've got a special girl. Anyone I know?"

"I'd ask how you figured that out, but I'm sure that it's obvious.

And, no, I doubt that you'd know her."

"You need to bring her in, so I can meet her. I take my role as substitute grandma pretty seriously."

"Wanda, that's not going to be possible right now," when he saw her expression he continued before she could ask. "It's complicated. Really. She's got very strict curfews." He figured that that was about the best that he could do to describe her house arrest without giving too much information out.

"Hmmm, she's met Brian and Deke, right?" Dom nodded, so Wanda continued. "So it's okay to let her meet cops, but not your florist?" she challenged.

"Wanda. I can't explain the reason that she can't come in to meet you. Maybe I can set something up where I can take you to her. Like I said, she's got really strict curfews."

Wanda looked at him suspiciously. "I'll figure things out. Now then, I suppose you'd like your order?"

Dom flashed a smile. "Thanks, Wanda."

As she took his credit card, Wanda smiled once more at him. "You take good care of her. I've never seen you so protective of any of the other girls that you spent time with before. She must be very special."

"She is," Dom said, wondering how Bridgette was going to react to getting flowers for the first time. If her reaction was anything close to what he anticipated, he would vow that he'd bring her flowers at least once a week for however long they were together.

"Oh, my...they're so beautiful," Bridgette said with her hand covering her mouth. Even then, the tears now streaming down her cheeks told the story. "Oh, Dom. I've never....no one's ever..." She could barely get the words out. She had read stories and seen movies where the hero makes a romantic gesture and brings the girl a special bouquet, but she had never been on the receiving end of those gestures. Until now.

She closed her eyes and reached for him. Letting her mind record every detail of this moment. His smell, his smile and the feeling in her chest where her heart threatened to leap out from sheer joy.

He set the arrangement on the counter and pulled her into his arms. "Just because no one's ever given you flowers before, is no reason that I shouldn't."

"I can't explain what this means to me, or what it does. But oh my, it makes me feel amazing." She pressed her cheek to Dom's chest and opened her eyes to glance at the arrangement once again. "They really are beautiful, Dom. Thank you." A dozen pink roses were arranged to form a heart around two small white lilies and a large white gardenia. "Where did you ever find such an amusing arrangement?"

Dom still held her close, his chin now rested on the top of her head. "My old apartment used to be directly over a flower shop. The lady who owned the building runs the shop, and has for nearly fifteen years. Anyway, I moved in to the building right after I got my appointment to the Organized Crime Taskforce. Wanda took me in under her wing, acting as my surrogate grandmother. She'd like to meet you, and will probably harangue me until I find a way to get you there."

Bridgette pushed back slightly, "Um, Dom, I don't see—"

Dom pinched her lips together. "I know that we have to work within the confines of stuff, but let me think about some ways that we could make it work."

The doorbell rang, and he deftly moved her aside so he could answer it. "Perfect timing," he said seeing the delivery girl from the restaurant. He took the folder with the bill, signed it and handed it back to her. Closing the door, he carried the bags to Bridgette's table.

"What's with all the bags?" she asked trailing slightly behind him.

He turned to stare at her. "When I said I wanted to celebrate your success tonight, what I really would have loved to do was to take you out to the finest place in DC. Since that's not a possibility, I decided to bring Enrico's to you. This way we get to share a romantic dinner that neither of us has to cook."

Bridgette dabbed at the corner of her eye. "I'll get the plates," she said turning to the cupboard, wondering how she had managed to find someone so well suited for her.

The rare steak melted in her mouth, and she wished she could try to talk the chef out of his recipe for the potatoes. They were like nothing that she had had before. "That was a fantastic meal. Thank you." Reaching across the table she took Dom's hand. "When this year is over, I'd like very much to treat you to a meal at Enrico's. Maybe by then, I'll have a car and I can even drive us over," she said with a wink.

"I'll put it in my calendar. Are you ready for dessert?"

She rubbed her stomach and shook her head. "I don't think I could eat anything right away. Will it hold for a little while?"

"Sure. I had them send over a few slices of their chocolate peanut butter pie. I put them in the fridge while you were grabbing the utensils and stuff."

"Good thinking. What's up next on our celebration, while we wait for room for pie?"

Dom rose and cleared the table. "Well, we could just sit on the couch and cuddle up and talk for a while. Doesn't have to be anything outrageous."

The room was bathed in soft light from the candles she had lit while Dom had finished washing the dishes. Dom had sat at the end of the couch, and she had leaned into him and was enjoying the feeling of his arm around her shoulder. "This has been an amazing end to a great day," she said.

"I'm glad that you liked it so much. I was a little nervous about taking such liberties with dinner. You know, ordering it, having it delivered to your place. I was afraid of stepping over that invisible line and have you think that I was pushy."

She smiled and tipped her head toward him. "That's okay. I was so nervous, that I almost cancelled on you. Of course, it wouldn't have worked too well, since you knew exactly where I'd be." Her eyes closed again. "I can't say thank you enough for what you've done for me. And I don't mean just tonight. If you hadn't broken some rules and come to the prison, I'd still be there. Instead, I've been given a wonderful second chance, I have a job that I'm finding very fulfilling, and I'm getting to spend time with you. I even have friends, which may not seem important, but I've really felt alone since my mom died. There just wasn't time for others in my life." She sighed, " I guess that makes me sound selfish, that I wouldn't make time for other people."

His arm squeezed a little tighter. "I think that everyone of us is a bit selfish. But how can you say that you didn't have time for others? The reason that we crossed paths was because you were doing what you thought you needed to do to protect others. That doesn't make you selfish, that makes you strong and brave."

"You make me sound like a hero, Dom, and I'm not."

"Maybe you don't see yourself that way, but that's what I see when I look at you. You took on an entire gang to try and save city. If that's not a hero, I'm not sure what is. But, let's not worry about heroes right now, and enjoy the moment we have right now."

"Okay," she said, wrapping her arms around his chest. "Are you ready for pie?"

"Sure," he said as he started to move.

"No, I'll get it," she said. "You took care of dinner, let me handle desert." Walking to the kitchen, she thought if he wanted to think of her as a hero, who was she to argue? In her mind, he was the hero. He was brave and kind and strong, and he did it all on the right side of the law. And because of who and what he was, she was going to push herself to work harder to follow his lead, and be a woman who was worthy of his affection.

CHAPTER 15

Dom watched her get the plates and the pie. She had had a look on her face when she walked out of the room that made him think she was in the middle of an internal debate. It only made him want to go to her more, to be there for her in any way that he could.

He was sinking fast, and he knew it. But, he admitted to himself, he'd be glad to go under for her. Of course, there were some details that would have to be worked out if this relationship went anywhere.

He was a cop, and as such, was required to have a side arm at all times. Technically, she was a woman with a criminal record, who was now forbidden to have a weapon in the house at all. Right now he could use the muse of being there to protect her from the Mamba threat, but that wasn't going to work forever. He had no idea of how they were going to resolve that issue, but he decided, that was a question for another day.

She was coming back in, carrying the two plates and two steaming cups on a tray. But it was the sparkle in her eyes that drew his attention. He'd seen eyes like that before. His mother's had lit up like that when ever she looked at his dad, even after they had been married for thirty years and survived the death of their daughter. She was a woman in love, he thought.

"I made tea to go with the pie," Bridgette said setting the tray down on the little table. "Figured it would go nice, and it's supposedly one of those decaffeinated versions, so maybe it won't keep me up tonight."

Dom accepted the tea with a smile, and he knew that it wouldn't be caffeine that prevented him from sleeping tonight. It would be the memory of her, and the way that she looked right this moment.

Her red hair glowed in the flickering candlelight, and her lips curved into a sensuous smile. But it was her eyes that captured his attention and took his breath. They sparkled like polished jade, dancing with excitement and desire.

He brushed her cheek lightly. Her eyes dropped slightly while her smile widened. It was hard to tell in the candlelight, but he would swear that she blushed.

"What are you thinking about?" he asked.

"I'm...I'm trying not to think too hard right now. I'm not sure what I'm doing, so I'm trying to fumble my way through." She raised her hand, "Sorry, that didn't come out right. It's just, I've never allowed myself to get to this point before, Dom. I don't know what's expected. Or what I should expect."

Dom set his cup on the table, and turned so he could face her. Gently, he lifted her face so she could see his face, so she could understand what he said next was the truth. "Bridgette, I need you to know that I have no expectations about our relationship only hopes and possibilities. I know that you've been through more than any individual should have to experience, and you've not only survived it, but you've excelled at it. You are absolutely remarkable. And I want—no, need—you to understand, that I will only go where you want us to go. You have the power here."

He leaned in and kissed her. Once. Twice.

The third time his lips touched hers, her hands gripped his hair and pulled him in. She couldn't be sure, but she thought that the soft moan that she heard very likely came from her, but she was too preoccupied in the moment to worry about it. Her heart was beating faster than she could ever remember it. Where had the fire in her belly come from? It was unlike anything that she had ever experienced before.

Her mind had quick flashes of other kisses she had had over the years. First with her family and then with her limited dating. Nothing she had experienced anywhere else had felt like this. Nothing had made her desire her partner in this way.

She felt his lips trace the line of her cheek up to her forehead, and thought that her head was going to explode.

His hands were now on either side of her face and he pulled back slightly. His breath had the faint aroma of chocolate and peanut butter. It was mesmerizing. He moved back in, again his lips on hers but this time his hands went to her back pulling her in closer.

A strange ringing sensation echoed in her head. "Do you hear bells?" she asked dazed.

"Hmmm? Do I what?" Dom answered.

She noticed that his eyes were glazed over, possibly from passion, and she wondered if hers looked the same. "I...keep... hearing...ringing," she managed between kisses.

Dom's eyes suddenly focused. "Oh for Pete's sake," he said shoving up from the couch and bolting to where his jacket hung on the back of the door and with the irritating phone in a pocket. "Franchini," he huffed.

Bridgette watched him from the couch. When he'd pulled the phone out, he'd been frustrated, perhaps even aggravated. But as soon as he had heard the caller's voice, he had become intense and focused. She listened to his side of the conversation.

"Yes, I'm with her now," he said tipping his head. "Okay, we'll be there in thirty minutes." He moved the phone away from his face and held it out to Bridgette. "It's the Director. He needs to speak to you."

Cautiously, Bridgette took the phone. "Hello?"

"Miss Mahoney, this is Assistant Director Meyers. There has been a development in the Federal Court Shooting case that is going to require your presence at headquarters. I have already made arrangements with the Department of Justice, and you have been granted permission to leave your residence tonight in the company of a Federal Agent for the purposes of returning to work to help us with this. As per my conversation with Agent Franchini, he will bring you in and return you home after we have dealt with this new situation. Do you have any questions?"

Bridgette took a deep breath. How was she to guarantee that this was legit? On the other side, these were the same people who had worked to get her into this program and given her this job and the director said it had been approved. "I don't believe I do at this time, Director. I will be in as soon as possible."

The line clicked off and she stared at the phone. "What's going on, Dom?" she asked handing it back.

He shrugged, "Don't really know at this point. About all I can tell you is that this happens every so often. We'll be working a case and then something unexpectedly falls into our lap that sends everyone scurrying back in to look at the new evidence. Welcome to the world of federal cops." He shrugged into his jacket. "Do you have everything that you'll need?"

Bridgette looked down at her outfit. She had chosen the pleated slacks and tailored blouse for tonight. It was a bit dressier than she normally wore into the office, but it would definitely work. "I need to grab my purse from the bedroom," she said heading down the hall.

"What's the status?" Dom asked as they rounded the corner into the conference room they had used earlier that day.

Bridgette tried not to notice the stares that were coming form around the table. They weren't focused on her. Or at least not exactly. They seemed to be concentrating on her hand, which was currently entwined with Dom's. She tried to convince herself to relax. Everyone in this room had known that she and Dom were involved with each other, this was just the first time that they had seen the undeniable evidence.

"Not one-hundred percent sure," Deke said. "Meyers said be here, so we are. But from past experience, he doesn't pull this very often, so I'm guessing that it must either very hot or very volatile."

"Sorry to pull everyone in tonight, but we've had a few things that fell into our laps in the last few hours," Director Meyers said as he entered the room and dropped a thick stack of papers onto the table. He efficiently moved to the computer keyboard and typed in a few codes. "As all of you are aware, we didn't get the data from the shooting until this afternoon. At our earlier meeting, Miss Mahoney deciphered a bit of their coded messages. The original intent was to let it run overnight, meet in the morning and look at what we have. And that was my plan until just over an hour ago, when Agent Jeff White called me about an urgent matter." Meyers held up a single sheet of paper this time. "For those of you who don't know White, he runs the watch in the evenings here. He often checks on the progress of the computer runs to see if anything is time sensitive."

Meyers pointed a remote at the screen and what Bridgette assumed was a scan of the letter that he held in his hand now appeared on the big screen. "As you can see here," Meyers said. "Our friendly gang is planning to hijack an arms shipment that is scheduled to arrive in Virginia at oh-seven hundred tomorrow. The fact that they are planning this is scary enough, but they way they have planned to do it is horrific."

Bridgette started reading the rest of the message on the screen. They were really planning to cause a commuter train accident to tie up traffic and reroute rush hour traffic? Her stomach curled at the realization that the Mambas were willing to sacrifice innocent people to cause a diversion so that they could carry out their larcenous plans. "Oh good God," she whispered.

Her insides were numb. She could see her father and Lisa walking up the street from the little diner they'd gone to pick up lunch. She had opted to stay with her mom to shop for Lisa's birthday present. The shopping hadn't taken long, so they were out on the sidewalk by the little gazebo in the town square where they had planned to have lunch.

She remembered looking up, seeing Lisa and their dad walking, arms linked, carrying several bags, both of them smiling and laughing. Then the world flashed intense white before she was plunged into darkness.

"Bridgette," Dom whispered while shaking her. "Hey, Bridgette, c'mon snap out of it."

She heard the concern in his raspy voice and blinked several times. Her eyes were wet, and no one in the room was talking. Instead they were all looking at her.

"Miss Mahoney, are you all right?" Director Meyers asked.

"I, um, I'm sorry, Sir. I had a flashback. The realization of what they're planning to do, sacrificing innocents to carry out their plan, brought back the way that they killed my dad and sister. It shouldn't surprise me that they'd do this, as it seems to be their typical way of doing business. It…just caught me off guard. I'm sorry."

Director Meyers only nodded. "I should have thought of that before I had you read this file. I'm aware of your background, and this probably should have been handled better." He let out a sigh.

"I'm hoping that you can help us stop this event before it happens. It was your knowledge that has gotten us in this far."

"I'll do what I can to save someone else the heartache that I live with, Sir."

"Okay, then," Meyers said. "Here's the game plan. Franchini and Kirkpatrick, you two are running with Moran and Mahoney. Get through the rest of the messages that are there. Find out exactly what their plan is. We've got the timing here," he pointed to the big screen. "Get us the details; where, who and when. While you four are doing that, I want Stevens and Manning to begin working on how we're going to interrupt their plan. I've got fifty members of the tactical team on standby. They'll be ready when we are. Start by figuring out how to prevent that train wreck. Once our computer team has the plan deciphered, we can continue to improve the defensive plan.

"Daniels," he said looking at Lucy. "I want you to get things organized so we can implement what ever plan we come up with in a moments notice. You know what communications we're going to need regardless of what we do, so that's a place to start. Again, once details become available, you'll have them."

Bridgette rubbed her eyes and wished for some ibuprofen. The wall clock said it was 4:38, but her body was no longer functioning the way she would have liked. Between the eyestrain from staring at the screen, the headache from the reading and worrying and the lack of sleep, she was about done.

She looked around the room. Dom, Deke and Brian all had their shirt sleeves rolled up, and none of them were wearing a tie, but they looked almost as fresh as they did during the regular day. "Is working without sleep something that they taught you guys in one of your training classes?" she asked trying to stifle a yawn.

Deke leaned back in his chair and stretched his arms over his head. "It comes after doing it so many times throughout your career. The adrenaline courses through you, your mind is working on the task and it's like taking a hit of something that makes you cruise. Don't worry, you'll get there eventually."

Bridgette shook her head in disbelief. "I don't think so, but hey, who knows? How are we doing so far?"

"Actually," Dom answered. "We seem to be doing fairly well. I know that it doesn't seem that we are, but look at the progress that we've made. We've been able to identify the inside man at the warehouse who was going to place the tracking device in the truck so they could follow it." He checked his watch, "And in a little more than two hours, he's going to get a very interesting wake-up call when he's picked up."

"That's going to mean that they're not going to be able to have the timing that they want. It keeps them off balance," Brain added. "I also think that we have a decent chance of keeping them from getting their guys in to pose as cops. You've got to admit, it's a pretty ballsy thing to do. Cause a traffic diversion and then have gang members pose as traffic cops to direct the flow away from the scene. But since we sent out the alerts to the various authorities they should be able to keep track of their people. May even be enough so we can keep the weapons from being hijacked at all."

"But what about the people on the train?" Bridgette wanted to know.

Dom placed his hand on her shoulder. "We're doing everything that we can on that point. You were the one who broke their codes. With that, we found that they were planning to hit the train with a rocket propelled grenade once the truck got to a specific point. The unfortunate part there is that they can fire that from wherever they choose."

"But," Deke interjected. "They have to have a clear path to the train, and they want the tuck to be in a specific locale. By preventing the tracking device from being planted, we should be able to keep them in the dark about the whereabouts of the truck."

"Maybe Meyers will be able to get the company to send the truck on a different route altogether," Brian said.

Dom continued, "We also have a list of the major players who are involved with today's production. Since each of these fine upstanding men have a dossier here, we have recent pictures which we've armed the tactical team with."

Bridgette slumped back in her chair and stared at the ceiling. "If only there were some way to know exactly where the attack was going to take place. I would feel so much better if we knew that we could prevent it from happening." She waved her hands, "I know, I know, we've got eyeballs out there looking for them, but I wish I could pin point it exactly."

They each nodded and continued to look at the reams of paper that were now strewn across the table. Somewhere in this mess was the answer they were looking for, she thought but where? What had she overlooked?

Sitting up, she grabbed a stack of the communications that had already been deciphered and began reading through them. What baffled her was the repeating code that no one knew, VSTM14B.

She culled out each sample that had that code on it. In each one, the phrase following the code had what she thought of as code words. Hotel-One, India-Fourteen, Oscar-Three. What was the connection?

Bridgette spread the papers out in front of her. Each code word was specific to an individual. Could this be part of their positioning? "Hey, guys, look at this?" she said and then showed them what she was looking at.

"VSTM14B?" Dom asked five minutes later. "I think Bridgette is on to something, but for the life of me I don't know what."

Bridgette sipped a cup of tea, "If we assume that these are

positions, how do we know where they—"

She sprang up, "Of course! These are locations on a map! Think about road maps. The have letters on one side, and numbers on the other, and points of interest are located by using the grid."

"I'll buy that," Deke said. "But what map?"

"They'd need to use a map that was widely available and easily obtainable. Everyone who was involved with the operation would need access to it," Bridgette said.

"What about a tourist map?" Dom asked. "They're available at every rest stop in the state and no one bothers to keep track of who gets them."

"But what about the code? The VSTM14B?" Brian demanded.

"Virginia State Tourist Map?" Bridgette suggested.

Deke nodded as he was tapping on his keyboard. "I think we have a winner." He spun his computer screen around. "The latest version is from 2014. Best guess would be that the B would indicate the back, or side B of the map."

"Let's take it to Meyers and he can get it to tactical," Dom said. He smiled at Bridgette, "How'd I get so lucky to be dating the smartest girl in the Bureau? You're the one who figured out how to save all those people. So, how's it feel to be a hero?"

CHAPTER 16

Bridgette slumped back on her couch, a cup of Earl Grey tea in her hand and closed her eyes. It had been too long of a day for her to function any longer, and now instead of being able to crawl into her bed and try to sleep for the next twelve hours, she was playing host to Lucy.

"How can you be tired?" Lucy asked as she walked back into the room with a can of Diet Coke.

Bridgette opened one eye and glared back. "Let me see," she said. "I got up yesterday before six to get ready for work. Put in a full eight-hour day, including having a few major breakthroughs in the case I've been assigned to—and yes, it's still a surprise to me to have been assigned to a case—then, after work, Dom and I had a date-slash-celebratory dinner. We were just, ah finishing desert when the call came in. I then pulled an all-nighter, which is something that I haven't done since college and even there I didn't do it often. I managed to come home long enough to grab a change of clothes and go back to work the details of the tactical team's interception of several members of the Mambas. I think I'm allowed to be tired."

"Baby," Lucy laughed. "I guess I figured that you'd be bouncing off the walls tonight. I know that with the adrenaline rush I am. I mean, heck if I'd been responsible for cracking the intel like you did, so that tactical could stop the entire hijacking event and prevent the deaths of untold numbers of people, I wouldn't be able to sleep for a week."

Bridgette sat up, and looked at her friend. "I guess I don't understand. Dom made some comment very early this morning, asking me how it felt to be a hero. But I'm not. I just put together some pieces of a puzzle. I didn't really do anything. So why is everybody so impressed, and giving me credit for all of these things that I really didn't do?"

Lucy set her drink on the table. "Let me see if I can set you on the right path here. You don't see what you've done as anything outstanding, is that it?"

Bridgette shrugged. "Well, not really. I was just doing what I was supposed to be doing. I mean, let's face it, I was ordered by the judge to work there. I didn't do anything extraordinary."

"Bridgette, my friend, you may not have done anything that you think is extraordinary. But maybe that's because you yourself are extraordinary. People in the Bureau have been trying to get into those files for years. You come in and get through things in just a few days. You figured out the way they tried to hide their communications by cracking their cipher—without the use of computers I might add—faster than any one else in the department has managed to do it in the last five years, even if they were using every available computer. When you got called in last evening, you didn't just hit the floor trying to keep up, you made connections that nobody, and I do mean nobody, else saw. Even after you'd given us the basics on what you'd found, I still had trouble tracking it.

"What I'm guessing is that you don't see yourself as everyone else does. We're all in awe of you because what you seem to think is simple is so far beyond the way we think, that we're running behind just trying to catch up." Lucy paused for a sip letting her words sink in. "So, when people like Dom or Director Meyers talk about your heroic efforts, they're being one-hundred percent honest. Remember, heroism isn't only something that is accomplished by great feats of strength or bravery. You used you mind and were able to save every life on a train that was other wised doomed."

"I guess I can see your point," Bridgette said. "But it still seems unreal to me. In so many ways. I mean everything that has happened to me over the past several months."

Lucy smiled wryly. "Well you've definitely had some experiences that the rest of us at the Bureau haven't. But I think that after seeing you in action over the last few days, almost everyone who was questioning the benefits of having you on board would have to be giving things a serious second thought."

Bridgette went to the kitchen and returned with a bag of cookies. "Would that include Tammy?"

"Well, she may be more of an exception."

Chewing on a chocolate chip cookie, Bridgette asked, "Is it because of her desire to date Dom?"

Lucy burst out in laughter. "Her desire? Let's be honest about this, shall we? She's been obsessed with Dom since the first day they met. Always going out of her way to do things for him, trying to win his affection."

"And then as far as she's concerned, I just happen to come along, a little con who steals what she thinks should be hers. That's just perfect."

Lucy reached into the bag for another cookie, then pointed it at Bridgette to drive home her point. "Maybe the bigger question is, who did Dom see? From everything that I can see, he's totally smitten by you. You've got him under your control right now."

Bridgette's face paled. "I don't want that! I don't want to control anybody. Heck, I can barely control me. He made the first move, not me. How's that for control?"

"Girl, he's under your spell," Lucy said shaking her head slowly. "Look, you said that he made the move, right? Why? Because you made him want you—"

"I didn't do anything! I was just being me. I, uh," she covered her face with her hands. "This can't be happening. I don't have that kind of power or whatever."

"Bridgette, honey," Lucy said. "It's not about doing anything special. He sees you differently than you do. It makes you attractive to him, and he can't help it. It does however put you in the driver's seat. I mean, tell me about what happened with your dinner date."

Bridgette looked over to the bouquet of flowers that still sat on the table. "He brought me flowers, which I'll admit to crying over. Nobody had ever done that for me before. Then he had dinner delivered, and the steak was exactly the way I like it." Bridgette sat quiet for a long moment and then shrugged. "But that doesn't mean much. Does it?"

"It means that he's taking this very seriously. Did you get into anything after dinner?" Lucy asked with a hopeful gleam in her eye.

"Sorry to disappoint you, but it was nothing more than some kisses on the sofa," Bridgette said. Liar, she called herself. If it hadn't been for that rotten phone call that sent them all back to the office, she had to be honest with herself, she had no idea how far things might have gone.

Bridgette pushed her hair back, and blew out a breath. She would have to find a way to prevent that from happening again. Oh, she liked the kissing and flirting just fine, but she wasn't ready to give herself to a man yet. One of the things her parents had instilled in her was the preciousness of that first time. It was meant to be shared with someone who was truly special.

Lucy sat in the chair watching with a careful eye. "Just some kisses, huh? From the look on your face, I'd wager that it was a bit more than that. Was it good?"

How much was she supposed to tell? "I don't know what I'm supposed to say," Bridgette acknowledge. "Okay, I'll admit that it was a bit more than just a few kisses, but I've never been in this situation before. I've never felt like I do right now, about any guy before, and it's still all so new." Her head came up. "To be honest, Lucy, since my mom's death, I really haven't had a real friend. At least not until Dom came into the picture. I'm so confused on so many levels, I'm not good at this."

Lucy set her partially eaten cookie down. "Why haven't you had any real friends? You've got a magnetic personality, you're scary smart. I can't believe that you couldn't meet people. What gives?"

Bridgette set her long cold tea aside. "When you're thrust into the world just shy of eighteen with no one there to act as a safety net, you do what you have to do. You don't worry about hanging out with girlfriends when you're more concerned about how you're going to put food in your belly. You don't have the time to let the complications of relationships get in the way when you're trying to figure out how to run a business and go to school at the same time. Everybody has trials in their life. For me, I was forced to face them early on and several at the same time. Maybe that's why Dom's unexplained attraction to me is so fascinating. For the first time in my life, I have the opportunity to be normal."

Across town, Dom sat in the corner of a booth in Clancy's with his back leaned against the wall. As had been their custom, they had descended on Clancy's for beer and nachos after the craziness of the day they had had. "I keep waiting for the adrenaline to wear off," he said to Brian and Deke who were seated on the other side.

"Know whatcha mean," Deke agreed taking another swig of his

beer. "But I've got to say this is kinda frosty, if you catch my drift. It's the first time in better than a week just the three of us are out."

Brian laughed. "Do you think Bridgette will give him parole once a week to hang out with us?"

Dom shook his head. "You guys know it's not like that, right? I mean, yeah we're spending a lot of time together, but she's not keeping me from drinking with you," he said gesturing with his beer.

"So what is going on between you two?" Brian asked.

"We're exploring the facets of our relationship. It's still new to both of us, so we're, uh, just feeling our way along."

Brian just grinned at him. "She's really coming into her own at the Bureau, isn't she?"

Dom set his beer down. "It's weird, you know. We see what she's done in the short time that she's been there, and we're absolutely amazed by it. Her? She doesn't feel that she's done anything unusual."

"What do you think?" Deke asked, motioning to the waitress for another round.

"I think she's absolutely amazing," Dom answered. "When I think about what she's been through. Losing her whole family, making her own way through it all and ending up where she did? I'm astounded. I remember what it was like when we lost Elaine. She lost so much more, and yet she didn't shrivel up and let the world keep her down."

"So, you're falling for her?" Deke prodded.

"No," Dom answered. "I fell for her. I'm head over heels about her and it scares the bejezus out of me. I don't know what to do or say. And…I don't know how to explain it."

Brian looked over to Deke with one eyebrow raised and then turned back to Dom. "What can't you explain?"

Dom sighed out of frustration. "My feelings for her are intense, but I need to be careful with her. She's been through so much, and I don't want to hurt her. But, last night, before we all got that call?

We were sitting on the couch and she went to get the pie for desert. When she came back, a single kiss led to many more. I really don't know how far we would have gone if it hadn't been for that call."

"You dog! Listen to you, figuring out how to get the girl and making the moves so seamlessly. You're going to need to give us lesser mortals some lessons," Brian quipped.

"No, no, no. You're missing the point, Brian. I don't want to do that with her." Dom stopped, "That didn't come out right. Of course I want to be with her, I'll even go as far as to admit that I've fantasized about it a bit. But I don't want to push her too far too fast."

"Dom, from what you said, she was right there with you," Deke offered.

"Yeah. But I think she was caught up in the moment like I was. I mean, as we were talking she told me about her dating experiences. She's never had anything that would even come close to resembling a serious relationship. I can't believe that she would just throw herself at someone because they liked her. Come on, you guys know her a bit. She's shy and sensitive and strong."

Deke nodded in agreement with Dom's assessment. "So what are you going to do next?"

Dom stared into his beer. "Well, I know that I'm going to continue to see her. And I think I'm going to try to figure out a way to bring this up. I…I don't want her to think that I'd pressure her into something. Besides, that's not how I was raised. In my household, my parents stressed that sex was something that should be saved for marriage. I think even with everything that Bridge went through that she'd feel the same way. I want to earn that respect and admiration from her."

Deke raised his glass in salute. "To having strong moral codes. May they help you find the blessings that you're after."

The three of them clinked glasses and continued to laugh.

"What do you mean that they didn't get the merchandise?" Antonio DePasquale screamed into the phone. "We had everything set up, there were fail safes upon fail safes. How could someone have gotten through it?"

"Listen, Tony, man, we're checking it out. Maybe that bum ran his mouth of to the cops trying to save his sorry rear-end. I've been going over everything from the site. The message board is secure. There ain't been any hacker attempts to break in or nothing. Our stuff is clean," Terry Martin reassured him from the other end of the phone. "We're probably taking more chances having this conversation on the phones than if we sent them over the net."

"You just remember, Terry, what happened to your cousin when that nosy broad figured out how to get through his devices. She cost us a cool million then." He grunted in aggravation. "There are just too many coincidences here to make me feel relaxed, you follow? First that whole cluster with your cousin not noticing that that Mahoney chick from the law firm was keeping tabs on us. Then we have Travis, that clown of a cousin of yours, who gets nailed not once, but twice in less than two weeks. We can't afford to keep having losses like that. And worse? That Mahoney woman is still walking and talking to the Feds. You know we got to keep the money coming in to keep things moving right here. But what happens when we ain't got no merchandise? All of our customers go somewhere else. And we look like dog crap."

"Tony, we'll get her. And we'll figure out what happened with the operation. When I find out who opened us up for this failure, I'm going open them up and choke them with their own intestines."

"Big words, Terry. Fix this bloody leak," Tony spat out before slamming the receiver down.

Terry lit the joint that he had rolled before Tony's call. Taking a deep drag, he leaned back in his chair and stared at the ceiling.

Somewhere, somehow, someone had tapped into the planning notes for the hijacking operations in Virginia. The full details were only known to maybe ten individuals, all of whom were in the upper echelon of the organization.

Taking another toke, he thought of his addiction to puzzles. Maybe he could have a bit of fun with identifying the leak. If he was to give each person a bit of information about the next op, each with a little twist, by knowing which version got out, he'd know who had leaked it. It was something that he was going to have to do a bit more thinking about.

But now, he decided, it was time to get serious about a woman he'd never actually been introduced to. Bridgette Mahoney had worked at the law firm that had represented many of the members over the past few years. Somehow she had finessed enough information out of the files to break into their computer system. His cousin Alex had been killed for that oversight.

Terry had actually liked Alex. He had been the only member of the family that had understood him.

Now that Alex was gone, it was time to exact payment from Mahoney.

Turning to his computer, he began a reverse telephone lookup for Mahoney. He didn't figure it would help much, since the number that had been obtained had been from before her incarceration. When she'd made her deal with the feds, he was pretty sure that they would have stripped that number away.

When the computer flashed its data, he was unsurprised. Time for plan C, he thought. Using the data that Travis had uncovered from the courthouse, he started with the case number. It took him less than twenty minutes until he was searching the files, and located the apartment number of the safe house where Bridgette Mahoney was staying courtesy of the FBI.

With an address, he could begin the next phase of paying

Mahoney back. He sent a quick e-mail to Antonio letting him know that he was going out of town for a few days for some recon.

CHAPTER 17

Bridgette reached over and turned off the alarm. It was amazing to her how much better seven hours of sleep could make a body feel. Following her new routine, she did her yoga workout followed by a quick shower. By seven, she was dressed and ready for her commute into headquarters.

Of course, she thought as she paced around the living room, today was Brian's turn to drive her in. And as usual, he was late.

The whole idea of needing somebody to transport her everyday seemed ridiculous. It was offset by the all-to-real threat that the Mambas were trying to silence her forever. A point, she was sure, that when they realized that she had managed to break their security again would move her to the very top of their hit list. She shuddered involuntarily and forced herself to think of anything else.

When Brian knocked on her door fifteen minutes later, she was relieved to be able to get out of the apartment knowing that her mind would be occupied for the next eight to ten hours.

"How're you doing today?" Brian asked as he guided her to his

SUV that he had parked near the entrance.

"I guess it's not too bad. I was surprised that I only slept for seven hours, not the twelve that I thought I would." Could she share the nagging thoughts that had worried her earlier?

"That happens with this job. Things hit, you go to the wall for twenty-four or more hours and then it just takes one night to put you back on an even keel."

She simply nodded as they weaved their way through the morning traffic. "Brian," she finally said. "How do you guys deal with this kind of stuff all the time?"

He glanced at her. "You mean the crazy hours?"

"No. It's just," she let out a sigh. "Maybe I'm not saying things right. I keep thinking about the fact that the Mambas have, you know, a hit out on me. I'm trying not to obsess with it, but it's there, you know? I never went through any training or anything before I ended up working here. So I'm wondering, I mean I can't be the first person in the bureau to get threatened like this. So, how do you handle it?"

Brian exhaled loudly. "That's a good question. For the most part, we try to ignore it, the fact that somebody has threatened us. We take all threats very seriously, but if you let your head get wrapped around the idea that somebody wants you dead, you tend to become paralyzed." He pulled the SUV into the underground parking area. "I think that everyone has their own way of handling the stresses of the job. Some turn to drinking and others focus on their relationships. But it's different for everybody. I guess if it was me that had received that threat, I'd probably talk about it with my friends but I'd throw myself into the job more. Try to run down every possibility that whoever made the threat could play. Does that make sense?"

She thought for a moment as she gathered her purse and other belongings out of the car. "So then, it's kinda like the best defense is a good offense, right?"

"That's exactly my kind of thinking. So, are you ready to go on the offensive now, Bridgette?"

"I think it's a great time to kick some Mamba butt."

Director Meyers leaned in the doorway of the little computer lab he'd created for this project, watching the two occupants focus so much on the task at hand, that they hadn't noticed his presence for the past five minutes. If only he could get the rest of the team to work with such intensity.

And, he thought watching Bridgette more closely, how lucky for him and the rest of the Organized Crime Taskforce was it that she'd interrupted their sting operation. After seeing her in action, he could now admit that Franchini had been absolutely correct with wanting to get her on the team.

"How's it going?" he asked, and nearly chuckled out loud when Moran and Mahoney both jumped.

"Ah, sorry, Sir. I didn't know you were there," Moran said. "I guess the answer to your question is it depends."

"What Brian is trying to say, Director, is that while we haven't found anything new regarding the shooting, we have intercepted a few intriguing e-mails."

Meyers nodded. "Can you give me a quick overview?"

"Sure," she said reaching over to a stack that to the outside observer looked to be a random pile of papers. "As I said, we haven't found anything new about our shooters. Nobody has taken credit for it. So, other than our trigger man, we don't know who else is involved. What we've got here..." she said shaking the papers in her hand. "...is a stack of e-mails that are from a running conversation that the head Mambas have been having regarding their finances."

Mayer's eyes widened. "Their finances? They're having online discussions about their money?"

Brian spoke up. "Actually, Sir, it seems if they are running it that way. From what we have gathered from the parts of the conversation that we've decoded, they've been hit pretty hard financially from our efforts over the past few months. Well, actually it's been our efforts and pure luck."

Meyers pulled up a chair. "We haven't actually hit any of their money laundering schemes, have we?"

"No, but when Bridgette screwed up our sting, she set off an avalanche of problems for them," Brian explained. "They had been planning to utilize that million for financing one of their other projects. When she diverted the money, they had to fund one of their drug shipments out of pocket essentially. When we add in Allen's arrests they're down another three million. From what we've gathered from the last few e-mails, they were depending on the hijacking operation yesterday to keep them afloat for a while."

"Did we hurt them significantly, Agent?" Meyers asked.

Brian shrugged. "Right now, we don't have a complete inventory of their assets so it's impossible to determine how badly we've hurt them. From the tone of the messages, I think we've really put a dent in their working capital."

"Any way we can figure out how much their base is, or how big of a dent we put in them?"

Bridgette looked over to Brian before she took the question. "I remember from my time at the law offices, that they had several legit businesses that are producing reasonable money each month. But I think, and this is based on conversations that I heard in the office, that they rely on the sales portion of their, uh, goods for most of their advancement."

Meyers turned slightly. "So what you're saying is that they have enough to fund the day-to-day things coming in from legit sources, but their illegal ventures fund most of their activities?"

"That would be correct, Sir."

"Okay, stupid question," Brian interjected. "What do they consider their day-to-day expenses?"

Leaning back in her chair, Bridgette shrugged. "Attorney fees, mortgage and rent on the various pieces of real estate, salaries to employees—"

"Employees?" Meyers gasped. "What do you mean employees? Are we talking about the flunkies who actually push their drugs on the street?"

"I'm not sure about them," she said. "But for example, in Bayview, there is a small clothing shop that is underwritten by the Mambas. Not all of the workers in the store belong to the gang, but they need to be paid. And I know that that's only one of their legit businesses."

Brain whistled. "I never thought about how far their reach was. If they've got a few of those places, they may have enough people on their payroll that any thing that we do might adversely affect more than just the gang."

"Definitely something to keep in mind, Agent," Meyers said. "Just as if the fact that they own and operate these facilities is widely known, it becomes an advertisement for them. It's like saying 'Hey come join us, we provide for the community' or some trash like that. Well, you keep plugging away at it, and be ready to report to the team at sixteen hundred in conference room B."

Brian watched him walk out of the room, "Jeez, just once, I'd like to get him to tell us that we did a good job. Since you've joined the team, we've done things that we've never been able to do before."

"I haven't worried about it in the past decade, so why start now? I just want to be able to look myself in the eyes and be happy with the job I did. Now, shall we get back to it?"

Bridgette followed the throng of people up to conference room B just before 4:00. She knew that she'd be able to look herself in the eye, the only question right now was for how long. There had to be another interpretation to the email that they had deciphered only an hour ago. She and Brian had looked it over several times, and it still made her blood run cold.

All she could do right now was continue to walk down the cream colored hallway to the meeting. The email didn't have anything to do with the shooting, or the hijacking for that matter. Therefore, she needed to put it aside and concentrate on what needed to be done.

"Bridgette?" a voice said softly as a hand touched her sleeve causing her to jump.

"Lucy! Oh, gosh you scared me. Sorry."

"You okay? You looked like you were in a daze there. I called you three times, and it wasn't until I touched you that you..."

Oh please, no. I can't afford to go out into my own little world right now, she thought. She hung her head down. "I'm sorry, Lucy. I've got a bit on my plate right now, with all of the data coming in from the site. Brian and I have been swamped," she said as they made their way into the room.

"You need to talk about it, let me know, and I'll come over and you can spew. Okay?"

Bridgette nodded and made her way to the back table to where Brian was sitting talking to Dom.

Dom's head turned and when he saw her, a smile flashed briefly before it turned to a look of concern. He rose when she got close. "You all right, Bridge?"

"I don't know," she admitted. Before she could go on, Director Meyers stepped in and began the meeting.

"All right people, let's get going. We've had a few advancements today, and I'd like to make sure that everyone is up to speed. As a quick overview, we've had a hit in the National Integrated Ballistics Information network that connects the gun used at the Federal Court House to another shooting that occurred six months ago. This was another known Mamba hit. The information doesn't help us much here, but it does provide a definite link." He checked his notepad, "Interviews with the victims and witnesses have been ongoing, and we've got some more there that we can work with as well. Our computer team has been busy, they've got a few hits regarding how the Mambas may be feeling a bit pinched monetarily. All in all, people we've made a good start."

He looked around the room. "Johnson? Why don't you start off with the ballistics information?"

Bridgette did what she could to pay attention to the reports from the others in the room. About the only thing that she could concentrate on with Johnson's report was the caliber of the gun and the amount of damage that it was capable of doing. Would it hurt much if that's what they used when they came for her?

Brian gave the report on their work. She was good on that data, so she only listened with half-heartedly.

"...the latest series of emails from Terry Martin aren't totally making sense to us," Brian said.

"What's the problem with them? Did they change the code?" The director asked.

"It doesn't appear so, Sir. It's that he sent the same basic message out to several of their top players. But each one is slightly different in tone, wording or some other small way."

"Conclusion?"

"We don't really have any conclusions at this time. We're going to keep working on it. Perhaps they're having an issue doing group emails, or maybe Martin was sending it from a mobile device. There are several possibilities."

Bridgette would never be sure if it was just the timing of Brian's words or maybe because she wasn't paying strict attention, but it was then that her mind showed her the most plausible answer. "I think they're looking for the leak," she said.

Several people looked to her saying, "Excuse me?"

She had done it again. Letting her mind wander at these meetings was entirely too hazardous to her health, she decided. Bolstering up her courage, she prepared to defend her thoughts.

"If we look at the messages that we found, as Brian said, they all have the same basic information in them. There are just very small variations of what they are trying to do. Why? As a guess, they suspect that there is a leak. How else would we have been able to shut down their operation yesterday? By giving out similar messages, but each one slightly different and, may I point out, we pulled these out of the individual mailboxes. This wasn't done as a group message. It's just a guess, but going out on a limb, I'd say that each person believes that they all got the same message. The exact same message. They could talk amongst themselves, and all be perfectly versed in the operation that it was laying out. But what Martin is doing is waiting to see how we react. Once we do, he can pinpoint the message that the data came from, which as far as he knows gives him his leak."

"That's an interesting theory, Miss Mahoney. I'd be curious as to why it didn't occur to you earlier," Tammy said.

Bridgette read the undertones that Tammy had not said. "I didn't realize that I was supposed to be infallible on this. The truth of the matter is, we've spent most of the afternoon going over these messages. Not much time was spent in batting around possible reasons."

"Bridgette may have another reason that she didn't spot this right out," Brian said.

Bridgette shot him a glance that pleaded not to divulge the last email that they had decoded. "Brian, no," she whispered. "It doesn't pertain to this at all."

Brian looked down at her, shook his head and turned back to the Director at the head table. "I think it does, Bridgette." He pressed a couple of buttons on the remote that he'd been using for his presentation which now brought up a copy of the last message on the large projection screen and now everybody was able to read it.

A- Bridgette Mahoney, 5994 Independence Ave, Apt. 301. I am taking a few days to head to DC. Plan to plug the leak we found there. This is personal. -T

"Director, this is a copy of the last email that Bridgette and I decoded today. As you can see, Terrance Martin has Bridgette's home address. We know that the message was sent to Antonio DePasquale, a known higher up in the organization. It has been traced from Terrance Martin. This combined with the earlier threat that was brought to us by the Metro PD, gives high probability that he, Martin, is enroute to the DC area with the sole intention of assassinating Bridgette for her role in the Mambas losing a million dollars. When we found this, she became quite concerned."

"Concerned, Agent?" the director asked nearly coming out of his seat. "My guess is she's scared out of her wits right about now. How the heck did they get her address? That's one of our safe houses, it's not supposed to show up anywhere."

"Sir," Lucy jumped in. "That address doesn't come from our data bases anywhere."

"I really don't care where it came from. They've got it. I want to know how." Meyers leaned back in his chair, and puffed out his cheeks. "We've got to work this problem in steps," he declared. "Miss Mahoney, first off, you look very pale. Are you feeling well enough to help us, or should we have you escorted to the medical center?"

"I'd rather work through this, Sir. I'll feel better doing something rather than just waiting for them to take their shot."

Meyers nodded. "Always figured you to have a strong will. Glad to see that I wasn't wrong. Okay, folks, this meeting is going into overtime. We're going to take a ten-minute break. While I'm working with the Department of Justice on Mahoney's clearance, I want everything that can be instantly dug up on this Terry Martin pulled up and ready to go. We've got an agent in trouble here troops and we can't let her down. Let's get moving."

Bridgette sat stunned. "He called me an agent," she said so quietly that only Dom heard her.

"Of course he did. You're an integral member of this team. And we're going to protect out teammate."

She smiled and nodded. There was more to it than that, she knew, but she wasn't going to dwell on it right now. "I can't explain how this makes me feel right now, Dom. It takes such a weight off my shoulders knowing that I'm not in this alone." She turned to Brian, "This was actually good for me, Brian. Having you tell everyone about that message had a different result than I expected. Now it's not just me against these bums. I've got help. Now, let's see what we can pull together on Mr. Martin in the next five minutes."

CHAPTER 18

"I don't like putting you out like this, Lucy," Bridgette complained as they climbed the stairs lugging up three bags of groceries to her second level apartment.

"We've been over this, Bridgette. Now, please relax for the next twelve hours. Meyers said that they would have this situation under control by morning. Until then, you and a few others are rooming here."

Bridgette stopped dead on the stairs. "A few others? Who else is coming over Lucy?"

"First off, Dom and the rest of the Three Amigos will be here shortly. They're going to be bringing hot food and files. This ain't no slumber party. So they were leaving the false trails from the bureau before they came here."

Bridgette thought to how she and Lucy had left the office. Lucy had been driving her standard issue government SUV while Bridgette crouched on the floor in the backseat. The plan that had been worked out was that several vehicles would all leave at the same time, heading in a variety of directions, and all taking random routes to their destination. The hope was that if any of them were being followed, the tail would be made.

"This is insane," she muttered as she followed Lucy into the small apartment. "How long are we going to have to keep up this cloak-and-dagger stuff?"

"Probably not too long. We just need to have a chance to nail this Martin fellow."

Bridgette stopped. "Do you really think that I'll have to do this that long? What if we don't get him anytime soon?"

Lucy set down her purse and the bag of groceries that she had hauled up. "Look, I know that things seem to be in the toilet right now. But trust me, people have your back now. As Meyers said, when we've got an agent in trouble, we'll all go to the wall for them."

"That may be true for most of the people at the Bureau, but I don't think certain people will do anything to help this process," Bridgette replied thinking of how Tammy had actively shunned her at every turn.

Two hours later, Lucy's cramped living room was littered with pizza boxes, empty soda cans and reams of paper. Bridgette looked up at the motely crew who had descended to help out in her time of need. Having Dom here wasn't a surprise and, she found, very relaxing. She felt safe with him there even though he thought of her as being very strong. Brian and Deke had both come over with Deke dragging Michelle, who happened to be a criminologist from the lab, along. The real surprise for Bridgette had come nearly an hour after the main group had arrived, when Lucy admitted Director Meyers and Judge Forsyth. It still made her shake her head to see the people who were standing up for her.

"What do we have on Terrance Martin?" the director asked.

"Vitals are straight forward. Born April 3, 1987 to Donald and

Pamela Martin. Parents divorced ten years later, he went with mom to live with relatives in Cleveland, Ohio. It was during his time there that he found his way into the Mambas. There is no record of him attending any schools after his high school graduation. Current address is bogus as it's the street address for Progressive Field where the Indians play," Lucy stated.

"We've got a mug shot from two years ago, when he was arrested on an assault charge. He's six-two, one-ninety-five, blond hair with brown eyes. Has a tattoo of a snake on his right forearm," Deke said holding up a picture.

"Do we have any information on what kind of car he's driving?" the director asked.

Dom shook his head. "Not as of yet, Sir. According to records, he owns a 2013 BMW Z4. We've given descriptions to Metro. We're also going through the video from the airports. It's possible that he flew into the area and rented a car. Either way, we'll have his location shortly I would think."

"Do you really think that you're going to find him that quickly, Dom?" Bridgette asked. "He's as slippery as an eel, and he doesn't exactly stand out. He can blend reasonably well. Unless we hit his car or catch him in the airport, I think he's got a better head start than we do."

"I don't see it that way, Bridge," Dom answered holding up his hands to give him time to explain. "We brought you over here tonight for several reasons. First, we wanted to make sure that you were safe. That was the top priority. But the second reason was we knew from the email that you and Brian intercepted, that Martin knew where you lived. We've put an agent who matches your basic shape and size in your apartment so that anyone watching will see you go in and out and having a normal routine—"

"You put a decoy in my place?" How could they do that? Arrange to move her out even for only a night, but then put someone else in there to be bait for Martin. "Why would you put her in trouble like that?" Tears threatened to fall, so she took a deep breath trying to steady herself.

"Bridgette," Director Meyers answered, "we pulled you out for your safety. You came to us through an unusual path. Normally, we have all of our agents go through a training program, regardless of what area they're going into. The agent that is currently staying in your apartment has been a field agent for nine years. She is highly trained for this, and also has another pair of agents who are watching from an adjacent building. She's safe as well, but more able to handle an attack that slips by. Metro police are also making sweeps through the area looking for him as well. That's why Agent Franchini believes that we will have him shortly."

She pulled her knees up and hugged them close to her body. There were just too many pieces of this puzzle that she didn't understand. How could she? "What happens now?"

"That depends on a few factors. Right now, we have teams that are waiting for him in several locations. With Judge Forsyth here, if we have any need of warrants, or for making other arrangements for you, we can do that in very short order. While everyone else is chasing things outside, we can brainstorm and see if we can deduce anything here," the director said.

By the time the director and the judge had left, it was pushing two in the morning. Lucy had been correct, Bridgette thought as she stared out the glass doors that opened onto the balcony, tonight had not been anything close to a slumber party. The group had sifted through mounds of data, trying to find some correlation of where Terrance Martin was and how he was planning to do her in.

"How are you doing?" Dom asked from behind her a moment before he pulled her into his arms.

She found comfort in the embrace, and laid her head on his shoulder. "I don't think everything has sunk in yet. It all seems to be moving in fast forward. This morning, when I got up, I was so happy with my little apartment, and now not even a day later, you're telling me that I'm going to have to move. It all seems so…" she searched for the word. "…outrageous, is the best that I can come up with."

"I know, Honey," Dom said softly rubbing her back. "But if they've got your present address, even if we get Martin tonight, the rest of them will still be after you. After all, if we get him, you would be the reason that he got picked up. They're not going to be happy to lose another member."

"Where will I go, though? I mean, part of my sentence was that I had to live in an approved house. If they could find out where I'm living now, what is to prevent them from finding out where I get moved to?"

"I don't know exactly what the plan is," Dom offered. "But, I know that Meyers and Forsyth are rightly miffed about what happened here. They're coming up with some angles that should be able to give you a reasonable amount of safety."

She nodded. She had heard the whispered conversation about where she should go, and knew that the director and the judge would be meeting to go over some options. She'd also heard them talking about something else. "Dom, do you think that Director Meyers was serious about getting me in for agent training? I mean, technically, I'm a…" she still had problems saying the word. "I'm a convict. Agent training would require me to be around firearms and other weapons. I'm not allowed to do that."

Dom smiled now, for the first time in several hours Bridgette recalled. "I think he was pretty serious about it, for several reasons. First, he thinks, and I agree, that it would be good for you to have the same training as everybody else so that you know how to protect yourself. Secondly, I think he's hoping that you'll like what you're doing so much, that after your time is served, that you'll be interested in staying on in this capacity. You've been a huge asset for us with what you've done in the computer area. I don't think he likes the idea of you slipping away.

"I also have a sneaky suspicion that he and Judge Forsyth are working on something that would allow your record to be expunged, or at least have a note in the file, that grants you certain privileges. Especially if those privileges are part of the requirement of your job."

"Well, I guess that could be something to look forward to," she said, trying not to get her hopes up too high. "I think we need to call it a night. Morning is going to come around too soon."

Dom walked her to the guest room. "Sleep well, my Irish Beauty," he said giving her a long kiss that made her blood rush hot before he sauntered away back to the living room and the couch that he was sleeping on.

Bridgette was roused from sleep by the smell of bacon. As soon as the smell had brought her to consciousness, her other senses kicked in as well. She could hear the snapping of the bacon on the stove, and the voices of the others who were probably already sitting in the small kitchen. The rumble of pipes told her that somebody was already in the shower. Yawning, she pushed herself out of bed and padded towards the sounds and smells of breakfast.

Dom was leaning against the kitchen doorframe, his hair still wet from his shower, dressed only in an undershirt and slacks sipping what she assumed was coffee. Deke was absent, but as he had left with Michelle by midnight, she wasn't surprised. However, the other face that she saw there did surprise her.

"Director Meyers," she said as she rounded the corner. Absent mindedly, she batted down the tufts of bed hair that she was sure were standing on end.

"How are you doing, Bridgette?" he asked in a fatherly tone.

"I guess I'm doing okay," she admitted and then waved in greeting to Lucy who was busy scrambling eggs. "You know you don't have to feed me."

Lucy smiled up from behind the counter she was working at. "Yeah, I know, but the truth is I really like to cook and stuff. But with it being just me, I never seem to get the chance or have enough of a reason. With everybody being here, it just seemed like the perfect time for me to have a bit of fun."

Bridgette grinned, to each her own she thought. Pouring herself a cup of coffee, she turned back to the director. "Did you have any luck getting Martin?"

He set his fork down, folded his hands. "I guess it depends on your point of view. We caught a visual of him last night, but Metro couldn't apprehend him. He apparently flew in and rented a car. So we know what he's driving and that description has gone out. Agents are currently talking quietly with the surrounding hotels to see if he's checked in anywhere. Most likely, he's used an alias, but we're hoping that we get a hit on the car."

This was about what she'd expected. "Where was he sighted?"

Dom answered this time. "One of the roving Metro units saw him as he drove by your apartment."

An unexplained chill went up her spine. Last night she had been upset about getting moved from her apartment. Now, she wasn't sure if she would ever be able to feel safe there again. Safe anywhere.

"You need fuel," Lucy said setting a plate, full of eggs and bacon and toast, in front of her. "You're going to have a long day today."

She thanked Lucy and dug in. Eating gave her time to think about what was happening. How was she supposed to put this on the backburner and not worry about it so she could do her job? There were just too many points that were aimed at her right now.

The noise from the chair next to her made her jump. Turning she saw Brian had joined them.

"You look like I've just tazed you," he said with a slight smile. "Am I that good looking fresh from a shower?"

She forced herself to swallow the eggs in her mouth. "Sorry to disappoint you, but you just don't send me over that way." She gave him a brief smile causing him to laugh. Which was exactly what she'd hoped for.

People were constantly popping into the makeshift computer room where Bridgette and Brian were trying to work. After the fifth interruption in an hour, she turned to Brian and asked, "How are we supposed to get anything done with the constant parade of people?"

"We've had people stopping by?" Brian asked deadpanning.

She snorted out a laugh, "I can see why Dom likes having you around. You always seem to know how to diffuse a situation."

Brian shrugged, "I guess it's just a matter of doing what we do best. Personally, I don't like working under stress, so I just tell myself that there is none, and move on."

"Kind of like a mind over matter thing?"

"Hey," he said with a big grin, "if I don't mind, it don't matter."

She tossed a box of Kleenex at him which he easily dodged before he stuck out his tongue at her.

"So have we made any real progress?" he asked.

"Not much chatter going on within the group. I'm still waiting for John to get back to me on the status of their financials that they were showing in their prospectus," Bridgette answered.

Brian shook his head. "It still gets me on how much they make themselves out to be a large business."

"In a way they are. They've got the hierarchy. It's more a case of their product just isn't always legal." Bridgette thought for a minute. "Maybe we can use that to formulate a plan that will take them all the way down."

"It'd be possible. The more we know about their operations,

the better chance we have of crippling them."

She may have been still looking down at the papers in front of her, but she could feel him looking at her. She had been hoping that she would be able to hide what she was feeling, but she knew— without so much as a glance—that he was aware that there was something else that was playing on her mind.

"You want to spill and tell me what else you're concerned about?" he asked finally.

She leaned back in the chair, crossed her arms on her chest and almost pouted. "I can't figure it out, Brian. How did they get my address? It makes me wonder if we have some kind of mole running around here. After the past few months, I was finally feeling good about things. I was looking towards the future, and now I'm looking over my shoulder. And I'm second-guessing myself. Is the person who's in line behind me at lunch, just a colleague or someone who is hoping to make a few extra bucks by selling me out." She sighed heavily. "My life is a mess."

Brian looked at his watch, "Come on, let's take a break and head to lunch a few minutes early." He rose and headed for the door.

They walked together to the cubicle where Dom sat shuffling through various screens on his computer. "What are you doing, Franchini?" Brian asked.

"Trying to track down how they got Bridgette's information. I can't find anything that indicates that it came out of here, but somebody knows how the Mambas got ahold of that information. I'm going to find it, and close it down with a clean sweep."

"See Bridgette," Brian said with a smile. "Your life may be a mess, but at least you're dating a guy who's pretty good with a broom. Who could ask for more? A guy who does housework."

Brian walked away laughing at his own joke. "See you guys downstairs in a few."

"You know that you don't need to worry about things, right,

Bridge?" Dom said.

"It's easy to say, not so easy to do. I-I guess that I'm overwhelmed about everything. I've got some sadistic gang that wants to see me listed in the obituaries, at least one stalker who is after me, and I still don't know where I'm sleeping tonight," she said, her voice getting higher with each phrase.

Dom looked around to be sure that no one was looking, draped an arm around her for a one-armed hug. "It will all work out, Honey. It may seem that there is no way that it could possibly happen, but somehow it always does. So what do you say about keeping our minds focused on one problem at a time, and not inviting problems in?"

"I'd say that would be a great idea, Franchini," Tammy said. "I'm sure the Director will be thrilled to know that you two are having some kind of weird and twisted romantic interlude here in the office. You both know that public displays of affection aren't allowed in the Bureau, right? Maybe after I see Director Meyers we can get back to doing some real work around here." She sneered at Bridgette as she dropped a pile of clipped papers onto Dom's desk. "Well, there you go, Franchini. The list of people who know, or knew, where your favorite convict was living. I still say do us all a favor and put her back in the pen where she belongs."

Bridgette watched her storm out, walking fast with her hips swaying exaggeratedly from side to side. "How much trouble are you going to be in if she tells the Director?"

"Don't worry," Dom said as he reached over and pulled his phone closer. Punching in the four-digit code, he spoke into the receiver. "Director, I'd like to give you a heads up on something. I believe that Agent Tammy Cipone is on her way to see you." He paused. "Yes, Sir. You see what happened is..."

CHAPTER 19

Bridgette slammed the drawer in her new kitchen. It had taken two days since the scare with Terrance Martin for the bureau to secure a new place for her to live. She looked out the stingy window over the sink into the small, enclosed courtyard, and forced herself to take a steadying breath.

"This is the last of it," Dom remarked as he along with Brian and Deke carried in boxes loaded with her stuff.

Boxes that she hadn't been able to pack. "Any idea what's in any of them?" she asked.

Deke and Brian shot a worried look at Dom, who casually set the box that he was carrying down and made his way over to her. Taking her in his arms, he tried to reassure her. "Babe, listen, I know that this all sucks sideways. One day you're thinking that everything is running fine, and then you're getting bounced all over the place. While they're playing the shuffle game, somebody goes in and packs up your stuff and ships it out. Meanwhile, you're being moved like a pawn in an elaborate game of chess."

The tears began to flow now, but she didn't care. The life that she had had before, the one where she was in control, was over and had been for a while. But, blast it all, she liked the way her new life had been going. Maybe she didn't have all that control like before, but she could deal with it. She had liked her little apartment. But somewhere up the chain, somebody had decided that she needed to be somewhere else.

She dabbed at her eyes, "I'm sorry, Dom," said between sobs. "I just don't understand what's going on. Why couldn't I go back and pack up things? I mean I get why I had to leave that apartment, but to have to let someone else go in and pack for me. Really?"

He rubbed her back while looking at his two best friends. The nod from Deke clinched it for him. "The cameras caught Martin watching your building yesterday morning. He's currently under constant surveillance. We got a warrant to tap the hotel phone, and subpoenaed the records from the hotel where he's staying. The problem is, he called in for reinforcements from his pals."

Bridgette's gasp was totally involuntary. "He's getting more help?"

Deke and Brian had dropped their boxes and now stood just behind her, each with a hand on her shoulder. "Yeah. We didn't get the entire call, so we don't know the exact data," Deke said.

"By the time we could get the tap, the only call that he got was just ten words long, 'Your request is approved. Reinforcements available in forty-eight hours.' Doesn't exactly tell us who is coming or what to expect," Brian added.

She buried her face into Dom's shoulder. "What am I going to do? They're going to find out where I am now, and this will never be over."

"No, Bridge. Nobody's going to find out where you are now. I promise you that."

"How? How can you be sure? We suspect that there is a mole in the bureau, and all it's going to take is for them to access my records, and viola! There's my address, and the entire Mambas organization knows where to find me."

"Hey, I'm going to take your lack of faith personally," Dom said. "Right now, only four people know where you are. And we're all right here."

"How? The director needs to know, and the courts, and—"

"Relax, Bridge. We talked to Forsyth and the director. Officially, the bureau is playing their game. We looked into the most likely suspects, and where they were likely getting their information from, and set up multiple dummy accounts for you. Each one has a different address."

This time she smiled. "You're running the same ploy they were, trying to figure out the leak, huh? Think they'll fall for it?" Her smile faded. "What about the people that actually live at those addresses?"

Deke grinned, "They're all Metro Police stations or empty safe houses. I don't think they're going to cause too much trouble there."

Bridgette looked around the apartment. It was nearly twice the size of her old one. The fact that it had a second bedroom and a bathroom that was big enough to actually dry off in after a shower were very nice features. The small balcony from her living room jutted off the front of the building, albeit at a height of five stories. From her bedroom, there was a second balcony, slightly smaller, that overlooked the shared courtyard. It could work she decided, especially if no one but the four of them knew where she was.

Across town in the Marriott, Terrance Martin paced around his suite. He had wanted to make a move on the Mahoney woman quickly, but there had seemed to be too many police cruisers going by to do it without getting busted.

She had to pay, but the cost had to come out of her hide alone. If he did anything that got him caught, or worse…well, he really didn't want to think about that. At least that moron over at the Bureau had come through, and he now had her new address.

Of course, that was going to push his timetable back a bit. But he needed to have the time to shore up his op.

He liked the sound of that, his op. Antonio would never let him run an op for the Mambas, but now, here? He was the boss, and he was going to make sure that nothing stopped him from getting his target.

He paused when his cell phone chirped. "Hello?"

"Davis, Moretensky, Wilson and Crewe will be arriving at Baltimore/Washington in the morning. Flight 952 arrives at noon. Don't let us down."

The line clicked off as Terry said, "Thanks."

He threw the phone across the room, hitting the sofa.

"Why?" He asked the reflection in the window. "I asked for five experienced guys, and what do I get? Four bozos who at the best held up liquor stores."

Standing in the window of his hotel room, he studied the traffic pattern below and cursed. There had to be a way that he could make this work. Sighing, he turned back to the table and the plans that he had laid out. He wasn't getting what he had asked for, but at least he had more bodies to work with. Now he just had to figure out how to use them.

It had been a rough night for Bridgette. She hadn't slept well over the past few nights, and last night had been the worst, she decided. It seemed that she had just closed her eyes and drifted off to sleep when the alarm went off.

Stumbling out of bed she headed for the bathroom in the dark. Or, at least she thought she had. Right up until she bashed her nose into the wall where she had remembered a door being.

Rubbing her nose, she blinked twice. "Right," she muttered,

"new apartment."

At least the new place had decent water pressure she thought standing in the shower. Letting the water pour off of her, she let her mind think about what had been going on over the past few days.

Dom had been able to share that they had ears and eyes on Martin, and that there was no way he could make a move without the Bureau knowing. But, she wondered as she wrapped a fresh towel around her wet hair, what was he planning to do? He was still going to be looking for her at the old apartment, so his plans would stem from there. And, she decided, as soon as he realized that she wasn't there any longer, who knew where he'd go.

By the time she was finished dressing, she'd come up with a few ideas that she figured that she would run by Dom on the way to work. Her phone sounded, letting her know that he was about a block away, so she grabbed her purse and headed for the door. Stepping out of the door, she noticed Dom—and didn't he look cute blushing like that—talking to the proprietor of the flower shop that was housed on the ground level.

"...so, I expect to meet this girl of yours, Dominic. Soon. Don't keep stalling me," Wanda scolded him.

Dom only laughed. "Wanda? Turn around for a moment." When she did, Dom continued the introduction. "Wanda, let me introduce you to your latest tenant, and the girl I'm infatuated with, Bridgette Mahoney. Bridge, this is Wanda James. She owns the flower shop as well as the building."

Bridgette swallowed hard, "Nice to meet you," she said with a quick nod before climbing into the passenger side of the SUV.

Wanda gave her a steely stare. "I think I might like you," she drawled. "You look like you'd be good for my Dom. You both come to see me later. I made a pie last night, lemon meringue, so you come after dinner, you hear?"

Dom shrugged, "You win, Wanda. We'll see you later."

Bridgette waited until they had pulled out into traffic. "Dom, is it safe? I mean I thought the whole idea of putting me here was that only the four of us would know where I was."

He reached over and took her hand. "I've known Wanda for five years now. She thinks of me as her adopted grandson, or something along those lines. I trust her. So do Brian and Deke. As I said, she owns the apartment, so she needs to have your name. You'll be safe. She actually has a higher security clearance than you do," he added with a smile. "She worked for thirty years in the department of defense. When she retired, she didn't want to leave DC, and invested in the apartment building. Wanda's Flowers came along as a way to have her hobby of playing with flowers pay a little.

"Besides, it's not so much that we need to keep your whereabouts quiet. We just don't want anybody inside the Bureau to know where you are. If Martin, or any of the other thugs try to locate you, we'll catch them in the act. Adds a few more years onto their sentences. I'm more worried about the leak that we have from inside."

Bridgette thought about what he was saying. So her landlady had security clearance and likely government training of some kind. Her life was definitely getting more complex each day.

By the time she managed to get to the cafeteria, the others were almost finished with their lunches. "Sorry I'm late. I had an, uh, unexpected meeting with the director. I guess I'm freaking out over several issues. All of which have me looking over my shoulder at every little noise." She huffed out a sigh. "I never used to consider myself a weenie, but right now, I think I'm definitely in the running for weenie of the year."

Lucy shot Dom a look that kept him quiet. "Whatever it is, Bridge, you are by no means a weenie. Clear?" She waited until Bridgette had nodded and her eyes had stopped bulging. "You've had more bumps in the road than most people twice your age.

You've managed, and quite successfully I might add. Now, what's got you all worked up?"

Bridgette looked at the sandwich that she was currently tearing into small pieces, shook her head and dropped it. "It's everything. The whole issue of Martin being in DC looking for me, the constant worry there and then we can add the complexity of Tammy breathing down my neck. It's almost like she's waiting for me to do just one little thing so she can run off to the Director and tattle on me. It almost makes me feel like I was in third grade again with the class bully waiting to attack."

"The Director's not giving you a hard time on things, is he?" Lucy wanted to know.

"Not exactly," Bridgette said. "It's...he called me into his office just before noon. He's a little concerned about some activities that he's hearing about around the division and my supposedly being involved in them. I haven't done anything...well other than those times with Dom when Tammy caught us. But somebody is spreading rumors that I'm sneaking off at all times of the day, and then coming back looking disheveled."

Dom placed his hand over hers. "It's small mindedness and somebody who's trying to get at you. I'd like to say just ignore it and it'll go away, but I'm not so sure about that."

"Bridge, I work with you almost all day. I know when you're in the mini lab and when you've taken a walk. Don't let this worry you. You've got solid alibis."

"Alibis? You make it sound like I'm being charged with some kind of crime. It's really not...Oh. I guess in a way it is, isn't it? They're trying to mess with my credibility and get me thrown out of here."

"Looks like it to me," Dom said. "Now the question is, what are we going to do about it?"

"Never was really into the cloak-and-dagger stuff, but I almost wish I could use a wire of some kind. You know have audio and visual of where I am and what I'm doing so that if it gets called into question, I have some protection."

Brian nodded, "I think I can set that up. We'll also start keeping logs, all of us," he said circling his hand around the table. "That way, you'll have the most protection that we can muster. Now, what do we all say about getting back to work? Personally, I'd like to find out what our old friend Martin is up to."

A woman? Martin was thinking to himself as he drove his new associates away from the airport. He'd asked for five experienced men, and they sent him four unknowns. Worst of all a woman. He'd heard the name Sam Wilson bounced around the HQ several times before, but he never, never thought it would be about the short, curvy Samantha Wilson who was now riding shotgun.

"Where are we going to set up?" the blond Wilson asked.

"I've got a suite at the Marriott. Figured we'd stay there. It's within sight of Mahoney's apartment."

Wilson's head nearly spun around. "You fool! How long have you been there? All it takes is for one of the do-gooder cops in this place to notice you, and they've got you cold. No wonder, Tony wanted me to take over here for you."

"Wh-what? What do you mean Tony wanted you to take over?" Martin demanded.

"Oh, you poor delusional fool!" she nearly laughed. "What experience do you have in killing people, hmm? Don't bother trying to lie to me. We both know that you've been involved on the periphery of things, but you've never actually pulled the trigger, and now you want to be the one to end this nosy broad? Let's be realistic about this, okay, Terry? Tony knew that you wanted to avenge your cousin's demise. But let's face it, when he let the feds get into our system, he signed his own death warrant.

"You did good finding Mahoney. So be happy on that part. But let's let the professionals take care of things from here on." She looked out the window at the passing monuments. "I'll tell you what, Terry. Help us kidnap her. If you really want to pull that trigger when the time comes, then you will have earned that."

Martin sneered at the window. How could Antonio do this to him? He'd been the one who had worked his childhood connection and found a mole in the Bureau. It had been his responsibility to redesign the web stuff to protect it. And how did they thank him? They send a self-satisfying broad and her three, as far as he knew, mute nit-wits.

Well, he decided as they made the last turn before the hotel, there wasn't much that he could do about it now. He needed their help to get through to Mahoney, so he'd have to just stuff his anger aside and do the job. Professionals? Hah! He'd show them all.

"Are we just going to check out then?" he asked, struggling to keep his voice in control.

Wilson looked at the set up. "I think for the next few hours, we'll hang out here while we plan our next move. It gives us a place to operate from until we can move to some place safe."

She nodded to the largest of the three men she'd traveled with. "David, you'll need to come up to the room. You stand out too much. And your experience with covert ops will be most useful. Carl, you and Todd need to position yourself in the lounge. See if you can determine what assets our friends have in place here. If it was me, I'd probably have an agent working the desk as well as a few in selected areas. Room service, security and such. Places where they'd be able to go almost anywhere in the hotel without attracting attention." She checked her watch. "Let's plan to meet at, shall we say six-thirty? We can all leave a few minutes apart from each other. There is a restaurant called Esquire that is two blocks north. We'll meet there.

Martin watched as the slim man with the mocha colored skin, Todd Crewe he thought, walked away and in seconds had almost disappeared from sight simply by blending in with the other business professionals who were scattered among the décor. Carl Davis grinned as he nonchalantly walked into the small attached bar, and settled onto a stool, again effectively disappearing.

David Mortensky was a touch taller than Davis, but his red hair was bright and would obviously prevent his blending. "I hate being so visible," he said.

Martin watched as Wilson strode up to the sulking man. "It's okay. Besides, I need you with me," she purred.

Turning to Martin, she smiled. "Now, let's get to the room and get things organized there."

CHAPTER 20

"I want to check the settings on this, and then we'll be all set," Lucy said as she tapped a couple of keys on her laptop. "See? This does double duty. It puts eyes and ears on you here like you wanted, but it also gives us a chance to play with some of the new toys. This device is accurate with your position to within one meter, and supposedly the quality of the optics in the camera will allow facial recognition from nearly half a mile away. For personnel carried gear, it's the tops."

Bridgette looked at the small button device that Lucy had secured to the collar of her shirt. So many things in her life just didn't seem possible, she thought. Everything that had happened to her prior to her eighteenth birthday, the horrible night when she made the decision to take the law into her own hands. Both were nightmares that shouldn't be possible in anyone's life. Of course, she mused, the final result of that night turned out to be pretty good so far, so maybe that would atone for the mistakes.

She could almost rationalize the idea of getting wired to keep her safe from Terrance Martin, but being wired up at work to protect yourself from a coworker's determination to get rid of you? That seemed to be a bit excessive.

"I've got to admit, when I suggested this at lunch yesterday, it was in jest. Well, more or less," Bridgette offered.

Lucy grinned at her. "Honey, we geeks love when we can play with our toys for good reasons. Anyway, your idea of being able to track your whereabouts to prove that you're not AWOL while on the job should be able to keep you on this side of a jail cell." She shrugged, "I've got to admit, I don't understand exactly why Tammy's got her sights fixed on you, but it sure seems that she does. I can say that over the past few weeks, she's been very outspoken about how she feels that everybody has overstepped their bounds giving you the access to the computers and stuff here. Me? Personally, I like you a lot. You've proven to be a very valuable asset to the team, so I'm not ready to let you go, so you're going to wear this transmitter like a good girl and when somebody tries to cause you grief, we'll be able to prove that you were telling the truth."

"I guess. I just feel petty about doing it."

"Let's see how long it takes before we have to use the data that this is recording," Lucy said engaging the system.

The answer was slightly more than two hours.

"Mahoney," Director Meyers said from the doorway.

Bridgette looked up to see a man that she didn't recognize standing with the director who was, to her mind, looking harried. "Yes, Sir?"

"Would you please come with us?"

She rose timidly, fighting back the tears that were threatening to fall. There was something in the expressions of both men that made her afraid. She grabbed her purse and followed the director to another small box of a room.

"Bridgette, this is Director Tom McQuaid. He's my boss."

Bridgette looked at McQuaid. He was probably in his early sixties she guessed, and looked like he had a bad case of constipation.

"Mahoney," McQuaid said, "we're going to cut to the chase. You were given what some may perceive as preferential treatment a few months back. Not everyone in the Bureau supports the idea of taking someone who has flagrantly worked outside the law and then rewarding them with a job inside. I did approve the request that was made by Assistant Director Meyers, and brought you in. From what I've heard from Director Meyers, you've certainly helped us in many areas."

He got up from his chair and paced the room. "However, it has come to my attention, that you are violating several policies within the Bureau. It should have been explained to you during your intake, that romantic liaisons during the workday are strictly prohibited. If you were a duly authorized agent, I would place you on a thirty-day suspension for the first offense. The second time it occurred, it would be an automatic dismissal. Am I clear?" he asked, turning to look at her.

"Sir, I've never—"

He simply held up his hand to cut her off. "I came in today to speak with you about the progress that you had made on the Mambas case, and find out that you were seen this morning entering one of the lounges this morning with an unidentified man. My source tells me that you remained there for nearly thirty minutes. Now, I can, and must, assume that this meeting was not for departmental business." His eyes flared with temper. "Right now, I'm not sure what our course of action should be. I am notifying you that at this juncture, you are hereby suspended until this is resolved. I'm instituting an internal investigation to look into the matter, and I will be talking to Judge Forsyth about the possibility of having your sentence reinstated. There will be no further discussions on this. Your actions have been brought to me by a very reliable source, who would have no reason to lie to me. You will be escorted out."

"That's fine!" Bridgette snapped. "I've reported people making up things about me to Director Meyers, and what's happened? Not a damn thing! Well, this is the last time! I've had it! I got myself wired so that every second of my day is on audio and visual recording. If you don't want to hear it now, that's fine. Tell me who is my legal rep for this matter, and I'll make sure that it makes its way to that hearing as well. I can prove that I was no where near any of those lounges today, and that except for the last ten minutes, I've been involved with decoding data from the Mambas."

McQuaid's head snapped at her tone, and she thought he was going to explode by the shade of red that he turned. But it was Meyers who spoke first. "Bridgette. Hold on a moment, and let's all take a step back," he said with his hands splayed in front. "Yes, you did come to me, as did Agent Franchini about some comments that had been made against you. I have been looking into them. To date there had never been a way to substantiate what was truth and what was hearsay. Now, am I correct that you took it upon yourself to handle the wire?"

Bridgette could feel her face flush. "When I left your office yesterday, Sir, I was angry. At lunch, several others got me to tell them what was going on. I jokingly said that I should wear a wire to be able to prove my innocence. This morning, Dom made sure that we got in early. Lucy was waiting for me. Apparently her group had just gotten a few micro recorders," she flipped her shirt collar so that both men could see the small button. "She said that they often would wire each other up in the building when learning a new system. We thought that this situation would be an interesting test. By using me as a test subject, we'd have the added benefit of me being able to have proof that I was where I said I was, and that whoever was telling you these stories was trying to get me in trouble." She hung her head. "I'm sorry, Sirs."

"Mahoney, you're telling me that you've got proof of your whereabouts today?" McQuaid demanded.

She risked looking up. "Yes, Sir. Agent Lucy Daniels, from the communications department, is recording the feeds."

McQuaid only glanced to Meyers before the Assistant Director was on the house phone.

"Agent Daniels will be reporting here in about five minutes with the data," Meyers said after he hung up. "Bridgette, I can't tell you how sorry I am about how things have been handled."

"I'm going to see that data first, before I'm going to go further," McQuaid said. " If what you state can be proven, then we have a real dilemma on our hands. This becomes more than just a human resources problem."

There was a soft knock on the door, and Meyers opened it to let Lucy in. She dropped the laptop on the table and went directly to Bridgette and gave her a hug.

"It'll be okay, Bridge," Lucy said. "I've been checking the progress on it all morning everything is good." Turning to the directors she said, "Sirs, what we have here is the newest micro recorder from SimCast, the SC-5602." She pointed at the screen of the computer. "Now, if we look at the current stream from Miss Mahoney's camera, we see all of us here now. Under your supervision, I am stopping the recording," she pressed a few buttons and the images on the screen stopped. "Backing up, we see that we have a continuous stream of data from Bridgette from oh-eight-forty-two until now. Can you specifically tell me what time we are looking for?"

She cued the recording up to the time that Director McQuaid specified, and then hit play. "As you can see, we have Miss Mahoney working in that tiny room she's been stuffed into with Brian Moran, and it appears that she's," Lucy squinted at the screen. "Ah, yes, it appears that she's working on an e-mail from the Mambas' organization."

McQuaid blew out a breath in a huff. "Well, if that don't just make me mad enough to skewer somebody. Someone I've known for nearly twenty years just lied to my face about this. I want to know why."

Bridgette sat in the chair in the corner, wishing that she could literally just become invisible. If she could just disappear, maybe things would settle down. But what was the old saying? If wishes were dollars, or something like that she thought. Pulling her knees to her face, she let the tears stream quietly. She needed to find a way to release this tension.

Her emotions began to blacken everything out, and the room started to spin.

"Miss Mahoney?" Director Mayer's voice softly called.

Bridgette opened her eyes to find that she was sitting in a chair, and someone was holding her head down so that it was almost between her knees. Looking through her eyelashes she could see the director was sitting directly in front of her. "I'm sorry," she tried to say but nothing above a whisper came out.

"Think you can manage to not pass out now," Lucy asked releasing her hold on Bridgette's back.

Bridgette sat up slowly. The room threatened to spin again, so she squeezed her eyes shut and drew in a deep breath. Opening them again, she focused on the others in the room. Lucy was still beside her with a hand gently resting on her shoulder. Director McQuaid stood at the table, scrolling through the record of her day.

Director Meyers was now sitting up straight in his chair staring into her eyes, almost as if to see her thoughts. "I think you've been under too much stress for too long. Why don't I get Agent Franchini to take you home for a while, so you can get some rest?"

When she started to protest, Meyers waved her off. "No, Bridgette. This is not something that we are going to discuss. You've been thrown into this business and have been burning things at all ends trying to keep up. It is now common knowledge that the members of the Mambas want you disposed of. We now have proof that there is at least one person here in the bureau that wants to cause you distress on the job. I think the best medicine would be a few hours down." He stepped away to make the call.

"Miss Mahoney?" this time it was Director McQuaid. "I need to apologize to you for my reactions, and to repeat that it does appear that somebody has it in for you. Everything that I had heard about you before the, ah, accusation this morning, was about how great you were doing. I really, truly wanted to congratulate you on your work. That was why I came down.

"I want you to know that the individual who came to me with this will be disciplined for their, um, part in all of this. Including a suspension if it is deemed necessary. I can't guarantee what will happen, but I can assure you that heads will roll."

Dom walked into the room minutes later, took one look at her and nearly vaulted the table to get to her. "Hey, it's okay, Bridge. I'm here," he said taking her into his arms and just holding her.

Her body shook with the ravages of emotion as the sobs ripped from her. Each time her body shuddered, he held her tighter, and whispered soothing words. When she was finally cried out, he led her to his car to take her home, hoping that he could contain his anger and not look for retribution from the person who had caused her this grief.

Bridgette woke suddenly, and cautiously looked around at the unfamiliar surroundings. Sitting, she studied the soft leather couch and the soft throw. She didn't remember anything past her and Dom leaving the underground parking area.

"How are you feeling?" Dom asked.

She looked to her left to see him silhouetted in the doorway, the light from the next room making it impossible to see his face. "I-I guess I'm okay," she managed to choke out. Her throat felt as if she'd swallowed glass shards. "Where are we?"

Dom smiled and came to sit next to her. "You about passed out as soon as we hit the road, and I didn't want to wake you, so I brought you here." He gestured with his hand. "This is my place. I bought it a little while back, and had if refurbished. It's bigger than I really need, but I don't rattle around too much. I figured it was a good bet to come here today, since it's all one floor. Made carrying you in a bit easier than trying to manage the elevator at your place."

Bridgette looked around again. Dom's house? "Dom, I don't think I'm supposed to be here. I mean the terms of my, ah, program state that I'm allowed to go to work and home. They even manage the amount of time that I'm allowed to take care of shopping and other household things." She frowned, "It's not that I'm not happy to be here, but I really don't want to blow things right now and have to go back to…that place."

Dom pulled her in. "Meyers gave me a direct order, remember. I was to take you home and make sure that you got the rest that you needed." He smiled. "When I called him and told him how you'd all but shut down, he agreed that this would work for a while. I'll get you back to your place before your curfew. But, in the mean time," he stood and held his hand out to her. "I fixed a nice pot of pasta e´fagioli. You need to refuel as well as recharge."

After a bowl of soup, Bridgette had to admit that she did feel better. Once she had finished the lunch dishes, she wandered around Dom's house while he was in his office on a call with the Bureau. She was mesmerized by the paintings that hung on the walls. She was squinting, trying to decipher the artist's name when Dom came back in.

"It's Maria Franchini," he said from behind her. "She was my Grandmother."

"I don't know much about art," Bridgette admitted, "but she

seemed to be quite talented at it."

"She did okay. Was never on par with the well known artists, but she made enough from selling her work to buy more canvases and paints. And," he admitted, "to pay off her house. I keep them because their sentimental value is beyond a dollar amount to me." He flashed her a broad smile, "She taught me how to paint one summer. I still play with it at times. Something to do to try and relax my mind."

Bridgette looked around the room. "Any of these yours?"

"No. I do okay work, but nothing that I'd want to show the world. Therefore my work stays in my workspace, kind of as a testament to my attempts at entering the art world."

"Maybe someday you'll show me," Bridgette tried.

Dom stuck his hands in his pockets and shook his head. "Doubt it. They're not very good."

"They've got to be better than what I can do. Heck, I can't even draw a stick figure. Every time I try, some part turns into a geometric shape and the next thing I know, I've got a flow chart." She grinned at him. "Please? Will you please show me your work?"

Dom huffed out a breath. "You really know how to get me, don't you? All right, come on. I hide them in here."

Bridgette followed him down the hall to the fourth door on right. The room was barely nine feet square. The floor was covered in a paint-splattered drop. An easel sat boldly in the middle of the room, a smock hanging over the corner of the current canvas. Canvases were stacked five deep all around the perimeter of the room. Landscapes and still lifes faced out. She bent down to look at one, a depiction of the view off of a mountaintop. "These are wonderful, Dom. It looks like I could step off this rock and climb right down into that valley." Turning she faced him. "Why do you hide them? They're gorgeous. I'd love to hang this in my living room."

"I guess I've never felt confident to show them to anybody. Or, maybe the truth is, there never has been anyone in my life before that I was willing to let into this private space in my life." He took the canvas she'd been holding. "I'll get this framed for you, if you'd like."

She wrapped her arms around him and held on as if her life depended on it. After the years of being alone, finding someone who would share their life intimately with her was a miracle. He may have been only offering a painting, but she realized that he was giving her the solid foundation to begin trusting life again.

CHAPTER 21

Dusk was settling over the DC area as Dom guided the SUV down the congested streets. "We're fine," Dom said looking over at her. "Remember, we got clearance from Meyers, so even if we're a few minutes late, no one is going to come knocking on your doors."

Bridgette fidgeted in her seat. She had thought that she had been hiding her anxiety well, but if Dom had been able to pick up on it, well she must not have done well enough.

"I know, Dom," she said. "It's just even the thought of having to go back scares me. And, to be honest, I really could use fewer tensions in my life, if you know what I mean."

Dom nodded as he pulled into the small lot by the building that served the tenants and the customers of the first floor businesses. "Well, heck. There goes the neighborhood," he muttered glancing up the street.

Bridgette turned to see where he was indicating and noticed Brian and Deke carrying what looked to be a pizza box. "I wonder what they're doing here?"

"My guess? Meyers told them what happened, and they brought over a pizza and stuff to try to help you relax." He took her hand as they walked. "It's what friends do."

"How did you make out with the message trail?" Bridgette asked Brian twenty minutes later.

Brian held up a finger, and then fought with the stringy cheese from his second piece of pizza. "We've made some progress. Between the emails and the phone taps at the hotel, we know that Martin was meeting up with some muscle. Unfortunately, we don't have video of the group coming in. The bigger disappointment was that they didn't remain in the hotel long."

Bridgette's eyes popped wide open. "What happened? Where did they go?"

"Not sure," Brian said, popping the top to another Coke. "We've got Martin going in alone yesterday at sixteen hundred, but almost nothing after that. This morning, Martin checked out of the hotel and they've moved on."

"I doubt that they've left the area," Deke added, waving his slice around in lieu of hand gestures. "As soon as they were out of the room, we had a team into the room to do a complete sweep. When we left the office, I hadn't heard if they'd found anything yet or not. But in any case, they don't seem like the type that runs away before the job is finished."

Bridgette sat staring at the pizza on her plate. "That doesn't exactly make me feel warm and fuzzy inside. What can we do?"

"For one thing, we keep our eyes and ears open. You and I keep working on getting through those messages that we've found. Especially looking at the new ones. We might get lucky there and find out where they're going," Brian said.

Deke finished chewing a bite. "I'll keep pushing with the locals and work with the lab boys. There may have been some trace or something that will give us a lead."

"Do we know what kind of car they were driving when they left?" Dom asked.

Deke shrugged. "Um, I think there's video from the surveillance cameras. Why?"

"Our intel shows that Martin was driving a rental, and we know that he picked up his associates at the airport. Odds would be that either they're in Martin's rental or they've traded it in for a different one. In either case, the car is most likely from a rental agency—"

"We can track them from the onboard GPS that the rental agencies would have used!" Bridgette nearly shouted.

Deke glanced at Brain and nodded. "I'll give the lab a quick call and see if we can get anything going tonight on that front."

"I'm going to try the rental agencies. We already know where Martin rented his car from, so I'll start there," Dom added.

"How are you holding up, Bridge?" Brian asked after the other two had left the room.

"If I said by one, very thin strand would you believe me?"

"Yeah. Meyers came in and talked to me after everything this morning. I'm not a hundred percent sure who is gunning for you, but I know that there was a lot of talk about an internal investigation."

Bridgette's face paled. "Oh no. I don't want to cause problems for everybody. I just want them to stop lying about me."

"What you need to remember, is that whoever is doing this is the one who is causing the problem." He paused to look out the window. "Do you remember when we first learned of the threat against you?" He waited until she nodded. "Meyers said that an agent needed help. Most people in that room would have done anything in their power to help you that day."

"Why?" she asked, her voice almost a squeak.

"When we take our oath and receive our badges, we know that we are pledging to risk our lives to protect the law abiding citizens in this country. When we say those words, we enter into a brotherhood with other like-minded people. In cases like this, where one of us is in trouble, we know that we have to be there for each other. Who else can we count on if not our brothers?"

"But," she hesitated, "I'm not an official member. I work with you, and Deke and Dom and the rest of the team, but I don't belong."

"That's where you're wrong," Dom said from behind her. "You may not have taken the oath, but your actions are very clear to anyone who bothers to pay attention. You've worked harder than most of the others. You stood up and did what you needed to, to protect others. You do belong."

She curled into his outstretched arms and clung to the hope that he was right.

"Did you find anything?" Brian asked as Deke was walking back into the room.

"Maybe. Seems the crew found some indents on the writing tablet that was in the room. They're trying to bring up the images enough to read from."

Dom nodded. "Well, I may have some better news. It seems that our Mr. Martin returned his car to the Hertz rental center on Constitution this morning. According to the manager who happened to take care of him, he was alone and on foot."

"And this is good news? I guess I'm not seeing it, Dom," Deke said.

"Ah, follow along, Grasshopper. Because in that section of town, there is the Hertz center and less than a block away is Alamo. Now, it's possible that our pal walked three blocks and hopped on the bus. But my money would be on them getting new wheels."

"I wish we knew what the others looked like," Bridgette said. "I think it would make more sense to have one of them renting a car while Martin was returning his. If we had pictures maybe someone would recognize them and we'd be on the trail faster."

Dom pulled out his phone again. "I'll get started on getting the warrant for the rentals from Alamo. They should also have video surveillance as well. Maybe we'll be able to get lucky there."

Bridgette nestled her head on Dom's shoulder as they cuddled up on the couch to watch a sitcom after Deke and Brian had left. They had done everything that they could to make her feel safe, but that didn't change the fact that she still felt scared.

"You're awfully quiet," Dom said before kissing the top of her head. "Anything that you want to talk about?"

She raised her head so she could look at him. "There's too much that I want to talk about and it overwhelms me. I'm not even sure where to start."

Dom flicked the remote and turned the television off. "Why don't you just pick a point and start. If we need to backtrack, we do."

"All right. We can give that a try," she said. "I can't figure out why—"

Dom's phone shrieking cut her off. Dom looked at the number and ran his hand through his hair. "Oh, boy. Now what?" he muttered. "Franchini," he said into the phone.

Bridgette watched him when he disengaged himself and walked to the window and stared out. She tried to be polite and not eavesdrop on his conversation, but she was worried that something had happened again.

"Bridgette?" he turned to face her. "I need you to get ready to go out. We're needed at the scene."

"What happened?"

Dom shook his head. "I need to make two calls first. Grab your laptop and your ID and anything else you may need to work a scene. I'll fill you in on the way."

Bridgette followed Dom's lead and draped her ID over her jacket. The flashing lights bounced off of every window on the small side street, so she just focused on the group of people that were standing just inside the yellow crime scene tape.

Ducking under the tape, she took a breath to steady herself. This was a first for her. She'd never been involved in the immediate aftermath of a crime. Well, she thought, that was true if one didn't count her little adventure from a few months ago.

Deciding that she was going to make the best of this, Bridgette scanned the area while Dom was talking to the uniformed officer. It was a narrow street, with cars parked only on the south side of the road. There were no spaces between the buildings, and they were all the same basic style. Brick fronts, with several tall skinny windows on each level.

The only one that stood out to her was on the fourth floor of the building in the very center of the block. Shredded and burnt curtains flapped though the broken glass, and smoke stains streaked the brick façade.

Her hand covered her mouth, "Holy cow. What happened here?"

She flinched when she felt a hand touch her shoulder.

"Sorry," Dom said. "Didn't mean to startle you. You okay?"

"Dom. What...who...how?" she said gesturing to the burned out apartment.

He sighed. "I can't tell you everything, simply because I don't know everything. As best as we can tell, someone launched a fire bomb through the window there," he said pointing to the second one in on the fourth floor.

"How'd they get it that high?" Bridgette asked. "It's got to be nearly forty feet above street level. To get it that high would take a very strong arm. To hit that window means that whomever did this was strong and accurate."

"Fire marshal has cleared us in, Dom," Deke said appearing from somewhere beyond the crowd of officers.

"Come on, Bridgette," Dom said leading her towards the doorway. "I can tell you that no one was hurt in this attack, and it may give us a few leads to work with."

The smell of charred wood became denser the higher they climbed, and Bridgette found herself feeling claustrophobic in the narrow stairwell. "Dom? What is the place?"

"It's one of the safe houses that we occasionally use," he admitted quietly. "It's not one that we frequent, as the access to it is limited, as is the security. There really isn't a great escape route from it either. It works well for a one night stay, or for somebody who needs to stay out of sight for a few hours."

Bridgette stopped on the step. "Who was here tonight?"

Dom turned to face her. "Actually no one was. But if you want to get technical about things, this is one of the addresses that we let out that you were staying at."

Bridgette could feel the blood fall from her face, and she would swear that the stairwell began to move. She squatted down to sit on a step, and pulled her knees to her chest and rocked.

"Bloody hell, Dom. Couldn't you have waited to hit her with that until we were actually in the room?" Deke snarled. "There's barely enough room on these stairs to walk up and down on. There's no way we can carry her up."

"You go on up, Deke. I'll sit here with her for a minute, and then we'll both be up to join you."

She felt the stairs shift slightly under his movement, and then his arms came around her. The pressure in her chest relaxed slightly when he held her, and she was able to gasp for a breath of fresh air.

"It's all right, Bridge. I promise you that it's okay. We're here to gather some data. The bad guys have already gone. I'm not going to let you be alone. We're all here to help you through this."

Bridgette sniffled. "I guess they really are out to get me, huh?"

"Yeah, I'd say so. But I want you to remember we talked about this. I told you that we were giving out bogus addresses to try and find our leak, and this sure looks like someone took the bait."

Bridgette shifted. "Does this mean we know who the leak at the bureau is?"

Dom frowned. "Not exactly. We know who shared the information. This person told somebody, whether it was another agent or someone outside, whose identity is still unknown. But we know where the source of the leak started. We'll get them."

Bridgette took another deep breath and ignored the smell. "Okay, so what do we do now, and why am I here?"

Dom smiled wryly. "We anticipated that something like this might happen. Each of the decoy apartments was set up with sophisticated monitoring devices that would record sounds and traffic, both pedestrian and vehicle. I'd like you to have a look at the video that we've got here. My guess is, unless the whole thing is burnt to a crisp, that we will have a video of who ever tossed this bomb."

For the first time in over an hour, Bridgette smiled. "Then let's get this done, so we can put him away."

The rest of the climb was made in silence, Bridgette taking in every visual clue that she could. She noted that there were cameras at each of the landings, and wondered how to get the feed from those as well. Had the attacker even tried to ensure that she had been in the apartment, or had they just attacked without regard for the lives of the others in the building?

Dom pushed the door to 401 open, and the scene changed dramatically. Instead of the lush carpet that had been on the stairs, the carpet here was melted and parts of the flooring were so charred that she wondered if it was strong enough to support anyone.

"This is what I want you to look at," Dom said pointing to a charred box in the corner. "Is the guts of the surveillance package. It should still be viable as it's encased in a water tight, shock-proof container."

Bridgette nodded and carefully made her way around to it. Pulling a screwdriver from her bag, she disassembled the outer box, exposing the hard drive inside. Using the cables from her laptop, she connected the drive and began working.

"I've got some images here," she said a minute later. "Appear to be real faint, though."

"That's during the fire," Dom said from behind her. He pointed to a smudge on the screen, "See that? That's smoke. And there comes the fire department," he said when the first truck with flashing lights came into view.

"Okay, then let's try backing up a ways and see what we've got," Bridgette said while pressing the commands on the keyboard.

She pressed play again. "According to the time stamp, this is roughly an hour before the first truck arrived." The screen showed the street below in early evening. There was almost no foot traffic, and only a single black Chevy sedan drove down the street. Bridgette pressed the scan feature, and they continued to watch as the time sped by.

"That's interesting," Bridgette said, pointing at the screen.

"What did I miss?" Deke asked.

"That's the third time this car has gone by in about twenty minutes," she offered.

"Looking for a parking place?" Dom tried.

"I don't think so. Watch again," Bridgette said. She went back a few frames before the sedan came into view. Pressed play and waited for the two agents to see what she had noticed.

The sleek black sedan came in fairly quick from the right side of the screen, slowed down just before it passed the apartment and then sped back up and rocketed out of sight.

"Did it do that in the other passes? That slowing down right in front of the building?" Dom wanted to know.

"Not sure about the first round," Bridgette admitted. "I picked it up on the second pass, and then again when he made this last run. I think if I go frame by frame, I can get a plate number to work with."

"That'll be a great start," Deke agreed. "Now let's let it play and see if we can find who made the actual toss."

Bridgette again cued up the recording and hit play. This time a tall red haired man strolled into the frame and stared at the building. He crossed the street before fumbling for something in his jacket pocket. With a glance in both directions, he swiftly pulled out a small gray orb, pulled a pin from the top of it and hurled it towards the camera.

The object went out of view and was immediately followed by the sound of breaking glass and the whoosh of the fireball. As the flames began to dance and distort the image, the black sedan pulled up, the door already open.

"It never stopped," Bridgette barely whispered. "They were doing dry runs before. He knew exactly how long it was going to take for them to come back around. He lobbed the bomb through the window, and they came to pick him up. And they did so without actually stopping."

"I'll admit, I'm impressed with his accuracy and moves. But I'm going to take this guy down," Dom said.

Bridgette went back to the point in the video when the unknown man was directly across from the building. She stopped the playback and zoomed in on him. "Hello, David," she said with a smile.

CHAPTER 22

"David?" Dom asked cautiously. "You know this guy?"

Bridgette nodded. "Yes. If I recall correctly, Henry Hyde who was one of the senior partners in the firm that I used to work at, represented him in a few cases. Again, if I remember right, his last name is Mortsky, or something along that. But I'm pretty sure his first name is David."

Deke peered over their shoulders, "I've never seen him before."

"Count your blessings. This guy was a real creep when I last dealt with him."

"Why did you have to deal with him if this Dewey guy was the one representing him?" Deke asked.

"Because I got to do most of the grunt work for the firm. A whole bunch of computer time. It seems that the partners felt that spending time doing research was way below their pay grade. As a result, I got to deal with many of the colorful members of the various gangs and troublemakers

"Anyway, I'm not likely to forget Dave, there. It's not everyday you get a proposition like he offered," she said with a shake of her head.

Dom's fist clenched until his knuckles were white.

Bridgette rested her hand on his arm, squeezed. "Dom, it's all right. I blew him off and never gave it, or him, a second thought."

Dom looked at her, and she could have sworn that she saw something in his eyes. Something that perhaps should have scared her, but instead it thrilled her. His eyes said that she was his.

Deke spoke again before anything further could happen. "If you've got a picture and a name, why don't you guys head into the office? I'll finish up here with the Metro guys and meet you there in a while."

As Dom guided the SUV away from the burned out building, Bridgette fought to keep control. There were too many aspects of her life that were in constant upheaval right now. The knowledge that a deranged group of gang members was trying to kill her, to the point that they had just torched an apartment without regard for any of the other people who lived there, the fact that someone whom she had had contact with in a previous part of her life was the one responsible for the attempt and, perhaps most interestingly, Dom's reaction.

Of the three, she wanted to spend time considering that reaction. No one had ever looked at her like that. It probably should have been a little scary, but she couldn't find the fear over the anticipation of what might happen next.

"Bridgette," Dom asked, his voice still rough with emotion. "I, uh, know that you're allowed time over the weekends to run errands and stuff. What do you have to do on Saturday?"

Whoa, she thought. That was a direction that she wasn't exactly planning to go. Why was he worried about what she was doing on Saturday?

"Well, most likely grocery shopping. I have this thing about having food in the house, and presently I'm running a little low. I need to run to the bank at some point and I'd like to take a run to one of the bookstores. Why?"

Dom drummed his fingers on the wheel as he thought. "Do you think you could make a list for me, and I could do the shopping for you tomorrow?"

Now she was confused. "May I ask why?"

He turned to her. "I really need to talk to you about a few things, and I'd really like to take you out for a real date. I...I just thought that if I took care of your errands before Saturday, maybe we could actually go out. Hit the bookstore, maybe a movie and then a nice restaurant for dinner."

Bridgette smiled. "I'd like that. We'll find a way to compromise with things," she said as they pulled into the underground parking area.

They walked into the building hand in hand.

"You two sure look chipper," Tammy snarled. She glared at Bridgette, huffed out a breath. "I don't understand why it's always my plans that get blasted when stuff like this happens. But it is, and I'm pretty sure that my date went back to his place and I didn't even get dessert.

"What did you find out at the scene?" she asked, pointedly looking at Dom.

"Crime scene located a few fragments of what looks to be an incendiary grenade. Deke is following up with the boys and girls from Metro and then will be bringing it in to the lab. We may have gotten a break with the surveillance equipment. It did survive the fire—always good to know that things work like they're supposed to—but more importantly we have the car that was used and a picture of the guy who tossed the grenade."

Tammy nodded. "Excellent. Do you want me to take the picture of the guy and I can start running him through facial recognition and then we can zero in on the car?"

"How about you start with the car? My guess is that it's going to come back to the Alamo rental fleet, likely rented at the Constitution Ave location sometime today. But we might be able to get a handle on who rented it. Bridgette recognized the guy. So we already have a name to start with, so she's going to run with that."

Tammy looked over at Bridgette in a way that made her skin crawl. The old expression about looks killing somebody was evident, she thought.

"I'll do my job, Tammy. You know I can. I...I don't know why you don't like me, or why you want me put away like you seem to. I can only guess, but I will promise you this; I will never intentionally do something that will put a member of this group in danger. Ever," Bridgette said before she turned and walked away.

"What's the status, Franchini?" Director Meyers asked walking into the conference room.

Dom checked his watch, "Sir, approximately four hours ago, the safe house on thirty-second street was fire bombed. Agent Kirkpatrick and myself went to the scene, accompanied by Miss Mahoney roughly ninety minutes ago. Kirkpatrick is in the lab now working with them on what we think is some type of incendiary grenade. He hopes to have some more details, specifically the make of the grenade within the hour. The surveillance video gave us two leads.

"Currently Tammy Cipone is working the car angle. When I last spoke to her, she had been able to isolate the tag on the car. Unfortunately when we ran it, it came back to a stolen truck. She's going through the video now, hoping to find something else that might lead back to the car. We still haven't received the warrant that I requested earlier this evening for the records of the Alamo rental in the city.

"Bridgette is in her lab working on the man who threw the grenade. Tentatively he has been identified as one David Mark Mortensky. He's got a rap sheet about two feet long, mostly for petty-ante stuff from when he was younger. He is also a known member of the Mambas.

"When I last spoke to Bridgette, she was running two searches at the same time. She was going through footage from the various airports, using Mortnesky's mug-shot for facial recognition, and she's trying to find who his known associates are."

Meyers snorted. "His known associates. If he's a member of the Mambas, then we have a fairly good idea who he associates with, don't we?"

Dom pulled out a chair and sank into it. "That's true, Sir. However it appears that as the Mambas have gotten bigger, they've begun to specialize a bit more. Bridgette's thought was that if we could find who Mortensky most often travels with, we have an idea of who else to look for."

Meyers slid into the seat across from Dom. "Hmmm. What you say makes sense. I just hope we can get this closed up fast." His fingers drummed nervously on the table. "We also need to decide how to play this with the media."

"The media, Sir? I'm not sure what you mean."

Meyers studied Dom carefully. "What do we let them think, Dom? Do we tell them that they hit an empty apartment knowing they'll try again? Do we put it out there that she's been hurt and is in the hospital? These are some points that we never got around to discussing."

Dom nodded. "We always thought that we'd be able to keep tabs on him and we would apprehend them before they got the shot off. But they got by us."

"Which puts her right back in their sights if we let them know that they missed." Meyers leaned back in his chair and scratched his chin. "What's going on with our leak?"

"I've turned the name over to Brian and Lucy. They were working on setting up a little session with our friend. I anticipate that ...wait. What if we let our leak know what happened? Tell the media one thing, but let the leak know the truth?"

Meyers' eyes popped open. "You're thinking about setting him up? Get him when he goes to make the trade? I like it. Call Moran and get that going. Have him and Daniels work on coming up with something for the press."

There was a knock on the door, and both men shifted.

"Come on in, Miss Mahoney," Meyers said with a wave. "Agent Franchini and I were just talking about a few things that involve you. Pull up a seat and we can fill each other in."

Bridgette was still struggling to overcome her fears that were caused by Director Meyers pulling her out of her office this morning—was it really less than twelve hours ago?— but knew that she didn't have a choice in the matter. She had to face him, and continue doing her job better than anyone else. It took a conscious effort to make her feet move and walk into the room.

"Sir," she nodded. "I did a bit of cross referencing checking airline manifest with David Mortensky's name along with other names that he was associated with. I hit pay dirt. Mortensky was on flight 952 out of Cleveland, which arrived at the Baltimore/Washington airport at noon yesterday. When I ran that manifest against other known Mambas, I found three other matches." She shifted so the others could see the computer screen. "Samantha Wilson. Age twenty-eight, and known Mamba since she was eleven. Her sheet includes doing time for robbery and assault. She is suspected of being involved with at least four homicides, but has never been formally charged."

She pressed a button and the picture changed to show a chunky man with a full head of dark brown hair. "This is Carl Davis. He's the youngest of the group at just two weeks past his twenty-second birthday. He's been with the Mambas since he was ten, and has done time in both juvenile centers and county lock ups, mostly for breaking and entering. It seems that he has a talent for getting around security systems.

"And last, but not least, this is Todd Crewe," she said again changing the screen. Crewe's face was expressionless but his onyx colored eyes spoke volumes. "He's thirty one and tends to be the lookout. At first glance, he's non-descript and can easily blend in without being noticed, but from what the reports say, he's lethal. He's done a little time for trespassing and tampering with security devices and suspected to having ties to a few other crimes, but nothing anyone can prove."

"That's good work, Mahoney," Meyers said. He looked across the table, "Okay, Franchini, brief Mahoney on what the current plan is, and then let's see if we can bag these buggers before the holiday weekend."

Bridgette's eyes were wide with worry. Dom tried to reassure her, "It's a pretty simple plan, Bridge. We'll get—"

"Holiday weekend?" she stammered. "I forgot. Lucy invited herself over for a picnic. What am I going to do?"

"What's the problem?" Dom asked hoping for some clarification.

"Everything. I don't have the stuff for a picnic, I just moved into a new space that she doesn't know about yet. What am I supposed to do? I haven't had a holiday picnic since I was fifteen. What do I know about hosting one?"

He reached over and took her hand. "Let's take one thing at a time. Brian, Deke and I will help you along every step of this. I'm going shopping for you tomorrow, I'll get the stuff. I'm pretty sure that between the group of us, we can make this happen. Now I need you to relax."

Once she had, Dom relayed what the next phase of the plan was.

Bridgette wasn't sure which concerned her more; the game that they were playing with the Mambas, or trying to get ready for a Memorial Day picnic. In either case, she was playing with fire and could very easily get badly burned.

Bridgette was staring at the computer screen and having difficulties reading it. It had been nearly fifteen hours since Dom had gotten the call about the fire, and she had yet to be to bed. "I think I need to catch some down time or some serious caffeine," she said to Brian.

Brian looked up from his own screen. "I hear you on that." He pressed a few keys and stood up, "Let's take a stroll down to the cafeteria and grab some coffee or something. Between the caffeine and the walk, we should feel better."

"Moran!" a voice called from down the hall causing them both to turn.

Tammy was running after them waving a sheet of paper. "Got something here that I think will be useful to everyone."

Brian sighed, "So much for caffeine," he muttered softly. Turning back to the lab he asked, "So what do you have for us?"

Tammy beamed, "I found the car."

"You mean the one from the fire bombing last night?" Bridgette asked.

"Yeah. I, uh, started following a few threads last night. Dom said how he thought this was from the Alamo rental place, so I scanned the car, and sure enough I was able to find the sticker they put on all of their vehicles. With that, I was able to give the warrant request that Dom had started last night a push.

"Turns out they rented a Black Chevy Malibu to one T.J. Crewe. The guy at the counter didn't remember anything about the guy. Said he must of come in alone."

Brian turned and smiled. "Good work, Tammy. Now did they give us the codes for the GPS tracker that would be installed in that particular car?"

Tammy frowned, "They tried to tap dance around giving it to us. I was able to access the file from the data that they did give us and found the manufacturer code and went with that instead.

"Got a hit on it in a little subdivision in Virginia. Doesn't exactly make sense to me why they'd be there, but that's where the car is pinging from."

"Do you have a physical address of the place?" Brian asked.

Tammy read it off of the sheet she held in her hand.

"It's deeded to a Rittenburg Enterprises. No way to tell for sure if that's a Mamba front or not," Brian said.

"So what happens now?" Bridgette asked.

"We take what you found last night, gather the pictures and all other data on our suspects, feed that with the information from Tammy to the Virginia police and hope that we get lucky. Between the agencies, we'll put the place under surveillance, and eventually we'll get somewhere."

Bridgette tried to doze in the seat of the SUV on the ride home. "I don't know how you guys can keep doing these kind of days. I grabbed a thirty minute nap at lunch, and I'm still exhausted."

Dom laughed lightly. "Maybe it's good clean living. I got my second—or is it third?—wind late this afternoon. I'll be good for another few hours."

She glared at him. "I'm going to sleep for a few hours when I get home. Can't think of anything else right now but catching some sleep."

"Can't think of anything else, huh? Not even what you'd like for dinner tonight, or what kind of chocolate I should pick up for you while I'm out?"

"You're mean," she pouted. "Now I'm going to be craving chocolate instead of sleeping. Then, tomorrow I'll be too tired to do anything."

"I'll surprise you with dinner tonight, and you can sleep while I get it ready, and the chocolate will be for just before I leave for the night. It'll give you sweet dreams."

He nearly had to carry her up the stairs when they got to her apartment. She staggered in the door and fell face first onto the sofa.

When she snored softly, Dom sighed and let out a laugh. "Guess you weren't kidding about being asleep on your feet." He leaned over, gave her a kiss on the cheek. "Sweet dreams darling. I'll be back shortly."

CHAPTER 23

Bridgette woke with a pain in her lower back and struggled to sit up. "What the…Why am I on the sofa?"

She looked around.

The blanket that was twisted around her feet was the one that was usually on her bed. Why had she brought it out here?

The light from the window captured her attention.

It was bright and sent a rainbow against her walls when it passed through the sun catcher that she'd hung.

"It can't be morning. There's no way that I slept that long."

Freeing her feet, she shuffled down the hall for the bathroom, and she hoped, some answers. Her reflection didn't have any ideas either, she decided minutes later.

In the kitchen, she headed for the stove to put on water for tea and saw the note on the table.

Bridge,

When I got back from running your errands, you were sound asleep.

Figured you'd had enough for one day. I'll make sure your doors are locked before I leave.

See you in the morning. Love you,

Dom

She clutched the paper to her chest and let the tears flow. No one had ever given her a love note before. It didn't matter that is was just a few lines. It was a first for her seeing those words written to her.

She took the note and put it in the little cedar box that her dad had given her the Christmas before he'd been killed. To her it was her memory box. She took the pictures of her family out and looked at each of them. Her Mom. Her Dad. Her Sister. "I wish you were all here right now. I so want you to know Dom. He's special."

She kissed each of the pictures before closing the box and placing it back on the dresser.

The growl from her stomach had her headed back to the kitchen when the knock on the door came.

Standing on her toes, she managed to look through the Judas hole and saw Dom.

"Good morning," she said pulling the door open.

"Good morning back—Bridgette, what's wrong?" he asked suddenly worried. "You've been crying." He scooped her up in his arms and rubbed her back.

"Nothing's wrong, Dom. Really. It's more...I'd guess I'd call it sentimental," she said pushing back so he could see her. "I found your note. It made me think of my folks. I miss them so much. I know that I should be over it by now, I mean, it's been nearly a dozen years since I lost my dad and Lisa. It should be easier. And it is most days.

"Today just isn't one of them. I, uh, found your note on the table. And I wanted to share it with them," she said with her voice trailing off at the end. "I really liked it. It's the first time anyone ever wrote that they loved me. It's special, you know."

"I'll be sure to write you a love letter at least once a week," he said kissing the top of her head.

They stood in the doorway, embraced together, each lost in their own thoughts.

Bridgette's stomach growled again, causing her to laugh. "I guess it's getting demanding. Come on in, and I'll fix breakfast for us."

"So any thoughts about where you'd like to go today?" Dom asked sitting at her table watching her.

She mixed the batter for the chocolate chip pancakes, shook her head. "Not really. With the time I lost while I was…um, otherwise located, I lost base with the movies and such. After coming to work at the bureau, I just sort of focused on things there.

"I would like to visit the book store, but other than that I am open to suggestions. Or we could just stroll around poking our noses into the various antique shops," she said.

"We'll see what happens. We can do the book store first and then I thought we could try Cecily's for lunch."

"That's kind of a fancy place isn't it? Why do you want to go there for lunch as opposed to hitting a fast food place?"

Dom grinned at her. "Apparently you forgot. The reason that I ran your errands last night, was so that I could take you out somewhere nice and we could have a real date. I'd like to spend some time romancing you, Bridge."

"Oh," was all she said before he pulled her onto his lap.

She turned her head up, and found his lips. Her belly tightened like it did every time he kissed her.

His hands found a spot on her lower back where her shirt had ridden up slightly, and the feel of flesh on flesh was disorienting.

She was intoxicated by his aroma, and drew in a breath.

"Oh blast!" she shrieked, jumping up. "The pancakes are burning."

She flipped the singed lumps. "So much for showing how good I am in the kitchen."

"I don't know. The little preview that I got sure whetted my appetite."

Bridgette walked out of Morgan's books with her arms loaded. "I never planned to buy this many books at one time," she complained to Dom.

"Hey, I mentioned the idea of getting them all in digital format, but you're the one who wanted to get hardcovers."

She stuck her tongue out at him, and he laughed.

"I don't know about digital books. There's just something about being able to curl up with a good ole' paper book."

Dom ruffled her hair. "I know," he said as he opened the trunk for her. "Let's put everything back here for now, and then we can go for lunch."

Cecily's was located right on the border of D.C. and Virginia in a little single story brick building. Walking in, Bridgette was immediately taken with the ambiance.

Soft glows from candlelight illuminated the whole main dining room. Speakers, which Bridgette guessed were hidden in the potted plants, piped in sweet romantic melodies, and the aroma reminded her of the smell of fresh baked cookies.

Dom took her hand as they followed the waitress to a table in the corner.

"It almost seems weird sitting in the corner in the middle of the day when there's almost no one else here," Bridgette said.

"I, uh, sort of requested it."

Did he blush? That was so cute, not that she'd ever tell him that.

But it was one more thing that endeared him to her.

"Are you that concerned about someone sneaking up on you?"

He shrugged. "I can't remember who said that it's only paranoia if they're not out to get you." He turned his head slightly. "I guess in some way, it probably is a bit of cautiousness. In my line, you never know who's going to come walking in the door so it pays to keep your back covered and your eyes on the door.

"Of course, today, I'm going to have difficulties keeping my eyes off of you," he added with a smile.

Bridgette was taking her second bite of cannelloni when Dom stiffened.

"I don't believe it," he whispered.

"What is it?" Bridgette asked before she started to turn.

"No! Don't!" he hissed. "Terrance Martin just walked in. If I'm not mistaken, David Mortensky is one of the others."

Bridgette's eyes widened with the realization of how precarious their situation was. They were in the back corner of the room. The only exits out were on the other side. That meant that they would have to walk right by Martin and the other Mambas.

Her stomach was suddenly filled with butterflies. "What do we do?" she asked.

Dom reached over the table and took her hand, but his eyes never left the other table. "I'm going to text Deke and Brian. I'll get them to send a team."

"What happens if they see me?"

"I don't know. I'd like to say since you've got your back to them, the odds are they won't see you. But I'm not sure we're that lucky. These are gang members, who've in the past have shown no compunction of opening fire in public places."

The phone in his hand vibrated, and Dom looked down to read the screen. "Deke has backup on the way."

Bridgette brought her phone out and held it with the power

off. The screen acted like a mirror, giving her a glimmer of what was happening. She concentrated on her breathing, fighting for the calmness that she didn't feel.

In the reflection, she watched the man with the mocha colored skin look at his phone. He whispered something to his associates, and the four of them stood and walked hurriedly towards the exit.

"Bloody hell," Dom said, as he watched Mortensky exit. "Somebody had to have tipped them off. But how?"

Bridgette turned to look at the door. "Do you think they know how they were made? Will they be waiting in the lot for us when we leave?"

Two Virginia State troopers came through the door, their eyes searching every table in the room.

Dom signaled to one of the officers, stood and pulled his ID out, laying it on the table. Bridgette followed his lead and stood as well.

"You call this in, Agent?"

"Not exactly, officer," Dom said and then explained how he'd contacted Deke for the call in.

"They must have been tipped off," the second officer, who to Bridgette looked no more than twenty, said.

"Good guess, Rookie," the older officer noted. He turned back to Dom. "Is there any chance that he made you or your wife?"

Bridgette blushed at the comment, but before she could say anything to straighten out the mistake, Dom answered.

"I don't think so. I noticed them as soon as they walked in. I kept my eye on them as I contacted Agent Kirkpatrick. More importantly, Bridgette never turned to look at them directly. So I'm pretty sure they didn't notice her either."

"What makes you think they'd make her?" Rookie asked gaining a nod from the older officer.

"Bridgette helped the FBI gain access to their computer system and as a direct result, cost them over two million in cash. The gang has a price on her head. If they'd seen her, with the place being as empty as it is right now," Dom paused for effect, "They'd have most likely blasted this room apart."

The older officer looked around. "Seeing as there were only you two and one other couple in here, yeah, I'd have to agree." He stood with his hands on his hips looking around the room. "They had you guys cornered, literally, didn't they? Any idea where they would be heading after here?"

Dom shrugged. "I know that our team has been tracking them using their rental car, but I don't know if they're still using it or if it had been dumped."

Bridgette jumped when a hand grasped her shoulder.

"You okay, Bridge," Deke asked.

She turned and saw that he'd brought Brian along as well. "Yeah. I think so, at least. I can't believe how close things were here."

"Keep hanging around Franchini there. He's got a real cool head when the chips are down and fur starts flying," Deke said before he moved over to speak with the troopers.

Feeling her legs giving out, Bridgette sank into the booth hoping that she would be able to control the shaking that she was sure was coming. It always happened after a traumatic event. She knew it, prepared for it, and was still always surprised by how badly it affected her.

Dom noticed her sitting with her legs pulled up and came over.

"Brian says they're tracking the car. We've got a team of agents that are alternating tails on the car so we can follow it back to wherever they're going. Relax now, Bridge, you're safe."

"Easy for you to say," she quipped. "Ever since I started working with you guys, I've had more than enough excitement. I guess, I'll never be able to claim that my life is boring again."

He pulled her into his arms and just held her. In that moment, she felt all of her tensions fade away, and knew that things were going to be okay.

"What the heck happened back there, Crewe?" Terrance Martin asked as they stormed into the little three bedroom ranch house that they were using.

"Hey, man, relax. All I know is that my contact in the dispatcher's office texted me and told me that a team was on the way to the restaurant to apprehend us. She didn't give me anything more than that." He ran a hand over his face. "Look, I know that things went crazy there, but at least we got out. The cops who were pulling in as we headed out didn't even look at us twice."

Martin hadn't stopped moving since they'd entered the house, and was now pacing the length of the living room puling at his hair. "How did they freakin' know that we were there? That's what we need to find out.

"I think we need to check that car for bugs. They followed us somehow, and if they found us at the restaurant, then they can easily trace us here."

Sam Wilson sucked in on the cigarette that she had just lit. Apparently forgetting that she already had one burning in the ashtray by the sofa. "I don't think they followed us. But I can't guarantee that they didn't trace the car," she said.

"There's no way that they could have bugged the car," Carl Davis said. "Heck, how'd they even know we had that car? I think some busybody cop must have made us."

Martin turned on him. "How? Think about it, where have we been? After we dumped our little present on Mahoney, we've been here. Inside. We haven't left other than to go to that place an hour ago. Who saw us?"

"I think I know," Moretnsky said solemnly. He turned his phone around so the others could see the screen. "When Todd said we had to get out, I videoed the others in the room as we left. Discreetly. Look at the guy at the back table."

"Cold eyes, man," Davis said. "That's a cop. How'd we miss that when we went in?"

"Because we've all been complacent sitting here," Wilson said. "But you know what I think is more interesting in your little video, David? Take a look at the cop's companion."

"She was there! My mole told me that she hadn't been home when we hit the apartment. Crap! That cursed Bridgette Mahoney was sitting there not more than fifteen feet away, and there would have only been three extraneous people to have silenced," Martin said. He exhaled loudly. "I'm going to go out for a walk and try to walk off this mad."

"I'll go with you. Tony's not going to be happy about either of these turns of events. We need to think of what we're going to say to him," Wilson said as she followed him out the back door.

"Okay, everybody clear on what's happening," Special Agent Kim Sellers asked, looking at the faces of her troops. They were the elite team, specializing in high-risk maneuvers, and the one they were facing today fit the bill.

She studied the blueprints for the ranch house and tried to anticipate every contingency, knowing that she was sending others into harms way.

"Warrant came through, Ma'am," a new member of the team said.

"Thompson? What's the word on location of the subjects?" Sellers asked.

"We haven't been able to sit on the house because of how open everything is. The unmarked cars have been doing drive-bys every few minutes and are equipped with heat sensors. It looks like two of our friends have slipped by us, but the car is still in the driveway, so they're most likely on foot. The other three gomers are just sitting there."

Sellers wasn't happy that two of the five had evaded her team for now, but concentrated on doing the job. "Let's go get 'em," she said.

The code word was given on the radio, and her four officers who had been handling the unmarked cars parked and made their way through the backyards off of the neighboring streets to cover the back door of the ranch.

When she received word that her team was in place, she nodded to the driver and the van began lumbering up the road. Just before they passed the house, she triggered the small explosive device that had been set up on the van's exterior. The loud bang followed by copious amounts of smoke gave credence to the illusion of trouble. The driver swerved the van across the yard sand stopped near the front door.

"Go! Go! Go!" Sellers yelled as she leapt from the van vaulting the stairs to the front door.

An agent with a battering ram knocked the door out of the way, and she led her men in. "FBI! Everybody down. Keep your hands in sight."

Carl Davis dropped the sandwich he was carrying, letting it bounce off of his shoe. His face was in complete shock as he raised his hands over his head and eased himself to the floor.

Crewe came around the corner, "Davis what the—"

"On the floor, Scumbag," Sellers said, gesturing with her gun. "We've got two here secured."

Her radio crackled, "We've got a runner! Back on the north side!"

Four staccato shots rang out.

"Blasted all," Sellers muttered as she made her way to the door.

David Mortensky lay in an expanding pool of blood. A nine

millimeter Glock was still curled in the fingers of his right hand. Two of her agents were walking cautiously toward the sprawled figure with their guns out aimed at center mass.

"Sorry, Ma'am. He took a couple of shots at Higgins, I had no choice."

They rolled Mortensky over. His eyes were wide open, but unseeing. "Stupid bloody fool," Sellers said. "He knew we had him, but he wanted to go out with a bang." She keyed the mic on her collar, "Control, SWAT two-niner. Location is secure. Two for transport to holding, one needs the coroner. Please advise all agents BOLO for Terrance Martin and Samantha Wilson. Suspects are assumed to be armed and dangerous."

Back at Bridgette's apartment, Dom hung up his phone and stared out the window. How did he tell her that they almost got them? How could he make her feel secure enough that she would relax and enjoy what she could of this holiday weekend?

He resolved himself that he would need help from his buddies and they'd give her a party that she'd never forget.

CHAPTER 24

"So there still isn't any word on where Martin and Wilson disappeared to?" Bridgette asked.

Dom looked up from the kitchen table where he was currently working on dicing potatoes for salad. "Not yet. Best guess is that they were near the house when the SWAT went in and have taken evasive action. There really wasn't much that announced their presence that would have alerted them."

Bridgette turned back from the counter where she was preparing the chicken that they would be barbequing for the party that afternoon. "Nothing like a few gunshots in a quiet suburb to warn off the bad guys."

Dom set down his knife and went to her. Wrapping his arms around her, he laid his cheek on her head. "Bridge, I know that this still has you concerned. And I'm not going to tell you that you should ignore it, or that we've got this all handled. The best that I can say is that we are working on it.

"Right now, we've got aerial teams searching the nearby wooded areas with heat sensing equipment. Every agent is on alert. We are doing what can be done. The best thing for us—you and me—to do right now is to get ready to have fun at the little soiree that we've got planned."

She scowled at him. "Yes, the little soiree, as you called it, that you planned and surprised me with."

He tried to look shocked by her reaction, but couldn't help but smile. "Hey, you were already planning to have Lucy and me over for the afternoon. And I wasn't going to make my friends spend the day closed up in their apartments. It just made sense to have everybody over. Besides, we'll have fun."

"Yeah, yeah, yeah. I'll forgive you for putting me on the spot… someday. But for now, since we've only got about an hour before this place is going to be overrun by hungry people, I think you'd better get back to work on that potato salad."

People were scattered around the Bridgette's apartment as she made her way through the living room. She noted Deke, Brian and Dom all standing on the impossibly small balcony gathered around a portable grill that was sending what appeared to be smoke signals.

She hoped that the burgers they claimed they were cooking tasted as good as they smelled. She wrapped her arms around herself and stood in the quiet corner of the kitchen watching everything.

There were eleven other people in her tiny apartment today, all because they wanted to spend the holiday together. They'd come here, she thought, because she couldn't go anywhere else. So instead of leaving her alone for the day, they'd brought the party here.

A lone tear dribbled down her cheek before she wiped it away with the back of her hand.

"Hey, you okay," Lucy asked pulling a Coke out of the cooler that sat against the wall.

"Yeah. I'm-I'm fine, really. It's just hitting me that's all. I haven't had a picnic like this since the year my dad and sister were killed. And then what everybody did so I could enjoy the celebration too. It humbles me."

Lucy handed Bridgette a Coke. "We like you. You're good people, if you know what I mean. Besides, by having it here, I didn't have to play hostess." She shot a sly grin at Bridgette.

"Believe it or not, I kind of like being a hostess. I haven't had much experience with it, and maybe I'll hate it in a while, but right now I'm enjoying it"

"That's good. Then I'll let everybody know that we're here for Thanksgiving too."

Bridgette's mouth dropped open before Lucy's face gave way to the smile. "Your face was priceless, Bridgette. Wish I had a camera," Lucy said before going back into the living room to join the others.

Bridgette made her way to the door to the balcony. "How's it going?"

"Chicken is done and the burgers should be ready in about five," Dom said.

"Dude, the way you're going, they're going to resemble hockey pucks in five. You need to keep turning them or you're burning them," Brian said.

Deke leaned against the railing laughing. "These two would argue about the correct way to fix a bowl of cereal, I swear."

"The only question I need an answer to right now, is should I start getting things set on the table so we can eat?"

At least all three of them agreed on that, she thought a moment later as she pulled out the salads that she and Dom had made earlier.

"What are we doing here," Terry asked Sam as they pulled up to the empty building. "I thought we were staying at the hotel tonight."

She reached over and laid a hand on his cheek. "You poor, ignorant fool. This is why Tony sent me here to save you. You're too predictable. How you were able to keep yourself out of a jail cell for those first few days is totally beyond me."

She slipped out of the car and deftly picked the lock on the door. "Are you coming in, or are you going to wait in the car?"

Terry hated feeling used, especially when it was a girl who was showing him up, but there was no way that he was going to sit in that car while she was in doing something.

He was still pretty miffed about the whole fiasco that ended with one of his associates being killed and the two others hauled out in cuffs. It had only been sheer luck that he and Sam had turned the corner just as the first SWAT member had jumped out of the back of the truck.

He remembered watching the events unfold in shock. Thankfully Sam had kept her cool and had ushered him away from the scene until they were a safe distance out.

He should have thanked her for that. But the thought of it only made his skin crawl.

Climbing the first step in the old building, he shook his head, as if trying to erase the memory so he could focus on the task at hand.

Of course, it would be easier if he knew what that task was.

"Sam, what are we doing here? There ain't nobody but the bleeding rats."

"And this is why you would have lost, Terry. You're too focused on one small facet of the puzzle. You forget that it's but a single battle on the way to winning the war. If we want to win, we can't do things that the cops are going to be able to predict that we'll do. We have to be one step ahead of them."

"And how are we going to do that while we're slogging through the rat crap?"

Her laugh echoed off of the walls. "You said that you had a contact in the Bureau, right?"

"Yeah. He's like my fourth cousin on my dad's side, or

something. Why?

"Well, think about this. He's been useful at getting us information, but how do you think he'd be about getting the feds some information?"

She'd stopped climbing stairs and was now picking the lock on one of the doors on the top floor.

"He'd probably prefer that. The only reason that he's giving me anything, is that I've got pictures that he'd rather his wife not find out about. If he could give them something useful, it'd probably help him out at work, and in the long run help us out too. The more data he has access to, the more we can get him to pass on to us."

He watched Sam as she wandered around the empty room, stopping at each window to peer out. He couldn't figure out what difference a window made. You still saw the same crap below.

"Yes," Sam muttered. "This will do nicely. We can set up our post here." She turned to Terry. "Okay, I want you to call this so-called cousin of yours and get him to find us," she made air quotes on the last two words. "If he does it correctly, they should plan to stake out our hotel within the next twenty four to forty eight hours, and then we can give them a little of our own brand of justice."

When Terry blanched a bit, she laughed louder. "Oh, please. Tell me you're not actually concerned about the idea of taking out a few cops. They took out Dave with about as much thought as you'd give to killing a flea on your dog. They deserve what they get from here on out."

As he walked back down to the car to make the call, he made a mental note that he had better stay on her good side if he wanted to see his next birthday.

Bridgette flopped back on the couch exhausted. "I never thought they'd leave," she complained.

Brain and Deke only laughed as they plowed their way through their third round of food for the day. Dom pulled out two Cokes and sat next to her. "They are an energetic bunch. Andy sure seemed to be having a great time."

"Was he the one who was hitting on every female here?" she asked.

Dom dropped his head and nodded. "That would be Andy. The only thing that could have made it worse is if his wife had been here. You'd feel for her. Luckily, she's a nurse and was on at the hospital."

Bridgette stared at him with her mouth hanging open. "He's married, and still doing that?"

"Well, not exactly. They're in the process of splitting. He's pulled that stunt a few too many times and she threw him out. To be honest, I'm not even sure how he got invited here today. I thought it was supposed to be a quiet event," Dom mused. "Oh, well, somebody here must have told him."

Bridgette shook her head. "Where does he work in the bureau?"

Dom shrugged his shoulders, "Not really sure. I've seen him around a few times, but I don't know which division."

"He's from the lab, but he's a good friend with, um, Truman. Doctor Kevin Truman, the shrink," Deke said. "I see them once in a while. From what I've heard, Andy has been having a rough few days with stuff going on with the soon-to-be-ex. Normally, he'd talk to Kevin, either as a friend or patient, but with Kevin being out of town visiting relatives for the last week, Andy's cracking. It's sad."

"When does the good doctor get back?" Dom asked.

"Not soon enough to keep Andy from making a fool of himself," Deke said. "Think I heard that he'd be back on Wednesday."

"Well," Bridgette said, "I'm going to be sure to keep away from Andy until well after Wednesday. And I think I'll have to pass the word that he's not invited to Thanksgiving if he's going to act like that."

"Thanksgiving?" three voices said at the same time.

"You're thinking of hosting Thanksgiving too?" Dom asked. "How did that happen?"

Bridgette shrugged. "I was talking to Lucy, and said that I was enjoying playing hostess. The next thing I knew she'd decided that we'd do Thanksgiving here too." She sipped her soda. "Actually, it'll be nice to have a bunch of people over for it. The last few years, I ended up going to Denny's or something. It's kind of lonely doing that."

Dom reached over and took her hand. "I wouldn't have left you be alone for the holiday, but I never would have volunteered you to host it for a whole group." He kissed her hand. "We belong together."

That night as she watched her friends go, Bridgette let herself remember what it was like so many years before. Her parents would have had a big party inviting all of their friends and neighbors over. Their house would have been packed with people laughing and enjoying life.

It was something that she hadn't done enough of over the past twelve years. She leaned against the window jamb and watched the D.C. traffic.

"I think you would have been proud of me today," she said. "I wish you could have been here."

She thought of her family often and spoke to their spirits freely, but only rarely did she ever feel anything after.

Tonight was special. She felt the pressure of hands on her back and shoulders. She knew she was physically alone in this world, but confident that they were still watching over her from theirs.

CHAPTER 25

Bridgette walked into the little office and stopped in the doorway to stare at the figure sitting at the desk. "Tammy. I didn't know you'd be here this morning. Can I help you with something?"

Tammy set down her Starbucks cup, raised one hand as if she was signaling for traffic to stop. "I know that we haven't exactly seen eye to eye, Bridgette. I...I need to apologize to you. I was jealous."

Bridgette dropped her purse on the desk and sat. "Jealous of me? Seriously? You look like you've just stepped out of the pages of some swanky magazine. At best, I look average. Why would you be jealous of me?

"Let's start with the obvious one. When you blew the sting that we were planning against the Mambas, I couldn't keep up with you. Your e-skills are like nothing I've ever seen. I've got the fancy degrees, and you bested me without even trying.

"I helped Brian with his search for the money right after the whole fiasco. And again after you told Dom all of the steps that you'd taken. Even with your map, I could hardly follow."

"Thank you?" Bridgette said, not sure if the admission was supposed to be a compliment or not.

"Then there was the way that Dom related to you." She sighed softly and shook her head. "I'd noticed him the first day that I walked into this building. But he never really looked at me. I know that he knew who I was. We talked, but we never really communicated, and believe me, I tried. But no matter what I did, he never showed any interest in me.

"Then to find out you'd won him, even when you were…how do I say it tactfully?" Tammy said suddenly looking perplexed.

"When I was in prison," Bridgette stated. "There is no other term for it, Tammy, so you don't have to beat around the proverbial bush. I'll admit that I made a serious mistake, and I have to face the consequences of that. My life will never be the same as it once was."

"Yeah, but even with that, you seem to have won. You cost the bureau over a million dollars, get arrested and Dom ended up getting raked over the coals for the screw up of the operation. Somehow, he managed to keep the fallout to a minimum, falls for you and then gets you a job working here? It really blows—"

She stopped, closed her eyes and took a long deep breath. "Sorry. I didn't mean to go off on my soapbox there. I promised myself that I would keep this civil between us."

"I can see your point of view, Tammy," Bridgette said. "You see someone who broke all the rules end up winning everything that you'd work so hard for. It would have to be frustrating. But I didn't plan any of this.

"My life got tossed into chaos when the Mambas killed my family. I did everything that I could to play by the rules, to make things better. When nothing seemed to work, I made a rash decision that ended with me getting arrested and convicted. I'd braced myself to accept the punishment that I'd earned when the judge gave me another option.

"I can't feel bad about taking the second chance that I was offered. I think anybody who was in that kind of a position would grasp at any lifeline. In the long run, I really do believe that my life will end up being better because of how fate has played this hand.

"But I've lost a lot as well. Besides my family, I lost my reputation, my house, the few people that I thought were my friends, and my rights. Things that you take for granted are now banned from me. Forever.

"When my time here at the Bureau is up, if they don't offer me a position here, I'll have to admit to my record on every application I fill out. These are things that will follow me for the rest of my life.

"I didn't come here to cause you problems, Tammy. I came here to work at closing down the Mambas, to help other people have a better life. And, to atone for the mistakes that I made."

Tammy studied her across the desk. "I think I can understand that. Or at least try to. And, while I can't say that I'm thrilled that Dom is with you instead of me, I'll try to remain civil. I'll also do my best to put the past behind me, and respect you as the outstanding computer tech that you are." She rose to leave and then paused at the door. "I think I'd like to try to be friends with you, Bridgette. I think under it all, we're very similar."

Bridgette walked to her, extended her hand. "I'm willing to try. Friend."

That afternoon, Bridgette was forcing herself to stay awake at the breakout session. It seemed that the bureau was no closer to catching Terrance Martin or Samantha Wilson than they had been a month ago.

"It appears that the pair of them ended up gaining access to another car. We have no information on this as of yet," Dan Manning reported.

"Would I then be correct that we still don't have any intel on where they are either?" Director Meyers asked.

"At this point, no." Brian answered. "Bridgette and I have spent all morning going over their email communications to see if there has been any further communications between the two of the them and the head honchos. Nada."

"I highly doubt that they're going to go running home at this point," the Director added. "What assets do we have in place right now?"

"I've got one team on the house. We've put dogs on the ground and we've got BOLO's out on both of them. Local agencies have been notified as well. We've been trying to track on their cell phones, but they're either keeping them off or, more likely, they've disposed of them," Kim Sellers said. "They'll make a mistake sooner or later. We're just going to have to be patient."

Bridgette watched the director. He was in one of his silent thinking modes, as she thought of it. He leaned back in his chair, folded his hands behind his head and rocked slowly.

"Has there been any information from the locals?" he finally asked.

"Nothing much," Sellers said referring to her notes. "They've responded to a botched burglary. Two teenagers were trying to lift some silver from the local apartment of one of the senators. They got nailed when one took a tumble spilling all of the silver and broke his leg.

"They responded to a break-in at Sampson Computers. Ah, thieves stole approximately four thousand dollars worth of computer gear. That's about all."

The Director simply nodded.

"What was taken from the computer shop?" John asked.

Sellers again referenced her notes. "They didn't take much that is going to be resellable. From what I can see here, it looks like it was mostly high-end networking and communication materials.

Commercial grade. Might have been a hacker of some sort, but most likely just somebody who didn't know what they were grabbing."

The meeting ended shortly a few minutes later with the attendees leaving in small groups.

Bridgette was walking with Brian and Dom heading back towards the small lab. "Do you guys often get cases where somebody steals networking stuff? I would have thought that somebody who was breaking into a store like that would have been looking for things that they could easily fence."

"It depends on why they broke in in the first place," Dom said. "You're right that many times a break in at a store like that would be for goods that could be quickly turned over, giving the thief some quick cash. Often they would use it for drugs or whatever. I'm not sure about this one. I'd agree with Sellers and the director, it may have been done by someone who didn't know what they were doing."

"Or maybe it was by someone who didn't want to take the time, or have the access, to buy these items through legitimate sources," Brian said.

Dom glanced at his friend. "Explain."

"If we think about this robbery as someone looking for cash, it doesn't make sense. But think about it from the point of view of a hacker who doesn't have the means to get the equipment that they perceive themselves needing. If they feel they need it badly enough, they'll justify stealing it."

"Can't say as that leaves a nice flavor, but it does make sense," Bridgette said. "How long do you think it will take to figure out which option it is?"

Brian and Dom both shrugged.

The answer came at four that afternoon.

Bridgette was running through the emails for the day, when she noticed the cursor on her screen jumping. "Hey, Brian." When he looked up, she motioned him over. "Watch this," she said pointing to the cursor.

The little arrow jumped a fraction of an inch left on its own. "Oh Mother of God," Brian said, keying something into his phone. "We've got a possible computer breach! Shut it down!"

"What do you mean a breach?" Bridgette asked wide eyed.

Brain's fingers were flying over her keyboard, "Right now I think somebody is trying to remote into your computer. And since I didn't authorize it, nor did you, that somebody is from outside."

She looked at him, "Do you think it's the guy who stole the computer equipment?"

He shrugged his shoulders. "I don't know, but it's definitely possible. With what they took, if they knew what they were doing, they'd have the basic tools. Obviously, they would need to have some knowledge of our systems to get through. But that could have been gained either through past trials or by talking to the right person."

Several people appeared in the door of the lab at nearly the same time. "Moran. What's the status?" Director Meyers demanded.

"Right now, Sir, I'm not sure. Bridgette noted the error, I've taken this computer off the network and ordered the rest of the system shut down."

"Sir?" Bridgette spoke up. "What data is stored on the individual computers?"

Meyers turned to Tammy, "I don't know. Do you?"

Tammy thought briefly. "Actually, ah, there really isn't anything on them. These drives are kept for the operating system files, and that's about it. Why?"

"What if we let who ever is trying to get in to this computer, manage it? While he's working on getting in, we can—"

"Right!" Brian snapped his fingers. "Let him in through the front door, while we follow him out through the back door. Let him lead us to where he is."

"I'll set up the search from here," Tammy said crossing to the second computer.

"That was quick thinking," Dom said as they were sitting at Bridgette's little table later that night enjoying a desert of left over cake from the party.

"I don't know about quick," Bridgette said before she sipped her herbal tea. "I just figured that if he didn't know that we'd clued in, we'd have a chance to follow him back to where he was."

"Too bad it didn't happen a bit faster. At least they we were able to retrieve the computer equipment that was stolen the other day. And it appears that Brian was right about it being a hacker who took it. Now, if we could only figure out who it was, why they took it and then just left it in an abandoned warehouse that would help things along."

"What confuses me is something else that Brian said. When we were trying to secure everything, he said something about the hacker having prior knowledge of the system. I didn't get a chance to ask him what he meant by that."

Dom poured another cup of coffee and debated on having a second piece of cake.

"As I'm not too familiar with the work that you computer nerds do," he said ruffling her hair playfully. "I can only guess what he meant. It seems to me that when they updated the system they mentioned that it had several firewalls that served as our protection from the hackers. The thing is, if I remember correctly, these firewalls changed in a specific pattern."

Bridgette tilted her head and waved her hands. "Wait. Just wait. You're saying that the order of the various layers changed daily. So if you worked out how to get through on Monday, it wouldn't work on Tuesday?"

Dom nodded. "Something like that. It's supposed to be super secure. But, as we all know, nothing is totally secured. There is always a way through."

"So in order for the hacker to have gotten through today, he either needed to have gotten through the individual layers in one shot, or had advanced knowledge of what order they were going to be in," Bridgette mused.

"I don't think it would be too likely that he got through on the first try, do you, Dom?"

"I wouldn't think so, no. I think our hacker had help."

She sipped her tea as she thought. "Let's see, what are the odds that we have two moles in the bureau right now?"

"Well, I'd like to say not, but I can't swear to it. Why?"

"Maybe I'm reading too much into this, or I'm projecting. But three days ago, Terrance Martin evaded capture. He's a decent guy on the computer. He's scum, don't get me wrong. But, he's decent on a computer. He'd know how to use that computer hardware that was stolen. We're pretty sure that he's got somebody in the bureau that has been feeding him information. If that person gave him the basics on how the layers changed, he may have been able to find his way in."

Dom was thoughtful. "Impressive. You've made a connection that the rest of us seemed to have missed." He pulled out his cell phone. "I'm going to contact the director on this now. He can get people looking at this tonight, and we can hit the ground running in the morning."

Bridgette rose to rinse her cup out and stood at the sink staring out the little window at the enclosed courtyard. She needed time to think. If she was right, and it was Martin who had hacked in, then she knew her opponent. This was nothing more than a game of chess on an invisible board. She wanted to review the moves that both she and her opponent had made in this match. Was this latest one a gambit or was it a real attempt?

Turning back she looked at Dom. He was right, whatever was

going on, they were going to hit the ground running in the morning.

If Terry Martin wanted to play chess, that was fine with her. She'd been playing that game for as long as she could remember, and was ready to flex her mental muscles in this contest.

CHAPTER 26

Bridgette sat at her computer sipping a latte and contemplating what her first move of the day should be. She had been informed when she and Brian had come in that there was nothing that could prove that Terry Martin was indeed the individual who had attempted to hack into her computer.

Was there a way, she wondered, to tie the Bandit's lead tech guy to the hacker who tried to get into the system yesterday? She knew from her own personal experience that she had certain techniques that she often used in her computing. Would proving that the hacker and Martin had similar styles be enough to arrest him?

Brian hadn't come back yet from the meeting that he had been summoned to almost as soon as he had walked in, so she couldn't run it by him. She looked at the phone on the desk, held a quick internal debate with herself and then dialed the number.

"Franchini," Dom's voice came through the receiver.

"Hey, Dom. Got a quick question for you."

She heard his chair squeak. "Okay," he said. "I'm listening."

Bridgette ran through her idea about trying to create a fingerprint from the code styles that Martin had used.

"I don't honestly know. If we look to an analogy, we can use serial killers. They often have a signature that identifies them. I would think that this could be the same. I guess it would depend on how unique the code signature was."

Bridgette frowned. "That's not exactly what I was hoping to hear, but I guess it's better than nothing."

"I would think that if you can prove that there is a strong resemblance between the two codes, it would be enough to perhaps bring him in for questioning."

"Yeah," she commented, "but wouldn't his association with Mortensky and the firebombing of the apartment be enough to pull him in too? For that matter, we've already got him saying that he was planning on coming after me."

"Once again, you are correct. We can't find him. But, once we do, every little thing that we have helps to build a tighter cage. Right now, we have him on conspiracy to murder a federal officer. Nail him with the hacking, and we add another federal charge."

Bridgette finished her latte, and closed her eyes as she thought. "Okay, Dom. I'm going to follow this thread and see if I can find something that will help. Thanks."

She turned to her computer and thought briefly of Terry Martin. "Let's see if I can out maneuver you on this."

Dom found her there two hours later hunched over the keyboard staring at the monitor. Quietly he came up behind her and started rubbing her shoulders. "Bridge, honey, you've got boulders in here."

"I'm only going to tell you this once, Dom. I'm giving you two hours to cut that out," she said arching into his hands.

"How's the search going?"

"I guess I'm making progress. I've located several areas that the style of the coding is exact. But I'm not sure if it's going to be useful to us. To be honest about it, if I were the one doing it, I'd have done it almost exactly the same way, so I don't know if it's any help. But the fact that both series are exact just seems to be too much. Something's not adding up."

"Well you had an idea and ran with it. If it doesn't pan out then we move to the next plan."

She turned to look over her shoulder at him. "That's exactly what Brian said a little while ago."

Dom smiled. "We tend to think along the same lines frequently. Probably why we're friends." He looked around the small room. "Speaking of him, where is he?"

"He left here about an hour ago, grumbling about how was he supposed to get anything done if they kept requiring him to attend all of these meetings."

"Ah, the curse of middle management, the meeting. Well, since he's not here, shall we head off and go to lunch?"

Bridgette folded her hands on the desk, and shook her head. "Might as well. I'm not getting any farther on this right now. Maybe the break will clear my head."

They reached the lunch table a few minutes earlier than normal, and Bridgette flopped unceremoniously into a chair. "There has to be a way to isolate the signature of those files. I'm missing it," she complained as Dom sat.

"Let's try this. For the next hour, why don't we forget about trying to find computer fingerprints and gang members and instead we can concentrate on breathing and getting your blood pressure back into the normal range?"

She cocked an eyebrow at him. "Are you trying to be funny or are you looking to get slugged?"

He grinned at her, "Your threat would be more believable if you scowled at me instead of smiling." He reached over and tapped her nose. "But either way, scowl or smile, I love you."

Hearing those words still made her giddy. "I can't even pretend to stay mad at you for long. Luckily enough for you, I love you too," she said leaning in to kiss him.

"Geez, why don't you two get a hotel room if you're going to make out over lunch?" Deke chided them as he pulled out a chair.

"A hotel room…" Bridgette said in a voice that wasn't quite normal.

"Bridge? You okay?" Dom prodded.

"I think that's it. I think we can get him with that," she said.

Dom glanced over at Deke, then shook his head before turning to Bridgette. "Ah, you want to try that in English perhaps?"

Bridgette's eyes snapped into focus. "I'm sorry. I know that we said that we were going to not talk about things regarding the case over lunch. But when Deke mentioned a hotel room, it made me think.

"I've located several pieces of code that are very similar. That's because they're coming from the same source. It's the hotel room."

"Okay. What hotel are they coming from?"

She waved her hands in frustration. "Ooh, I'm doing this all wrong. Let me try again. If you went into a hotel, almost every room is the same. They are all set up in approximately the same way, right?" She waited for them to nod. "Now, if we were to take a picture from inside the room, you might be able to identify what hotel chain it was from, but you wouldn't be able to identify the exact room. They all look alike.

"When I was searching for the fingerprint, I was trying to compare the information that we had on the Mambas to where they went on my computer. I'm heading in the wrong direction. I think what's happened here is that they didn't use the network hardware to break in here, they used it to tie into their normal network."

"So you're seeing the image of a computer on the same network, so of course it would look the same," Dom tried.

"I think that's it exactly. I haven't been looking for a connection between the stolen network equipment and the Bandit's network. I was focused here. Maybe we can prove that he used the equipment to connect to their network and made the attack that way."

Deke looked at her with a blank expression. "You computer geeks get turned on by the strangest things.

"I've got something here," Bridgette announced an hour later. She pointed to the screen, "See that? That's the echo from the stolen network machine. Martin used this to tap into his own network before he came at us here."

"That's kind of stupid don't you think," Dom asked looking up from the files he'd been working on. "I would think that if you were going to commit a felony like breaking into the secure computer system of the FBI, you wouldn't want to leave the copy on your home computer."

"I wouldn't think so, but I don't think sane thoughts are his strong suit. He likes puzzles, but..." she paused to bring her memory of Martin in the old law offices back into focus. "...it seems to me that he liked coding problems. He was good with puzzles where one letter stood for something else. Maybe logic isn't a strong suit either."

"Well, either way, it sounds like you've got enough that we can charge him with the hacking."

"Yeah, all we have to do is catch him," Bridgette said.

"Well, maybe this will help," Dom said offering her a file.

"What is it?"

"I had the thought that after Martin returned the car and SWAT missed him, that he was going to need a new set of wheels and a place to stay. I pushed a warrant through to track his credit card use on the off chance that he tried to use it. He did. The company has a record of him checking into the Wayfarer the night that he and

Wilson evaded the SWAT team.

"They stayed there for two nights. Yesterday, they checked into the Hilton. Appears that they're still there."

Bridgette fought back her concern. "You're going to go after them? Now?"

"I'm going to go stake the place out. No sense hitting a room if they're not there. They've already gotten lucky once. I don't want that to happen a second time."

She swallowed hard. "Please be careful, Dom." She held up her hand when he started to speak. "I know that it's all part of the package, you being a cop. But I'm asking, please be careful. I don't want anything to happen to you."

She reached over and touched his face. He held her hand on his cheek briefly before kissing it.

"I'll be careful. I promise. I'm not going to play hero or anything along that line. You…you mean too much to me to take unnecessary chances." He bent down to kiss her cheek. "I'll come by after the shift. I'll grab some take-out and we can have a late dinner."

"Don't bother with the take-out. I want to try a new recipe. I'll talk to you later," she said before he walked out the door.

She clutched her stomach and squeezed. She couldn't let him see how much this worried her.

Dom sat in the SUV a block away from the Hilton, watching the door. He knew that another pair of agents were two blocks away watching the door from the opposite side, and there were two more inside the building. If Martin and Wilson were using this as their hide out, they'd be apprehended—and soon.

The door of the SUV opened, and Deke slid back into the passenger seat. "Got you a coffee and doughnut," he said holding the items out.

"Thanks," Dom said, never taking his eyes off of the building.

"You really think he's in there? It doesn't make much sense to use your credit card if you know that every law enforcement agency is looking for you."

Dom sipped the coffee. "Bridge sort of agrees with you. She didn't think that sane or logical were Martin's default setting. But you never know."

Deke took a bite of his chocolate doughnut, "You know anything about the woman that he's supposedly hanging out with?"

"Not much on her. I know that Bridge said that she was suspected in being involved with several…" He stopped and thought about what he was going to say. "Oh bloody hell. My spidey sense is slow today." He grabbed the radio, "Two-four-kilo do you copy?"

"Yeah we—"

Even from two blocks away the explosion was blinding and the concussion set off car alarms.

"Oh good God," Dom muttered as he watched the SUV explode and flip over. "Dispatch! Seven-niner-bravo. Officers down on the three hundred block." Officers down my foot, he thought. They weren't down, they were gone.

He'd sent men into a situation, into harms way, for this stake out, and now he'd have to face the families and tell them that their loved one wasn't coming home.

It was much later than he'd planned on when he knocked lightly on Bridgette's door. It swung open and he saw her there. Her face red and splotchy, tear stained cheeks. He hung his head, needing the release of emotions that he'd bottled up inside. He needed to mourn for his friends.

She wrapped her arms around him, and pulled him in tight, with her hand rubbing his back like he often did for her. "I'm so sorry about your friends, Dom. But I-I'm so thankful that you're okay," she said into his shoulder.

He couldn't say anything without losing the single strand of control that he was clinging to. He only held tighter.

She gently tugged him towards the open door, and he blindly followed.

"I made zuppa toscana, so it's been simmering. Sit on the couch, and I'll get you a bowl," she said helping him down.

It was all wrong, he thought. He was supposed to take care of her, and somehow, the roles had been reversed and she was caring for him. He loved her more than he ever had imagined possible.

She brought him a bowl of the spicy soup with a hunk of fresh garlic bread. "Here, eat now. When you're ready to talk, we can, or we can just be here for each other for now."

He tasted the soup and appreciated the flavor. "This is good, really good," he said his voice strained.

"I just found the recipe. For that and the bread. It is good," she acknowledged. "May I ask what happened?"

He set his spoon down on the little table. "I screwed up. I didn't think everything through. When we found the information about how Martin had used his personal credit card to check into the hotel, I got anxious. I wanted him behind bars."

He turned to her, stroked her cheek. "I wanted for you to be safe. We'd talked about what kind of mind he had. I just never thought about the personality of Wilson. I fully believe that she was the one behind this."

Bridgette nodded. "When the director came over and told me what happened, I pieced it together and come to the same conclusion. He may not be logical, but she is. I think she's the planner in all of this, and she'll be the one who will be directing the attack on me."

Dom's eyes went dark. "I'm not going to let her get anywhere near you, Bridgette. I'll kill her if I need to, but so help me, I'm going to protect you."

"I don't want to argue right now, so I'll accept that. For now.

When you're feeling better we may have to negotiate a little on it, but for now we'll let it be." She pulled him in close.

He needed to be held. He couldn't remember a time in his life when he felt so breakable. But somehow she had known what he needed right now. He found the comfort that he was longing for in her arms. And with it, he knew that he had found something much more important.

CHAPTER 27

Dom woke with a start. He wasn't in his own house or in his bed.

He squinted at the light that streamed in from a window. He recognized the furniture. Bridgette's apartment.

As he went to sit up, he discovered that he was covered with a thick blanket. He tried to remember what had happened after he'd arrived last night, after the nightmare. She'd made him soup and had been there to comfort him.

He heard something, and spun enough, that he fell off of the couch.

"Oh, you're up," she said standing where the little hall met the living room. She stared at him. "I'm sure there's an excellent reason why you're sitting on the floor. So, while I'm trying to guess what that reason is, is there anything that you'd like for breakfast."

He was flummoxed. His eyes couldn't focus on anything but her.

The way the robe wrapped around her slender shoulders and left plenty of leg exposed made his breathing quicken. He was so lost in his thoughts of her, he barely noted the electronic bracelet on her ankle.

"Dom? You okay?" she asked crossing to him. She squatted down, placed a hand on his cheek. "Did you sleep okay?"

He nodded. "Yeah. Thanks for the blanket and such." He ran a hand over his unshaven face. "Why did I sleep on the sofa?"

"It's where you crashed. You were having a bowl of soup. I went out to the kitchen to get some soda, and when I came back, you were out. Figured that you were absolutely beat, so I just let you sleep." Her hand covered his. "Are you feeling better?"

"Yes. No. I guess, I don't really know. I'm better knowing what happened, but remembering why I was so out of it isn't helpful. I don't think I'll ever forget that explosion. Knowing as I watched, that friends of mine were dying and there was nothing that I could do to stop it."

"I'm sorry," she said pulling him into her arms. "I understand. I remember the horror from when my dad and sister were killed. To this day, I can still see it as a slow motion scene. If I could draw, I could create a perfect animated version, I see it that well.

"I'm here for you if you ever want to talk, okay?" she asked, giving him a squeeze."

She fixed a breakfast of French toast with bacon. As she stood in her robe dancing to the song on the radio, Dom felt something that he'd never felt before. He knew that his life would never be right unless he could have more mornings like this. He wanted her to be the last thing he thought of at night, and the first thing in the morning.

He was totally in love with Bridgette.

Not just in love with her, it was all in capital letters. He'd always thought that someday, when he met the right woman, he'd get married and settle down and hopefully have a family.

Right now, he was single. He'd finally met the right woman,

when he'd arrested her, he thought with a sly grin.

"What's so funny?" she asked as she set a plate in front of him.

"I'm thinking of ways to tell you how much I love you."

He was going to have to find a way to locate and apprehend Martin and Wilson, so he would have some time to do some jewelry shopping.

After breakfast, Bridgette rode with him to his house and waited while he dressed for work. Walking into his kitchen, he took one look at her sitting at the small breakfast bar engrossed in a novel and knew, beyond a shadow of a doubt, that she belonged there. He needed her here. At home with him.

Everyone was quiet when Bridgette and Dom arrived at the office, and she understood that while no one had told her explicitly, they mourned for the agents who had been killed. She was also sure of one thing. No matter what happened for her in the future, she was sure that she would never forget how she had felt when the first call had come in.

Her world almost ceased to exist. She had survived losing her family when she was a teenager, but last night she almost crumbled. She had thought that she had lost Dom.

It was then that she realized how important he had become to her, and how much she loved him. Now, she was trying to figure out how to tell him.

She was thinking about the possibility of fixing a special dinner for him tonight, and then telling him when she rounded the corner into the lab.

"Good. You're here," Brian said never taking his eyes from his computer.

"Yeah, I'm here. What's up?"

"I think I may have found something that's going to require your personal touch." He looked up, "I found some kind of encrypted message."

"Where?" she asked, circling around the table to look over his shoulder.

"At first glance, it looks like a normal one of their emails. I started to run the decode program on it, but it stuck. When I went to see what had caused the blip, figuring that the computer had a hiccup, I discovered this." He hit a key combination, and the screen showed an attached picture.

"Great. It's a picture of some half naked girl lying on a car. So what?"

"First, the 'car' that you so quickly dismissed is a Lamborghini. Second, the subject of the picture isn't what interests me. Well, okay," he admitted, "I spent a few seconds as both subjects in it are drool worthy. But the real interesting part is this." With a click of the mouse, he brought up the information on the picture.

"Whoa!" Bridgette gasped. "That file is almost twelve gigs in size. Why?"

Brian smiled now, "There's an embedded message within the picture. I'm guessing here, but I think the message is quite lengthy. Figuring that the image is only supposed to be at three-hundred dpi, all I can guess is that it is a layered image. But I've got no idea on how to decode this."

"I've never done it myself, but I have a basic knowledge of steganography. Can you send me the picture?" she asked making her way to her computer.

"Done. Can we project it on the screen so we can go at it together?"

Bridgette nodded as her fingers ran over the keyboard. "I'm going to start by finding the hidden watermark in the file. From there, we'll have to unhide it, find the password and then decode it. We may be at this a while."

Across town, Terry Martin was sprawled out on a couch with a whiskey in his hand staring at Samantha Wilson who was studying her plans while she nursed a rum and coke and nibbled on Doritos.

"Whatcha doing, Sam? You've had your head in that notebook for the last two hours," Terry asked when the boredom became too much.

"I've never had a miss on my watch. Tony said this Mahoney chick was to be eliminated, so I'm working out the best way to make that happen."

"Don't you think the feds are going to be all over you? I mean you wasted two of their kind when you blew 'em up with that little bomb."

Her head came up and she smiled at him with a big toothy grin. "Yeah. That was freaking cool watching them do a flip like that. And the fireball when they landed? That was the highlight of my day. Personally, I'm not too worried about the cops. They're going to look where I send them. They don't have any idea on where we are."

She took a long sip of her drink. "Think about what we found out. They've found a way to get data from the organization. How they're doing that isn't relevant at this exact point right now. We know that they're trying to figure things out. So we feed them a line of crap, and they go right where we want them. It's simple."

He laughed, "Yeah, hitting that group outside the hotel was like shooting fish in a barrel. Almost too easy. But don't you worry that they're going to figure out what's going on?"

"Nope. They're going to look for the obvious info. We hide everything so it goes under the radar, they'll never be any wiser.

"Now, since you've gotten me out of my notes, have we had any luck on finding out where Mahoney is living? I really don't want to have to waste my time hitting another abandoned building," She said.

Terry shrugged. "I've got my guy inside working on it. He knows that another false report like that, and, uh, he'll be looking at grass from the other side. Tony's already made that pretty clear.

"From what he's pieced together, once they got wind that we were looking for her, they moved her to a secure location. Nobody seems to know exactly where that is. He's trying a different route, going to the court system to find out. Since she technically is a convict, her whereabouts has to be in her file, and the apartment approved. He hoped to have that information today."

"Well, it's still early on," Sam said. "The sooner we get this over with, the sooner we can blow this popsicle stand and go home." She stared out the small window of the apartment. "I've gotta hand it to you, Terry. It was a good idea to lease this apartment. Using the ID from somebody you know is currently out of the country, and will be for three months, gives us a place to relax without them watching.

"Of course I may need to keep it a bit more than the few weeks we had planned. I need to figure out what to do to get Carl and Todd out," she stated.

"I'm trying to tap in for you there," Terry said. "Again, going to my source inside, I'm working to have the evidence's chain of custody screwed up. All it takes is for one little blip, and they can't use it. Should have that tied up by the end of the week, I'd think."

"That's good to know. Good to know. Since you've done that preliminary work, I think that I should get back to working out the best way to raise a little havoc with those feeble minded feds so we can get to your little friend."

"Sounds like a plan. Think I'll turn the tube on, catch a ball game—"

He was interrupted by the ring of his phone. He glanced at the readout and smiled. "It's my friend from the FBI. I'm going to take this in the other room," he said rising and heading out.

"How are you making out on the embedded data, Bridgette?" Dom asked as they were sitting with the normal contingent at lunch.

"A whole lot more than slow, that's for sure. I've been able to lift three separate watermarks from the image. All three show some signs of having data encrypted into them. The problem is that I can't tell which one, or ones, have something that is meaningful. I'm going to have to find the password for all three, and then find a way to decipher each one. Until then? No way to tell what's on any of them."

"Sound's like a bunch of fun," Tammy said a bit awkwardly.

Bridgette noted that she had opted to sit with them again today, and was really trying to interact with everyone while acting like everything was fine. It was hard to tell if it was real or just a pretense.

"It's obviously going to be keeping us busy for a while," Brian said. "I've been taking short breaks to run the new emails through to make sure that we keep up on that end. But, I've got to admit that I think we may be in over our heads on this one."

"Brian!" Bridgette snapped. "I wouldn't say that we're in over our heads. We've just got to figure out what game they're playing right now. Once we do that, we'll be able to beat them at their own game."

Dom looked down at his empty tray and back to his friends. "Is there anything in the emails that might help us right now?"

Brian shrugged. "We've had a few things. I passed along the information about a few drug transactions over to John."

John nodded. "I've got things started there. From the surveillance we were able to get on the supplier, we're going to be able to take out several key people. We've got the mule from the cartel that's bringing the pure heroin in and we know who they're meeting from the Mambas. So, we should be able to take a few pushers off the streets, along with nearly five million in drugs..." he checked his watch, "...oh in about two hours or so."

"That's something," Dom said. "I was really hoping that we'd be able to get a fix on that Martin and Wilson. I guess I'm getting antsy about this. I want the threat on Bridgette's life, behind us."

After lunch, Dom walked back to the computer lab with Brian and Bridgette. "Can I see the embedded message that you're working with?"

"Sure," Bridgette replied tapping a few keys to bring it up on the big monitor. "This is the original."

"Nice," Dom said.

"Hey be careful pal, or your girlfriend might realize her mistake and decide to leave you for me," Brian stage whispered.

Bridgette laughed, but Dom only took a step closer to the screen. "Dom? What is it?" Bridgette asked stepping up next to him.

"I was just looking. I think this picture was taken just outside of D.C. over in Maryland. See that building there in the background? I think that's the Washington Monument."

Bridgette looked confused. "I thought that the Washington Monument was here in, you know, Washington and was kind of brick building with a pyramid on top."

"That's one of the Washington monuments," Dom said. "There's another one in Baltimore. It was the first one built, back in the 1820's if I recall correctly. As you can see, it's a large column with a statue of George Washington on the top." He edged a little closer, "I'm pretty sure that's it."

Brian flopped into his chair, and started drumming his fingers on the table. "Okay. If that's the Washington Monument in Baltimore, what does that tell us?"

"It could be nothing but a coincidence," Bridgette said. "They may have just used the picture as a blind to put the real message into the watermarks."

"Maybe. Or maybe they've put the watermarks there to mess with your mind," Dom offered. "Think of it like this, if I knew that someone with pretty good computer skills was likely reading my emails, and I didn't want them to know where I was, how could I get the information to my friends. Put all of the information in an innocuous picture and then embed it with a bunch of nonsense that will keep the e-geeks running in circles for days."

Bridgette leaned back in her chair. "I guess that kind of makes sense. But we still need to go through the steps of deciphering the watermarks, don't we?"

Brian glanced at Dom. "You're absolutely correct, Bridgette. Why don't you continue on that path, Dom and I'll take a closer look at the picture?"

"All right," she sighed. "I'm going to go to the other lab and use my workstation there. It has a bigger screen and better lighting than we have here."

They watched her leave. "Something tells me she's not to keen on the idea that she's heading down the wrong track," Brian said after she'd left.

"Do you think she is? I'm not one hundred percent sure on this, but as she said, it's an angle that needs to be checked out. She didn't pick up on the location, most likely since she's never been there before."

Brian huffed out a breath. "Yeah that's good excuse for her, but what about me? I grew up just outside of there, and I didn't pick up on it."

"You were too focused on the girl or the car to notice the background." Dom turned back to the screen. Can you enhance it any more without distorting it?"

"Sure," Brian agreed. "Any where in particular?"

Dom thought about the picture, what they were trying to find. "If we go under the assumption that they did this intentionally to tell someone where they were, what information would they need to transmit?"

"Well, obviously a city, the place where they were staying, or a number to contact them at."

Dom nodded, "So if we've located them in Baltimore, where on this will we find numbers?"

"There looks to be a sign of some sort, on the left," Brian noted as he zoomed in.

"It's frustrating," Brian said. "We've spent more than an hour looking and I really thought that we'd find something here."

"I still think we may. It's going to be obvious when we—"

He broke off and stepped closer to the screen. "Brian, come take a look at this," he said pointing to the screen.

"What'd we miss?" Brian asked following him.

"We've spent the time looking for something hidden, but what about what's right in front of our noses? Take a look at the license plate."

"M-V-H- two-four-six. So?"

Dom picked up the phone and hit a few buttons. "Get ahold of the Mount Vernon Hotel in Baltimore. Check and see if they have either Terrance Martin or Samantha Wilson registered there, as well as the occupant of room two-forty-six."

"It couldn't be that easy could it?" Brian asked.

Dom shrugged as he made the next call. "Bridge, we may have something here. Can you come on back?"

He hung up. "She'll be back in five," he told Brian. When his phone rang, he answered quickly and listened for thirty seconds. "We've got a Sam Wilson registered in Baltimore. I think we found them."

CHAPTER 28

Conversations flowed around the table in the conference room, but Bridgette leaned back in her chair, pinching her nose as if to ward off the impending headache. She had been making progress on the embedded messages from the image, but everything had been shelved when Dom had made the connection between Samantha Wilson and the Mount Vernon Hotel.

It was too predictable, she thought. She knew some of the Mambas. They'd talked to her when she'd been working for their attorneys. And, she was positive that putting a false message was something that they'd do.

"All right, people," Director Meyers said walking briskly into the room. "We've had a few new developments in the case with the Mambas. Franchini, give us the update on what you found."

Dom nodded, walked to the front of the room and took control of the computer. "We intercepted an email among the Bandit infrastructure. It appears that the sender was most likely Samantha Wilson, and the recipient was Antonio DePasquale."

He clicked the next button, and the image appeared on the screen.

Bridgette watched for the other's reactions. "Wouldn't mind taking her for a spin," an agent across the room commented and his neighbor agreed.

"When we found this image, it gave us a few threads to tug at. First, it was noted that the file size was abnormally large for an image of this quality, hinting that there was some kind of message that was layered into the image, likely in a watermark or something. Presently, Miss Mahoney is working on breaking that code. Agent Moran and I noticed some other odd occurrences."

Over the next ten minutes, Dom explained what they thought the symbolism of each part of the image meant, and what data they had collected.

"Do you believe this is where they're hiding out, Franchini?" Meyers asked.

"Sir, it's hard to know for certain. This is the same group that gave us information that led to the deaths of two agents less than twenty-four hours ago. I think that it is likely that since the image contained two messages, that we need to consider our positions carefully."

"Why would they give us two messages?" Dan Manning asked. "I mean, if they're trying to hide from us, whey give us more than they need to?"

"Bridgette? Would you want to try answering this?" Dom asked.

Bridgette sucked in a breath. "We're not sure what messages they're trying to send. What we've found are two areas that require further analysis. As agent Franchini has already demonstrated, there is sufficient evidence that points to them being in Baltimore. But the question becomes, is that where they are or where they want us to be?

"I've been working at decoding the embedded messages. At

this time, we haven't gotten too far. The parts of the image that we think contain the message are buried under several layers and are coded in such a way that extraction is proving to be difficult.

"Agents Franchini and Moran have both opined that it is possible that these 'messages' were embedded like this so that our time would be wasted chasing after a wild goose."

Dan spoke up again. "From what we've seen with these guys, they're not that advanced. They're lazy. They're not going to go through all that trouble to make the photo and embed a message. If the info that was pulled from the photo, everything being in Baltimore, is legit, I say that we load up and head to Maryland."

Director Meyers held up his hands. "Hold on, Manning. We've still got several pieces of this puzzle that don't exactly fit well. It very well may be that the embedded messages are there to keep us busy, but we need to verify the authenticity of the image before we go charging in."

"The authenticity?" the agent next to Manning sneered. "What do we need to do? We've seen the picture? We've got confirmation that they've checked into the hotel. What more do we need?"

Bridgette shook her head, and kept silent. There was no use voicing her opinion when she wasn't fully behind the photo being exactly what it looked like. A photo.

She closed her eyes and tried to put herself in Wilson's shoes. How would she get a message to her leader? She knew that she'd go for the wild goose chase, but that she'd make the chase the more obvious set of clues.

Voices from all sides were giving their opinions of what actions should be taken. "I still think we need to decode the watermarked images before we do anything," she said conversationally.

"Excuse me, Bridgette. But what did you say?" Dan asked.

"I've never met Samantha Wilson, but I have had interactions with several other members of this gang, especially the higher ups.

They know who they're up against. I think," she stressed that word. "They're going to put the trap where we are most likely to find it. That's what the parts of the picture are. I'm almost positive of it."

"But...data...action," Dan spluttered, his face was nearly beet red. He took a calming breath. "We've got data that indicates that they're there. We've got to check it out."

"I think what Bridgette's saying is that we need to have all the data before we rush into something," Brian said.

Director Meyers nodded in thought. "I think the best thing to do right now is to get that data. From both sides," he said quickly stifling the brewing argument. "Manning, I want you and Thomas to head up to Baltimore. Carefully. I'll have the blueprints and floor plans for the Mount Vernon sent to you. Get into one of the surrounding buildings that faces room two-forty-six, and observe. Make sure that they're really there.

"Mahoney? I want you on breaking that other message. Moran can keep up with the email duty. We need that data."

He looked around the table and got nods from the participants. "Okay, in a related matter. I hate to discuss this, but it needs to be done. We've known that the Mambas had to have had some kind of mole inside the bureau for a while. Through a joint effort with the Metro police, we were able to discern who the leak was. Kevin Truman was arrested this morning at his home.

"While we hope that this will be the end of the leaks for now, please remember that it is entirely possible that there are more. Be careful of what you say to whom."

"If there's nothing else, let's get back to work people," the director said before he left the room.

Dom sat at the small table in the communications center with Brian and the Director. "What's the status?" he asked Manning.

"We're in a building across the street on the third floor. We've got a clear view of the windows for their hotel room. Right now the shades are pulled, but according to the infrared, we've got two heat sources in the room," Manning said.

Dom looked over at Brian. "Heat sources don't necessarily mean that we've got people there. Thoughts?"

"Any way they could try to get a visual? Maybe they could pose as room service or something?" Brian offered.

"That's not going to work too well, Moran," the director said. "In order for them to gain access that way, one of the two suspects would have to call down and request service. From the records the hotel sent us, there have been no such calls. The computers show that the locks of the door are opened a few times per day, but so far we haven't been able to confirm their presence with any of the security feeds either."

Dom leaned back in his chair. "Is it possible that they're using their cells to call for food delivery. The security cams are going to pick up the delivery guy, but as they often are in hotels, no one is really going to pay too much attention to them."

"It's something that we're going to have to look at," the director agreed. "The question now is, what do we do next?"

Brain shook his head. "I talked with Bridgette just before coming down. She's making some progress, but I believe her exact words were that it was going a tad more than slow."

"Would it be possible to bug the room?" Dom asked.

"Perhaps," the director admitted. "The warrant definitely covers this, but how do we get it in if they're inside? If we go to sneak in to plant the bug, and find them in there, then we've kind of screwed up our element of surprise."

"Why not use the Uzi Pro Spy?" Lucy asked.

Dom turned to face her, "The what?"

Lucy sighed, picked up a small device that looked like a radar gun with a clear parabolic dish on the end. "The Uzi Pro Spy. This little model will pick up sounds from as far away as three hundred feet. If they're only across the street and a few floors up, they're most likely only a hundred feet away or so. They'd be able to hear what ever is going on in that room."

Brain and Dom looked at each other. "Would that be enough to get an operation set?" Brian asked. "Even if Bridgette hasn't finished her end yet?"

The director thought briefly. "If we've got confirmed heat sources inside the room and can confirm voice print analysis, I'd say that I'd give that a big go."

After the meeting, Dom walked down the hall to see Bridgette. He stopped in the doorway to watch her, and felt his heart stutter. It should have annoyed him, he thought, that after everything that had happened with them, that just the sight of her would cause him to have that kind of reaction. He was amused at how he acted like a man in love seeing the object of his obsession.

Quietly, he walked up behind her, leaned in and kissed the top of her head.

"What the…Oh. Hi," she said spinning around and out of her seat.

"Sorry to startle you, but you looked like a picture and I couldn't resist. How are things going?"

She sighed, "Not as well as I'd like or hoped for. I've been able to isolate the different—for lack of a better term—watermarks and get them to a point where we can view the data."

"What does it say?" he asked hopefully.

"Not there yet. It's still raw. We've got the characters, but as of yet, I haven't' been able to figure out the cipher that was used. Unfortunately, it's not the same one that they used on the web site, I've already tried. Tammy's been helping with this process, but unless we get lucky and figure out part of the code word, it's going to take us a while."

She studied his face. "Something else is going on. What's up?"

"Manning and Thomas are in Baltimore. Using IR detectors, they've got confirmation of two heat sources in the room. They're going to be working with a guy out of the communications division with a listening device that should be able to pick up voices in the room. If they get anything, it's likely to mean a 'go' for an operation in Baltimore."

He rubbed his hands on her arms. "I know that you think Baltimore is the wrong direction, but if they say go, we're going to be heading there. I wanted you to know."

She pushed away and paced the room. The thought of him going to Baltimore was more than she wanted to think about right now. She was sure, deep in her gut sure, that Baltimore was a diversion. Or worse, a trap.

Thinking of the leak that the director had talked about this morning, she had to believe that the gang knew of her relationship with Dom. And, if the Mambas really wanted to get to her, she was sure that they wouldn't even hesitate to go after Dom. She couldn't let that happen, but yet, she felt powerless to do anything.

"Dom, please, I…I hate to ask. To beg, if needed, but please don't go to Baltimore unless they're one-hundred percent sure that Martin and Wilson are there."

"Bridge, it'll be okay, I promise. The only way any of us are heading that way is if we get confirmation. Now, it may not be the hundred percent that you asked for, but we're doing everything that we can. If we go, it'll be with a high probability that we'll get those two."

The words made sense, but they didn't ease the feeling in her heart. But, she reminded herself he was a cop. This would be part of his duty. She'd chosen to become involved with him and had to accept the good and the bad.

"If you have to go, please take every precaution."

He glanced around the room before leaning in and kissing her gently on the lips.

His phone vibrated.

"Before I get this, I wanted to let you know that I need to find some private time with you. Soon. There's a couple of things that I need to talk to you about," he said with a smile.

Watching his body language as he talked on the phone, she knew. He was getting ready to head to Maryland.

They were all called to the conference room to go over the operation. Bridgette sat quietly wishing for more time to finish her analysis of the message, but she understood that the computer was chewing on it now, and it didn't have the same urgency as before since they had recorded proof that Martin and Wilson were indeed in room two-forty-six.

"It's going to be a pretty straight forward op," Director Meyers said. "Once we have the teams in place, two groups will be clearing the floors, getting the innocents outside. Once the building is secured, we can move in. I'm sending Manning and Thomas in, as they're already on site and have been going over the video surveillance. They'd have the best chance to make any one who has had contact with the perps. Franchini and Kirkpatrick, you two will be going in from this entrance here," he said tapping the screen displaying the building blueprint. "Moran you'll be working the computer video from the hotel security room. We can't know for sure that they don't have the feed tapped, so we'll take precautions.

"We go in fast, strong and efficiently. We don't want anyone to get hurt, and we want these two for a variety of charges. I personally don't want to see them end up dead so they can skip out of paying for them.

"Any questions?" He asked, looking around the room. "Good luck gentlemen. Let's get this taken care of and shut them down."

She took a few moments to say goodbye to her friends before she made her way back to the lab. When she heard footsteps running up behind her, she turned to see Lucy.

"You're not looking too good, Bridgette."

Bridgette shook her head. "I've got a bad feeling about this whole operation. I really hope that I'm wrong, but I can't shake it."

"So, I'd guess this would be a good time to ask if you wanted me to grab some food and come over and hang out for a while. Kind of help keep your mind off of things for a while."

Bridgette shrugged. "I don't know what I'm going to do tonight. The director gave me permission to stay here a little late to work on the message, but I've still got to be back to my apartment by nine. I just figured that I'd order some food and work in the lab."

"Well then, come on. As it happens, I like to nibble on pizza while I play with computers. So let's go do what we can here tonight, and then we'll go back to your place to wait it out."

She felt a little better walking with Lucy to the lab. Things still didn't seem settled, but having someone there to talk to definitely helped.

CHAPTER 29

Dom walked up the three flights of stairs instead of waiting for the elevator, claiming that the car ride up from D.C. had put his mind to sleep. The reality of it was he was thinking about Bridgette and her warning.

"Trying to get some extra exercise there, Franchini?" Dan asked.

"I'm not going to answer that, Manning. Just wanted to clear my head before we go after these guys."

Dan studied Dom's face. "You sure you're okay for this? You're not looking like your usual cheerful self."

Dom leaned against the wall. "Lot's on my mind."

"Let me guess. She's got long red hair and green eyes, right?"

Dom smiled weakly. "She's on my mind too. But she's not all that's there. I...I can't help but think of what happened last night. We got snookered into thinking that they were in the hotel. We set up the watch and only a few people knew we were going to be there. Yet somehow they knew.

"One minute everything was going fine and then Deke said

something, and it all clicked for me. I knew it was a setup. But as soon as I called them, that's when everything went to hell.

Dan put his hand on his friend's shoulder, "Life can be like that. It's fickle, and when it's your time, it's your time. But remember, it's what you do while you're living that makes the difference. You make a difference, Dom."

Buoyed by the thought, Dom nodded. "Yeah, I guess I do."

"You ready to go capture some Black Mamba Booty?"

"I want to listen in to their conversation before I do anything else."

"What? You think I made things up?" Dan shook his head and led Dom into the room.

It was a small office, Dom deduced as he stepped in. The walls were a drab color and the windows were grimy and small, but they served their purpose. Looking out, he could easily see the Mount Vernon Hotel. It didn't take much to guess which room was the one in question. It was the only one on the second floor with the windows completely covered. Fred Thomas stood by the window pointing the listening device out the window while the other agents sat around a small round table with a speaker in the middle.

Voices came through the speaker, and Dom closed his eyes in concentration.

Yes they sounded exactly like the samples he'd heard back in D.C., and they had been verified as being those of Terrance Martin and Samantha Wilson.

The laptop that the agents had set up on a counter showed the output of the infrared scanner.

Two figures moved around in the room. Everything looked normal.

But there was a niggling sense that Dom couldn't shake. Had Bridgette's plea affected him this much so that he couldn't concentrate on the mission at hand?

"Okay," Manning said. "The warrant just came through so we're clear to go in. I'm letting the Baltimore Police know that we're ready. They've given us four plain clothes to help get people out of the hotel. I'm going to have them get started"

"You look jumpy, bro," Deke said softly from beside Dom. "Everything okay?"

"I can't shake this feeling. You know how you start to trust your gut in this job? Well, right now, mine is telling me that something isn't quite on par with this one."

He'd wandered back over to the speaker and was listening to the conversation between Wilson and Martin.

"Look, Terry, when we get her, if you really want, I'll help you. I don't know why, but I like you. So if you really want to earn your mark I'll tell you what to do. But you've got to trust me okay?" Wilson said.

"I don't care what I've got to do," Martin said. "I told Tony that I was going to kill this broad, and I want to. I'm not that concerned about getting my mark. I'm already a full member, and killing others don't exactly turn me on. But with this chick? It's personal. She's responsible for killing Alex."

"Now that's not true, Terry. She only breached the system. It was Justine who took care of Alex. But I understand your sentiment." There was a pause. "I'm going to go read for a bit, and I, ah, want to check on the other item as well."

Dom glanced at the monitor, and saw one of the heat sources move to the bed. "What was the faint whirring sound?"

"Not sure," Thomas remarked. "Heard it a couple of times throughout the day. Probably some kind of electrical static or something."

Manning turned back from the window. "BPD has the other occupants moving out in a fairly orderly system. The plan was for them to go out the back doors into the lot. Got a couple of coach buses to take them away from here until we're done."

Dom tried to settle back and relax. He'd done everything that he could, now all he could allow himself to worry about was keeping himself safe.

"Are we making any headway?" Tammy asked leaning over the desk.

"Some. It seems like we're getting a few letter combinations here and there, but it's not the right algorithm. It's frustrating," Bridgette complained. She lifted the slice of pizza, and tried not to think about what Dom was doing. She was pretty sure that if she actually knew, she'd be terrified instead of just plain scared.

Lucy sat next to her playing a game on her phone. "You know, when this all turns out to be a hoax, we're going to feel real silly for sitting here for so long." She sighed. "It really stinks that we're stuck here instead of going into Baltimore tonight. I mean that's where all the action is, right? And where are we? Stuck in D.C. like some losers."

Bridgette sat up straight. "I wonder," she said and started tapping on her keyboard.

"Your mind just clicked on to something," Tammy said reverently. "I have to admit that I love seeing you do that. What are you thinking?"

"We know that the last time that the Mambas used a Vignette cipher, they used the gang name as the key. I'm wondering if they would have used a similar phrase or something for this one," Bridgette said pointing at her screen.

Tammy nodded. "Okay. I can't tell you how much it hurts me to tell you that you were right last time, so let's follow your thoughts on this as well. What kind of phrases would they use?"

"What do they want people to know?" Bridgette asked.

"I'm not sure about wanting people to know, but I know what they want," Lucy said. "They want you dead. But we're not going to give them what they want."

Bridgette was already tapping away on the keys. "I think we're getting closer," she said.

"What are you doing?" Tammy asked.

"I'm trying to think of all of the variations of that kind of phrase about me getting it here. Lucy's right. It's what they want, so they'd be able to make it into a key phrase so they'd all know."

"You're thinking that this is kind of like their password for this mission?" Tammy asked in disbelief. "You've got to have ice water in you veins if you can be trying phrases about meeting your demise without flinching."

Bridgette sent her a quick smile. "Lucy's right. We're not going to give them what they want."

A sound beeped from the computer. "We've got something!"

"We should be ready to go in about an hour or so," Manning said.

"Wonder what's taking so long for things to get through. I figured they should have been able to send the warrant over via the smartphones, but something has to be blocking the signal."

"It's probably the old building. When they built this place, they weren't exactly worried about cell phones. It's probably some weird building material or something."

Dom looked over to Deke with a raised eyebrow. Too many little coincidences, he thought. He strolled over so he and Deke were only separated by a few inches. "My senses keep telling me something's not right here. There isn't any building material that's going to cut off cell service that well, is there?"

Deke shrugged. "Not that I'm aware of, but you never know. But I tend to agree with you that something seems very fishy to me. I'd like to be able to call Meyers and get an update."

"Well, it looks like we're kind of stuck with things for now."

"Why don't we go down and start getting in position?" Manning asked.

Dom and Deke followed along, their orders said that they had to. With every step he took, Dom's stomach contracted another notch.

"Dan?" Dom finally said. "Something's way wrong on this. Let's call it off before someone gets hurt."

"Dom, will you stop worrying? Look, I know that you're antsy after what happened last night. Heck, anybody would be a bit shaken after that. But right now, we're getting ready to go nail these guys. In less than an hour, we're going to have them in custody." He slapped Dom's shoulder before he walked away.

"We don't trust our backs to anyone else right, pal?" Deke whispered.

"Roger that one. We're going to need to be ready for what ever happens next."

They tried to focus on the pre-mission briefing that Manning was setting up. But all Dom could think about was what he was going to have to do to ensure that he walked out alive.

"What does the message say?" Lucy asked leaning over Bridgette's shoulder with Tammy right on the other side.

Bridgette scanned the message. "Oh, God. Oh, God, no!"

Tammy grabbed the paper out of her hand, "What is it?" She went ashen. "They're walking into a trap."

Lucy looked from face to face. Tammy was pale, but still standing, while Bridgette looked as white as death. "Hey! Come on Bridgette. Snap out of it. Let's go," she said shaking her lifeless friend.

"I'm calling the director right now. You keep on her. If she doesn't respond in two minutes, you call for an ambulance, got it Lucy?"

Lucy kept shaking Bridgette lightly. "Come on. Let's figure out how to help them. If you play possum, you're not going to be able to help any of them, Bridge."

Tammy burst back into the room. "I can't get the director. Either of them. I'm heading to Mayer's house. I'll call in when I'm with him," she snapped before racing out of the room.

"Oh, of all the times to panic, Bridge, this isn't it. If we know what's going on, we have a chance to help them. But we've got to move quickly.

"Dom wouldn't hesitate. He'd take some kind of action, and he'd do it right now, Bridge."

Bridgette's eyes focused, and she gasped for breath. "No, no, no, no. I begged him not to go to Baltimore. Don't you see? He went there because of me. He's there because those two threatened me. And now he's going to be killed because of me. I never got a chance to tell him how much I love him. To share my dream with him."

"Bridgette, I'm only going to say this once before I get real strict. I'm glad you're in love with him. But right now we need to get our butts in gear and find a way to help them. And then you can tell him when you see him, okay?"

Bridgette fought for control of her breathing. The wild in her eyes slowly retreated to mild excitement. "I'm going to call him she said," pulling out her phone.

Lucy watched her friend dial and then decided she'd make a couple of calls of her own. When she turned around, Bridgette's face was scrunched up looking at her phone.

"What did I miss?" Lucy asked.

"I don't know. But the call went right to voice mail. Dom never turns his phone off, or has it go right to the message. Something's up, but I'm not sure what."

"Hmmm. My call went right through, no problem. I'll try Dan and see if I can get him."

They tried all of the guys on the team. "There's got to be some weather phenomenon or something that's causing the whole system to be down," Lucy said.

Bridgette was pacing the lab, with her arms folded tightly around her body. "No. I don't think that the whole system is down. I think that the Mambas must have gotten some kind of signal jammer to block cell usage."

"Why would they do that?" Lucy wondered.

"So we can't tip them off."

The phone on her desk rang. "Hello?"

"Bridgette, it's Tammy. Put me on speaker. I'm with the Director."

They outlined the situation in under a minute for the director.

"This is beyond bad," he said. "The operation is to begin around seven. We wanted to catch them at dinner time."

"It's a great thought, but they're not going to be there. If I'm reading things right, they're in the same building as our team is in, on the top floor. They're waiting for our guys to be inside before they start the fireworks," Bridgette relayed, her voice sounding stronger than she felt.

"We can try to call the city police," Tammy said.

"Not going to be much help," Lucy answered. "I called a friend at the phone company. They've lost a whole bunch of phones, both landlines and cell in the Baltimore area. There's also some kind of interference on the airways, she said it was almost like somebody had a stuck mic. Communications to our team in Baltimore is pretty much out of the question."

"Somebody's got to get there to warn them off," Bridgette said. With out thinking any further, she grabbed her purse and turned.

"Where do you think you're going?" Lucy demanded.

"I'm heading for Baltimore!" Bridgette answered.

"Miss Mahoney, I can't condone that," the director's voice came over the phone. "The conditions of your release required that you have permission before leaving the D.C. area. If you go before we have that, I'm not sure what's going to happen."

Bridgette closed her eyes. Memories flashed back for her. Her mom, her dad and her sister. How it felt when Dom held her. How he'd risked everything for her, potentially sacrificing his career to help her. Now he was in trouble.

There was no question.

"Sir, I respect your advice, but right now the lives of agents, our agents are in mortal danger. I was told that day in court that they would be able to track this bracelet no matter where I went, and that the only time I could leave my apartment after hours was with permission or if there was a danger to my, or another's, life. I'd say that this counts. I'm heading for Baltimore. They can track me as I go. I'll deal with the consequences later, but I don't know if I can survive having someone else I love killed by this group. So I have to go, and I need to leave now."

She turned and headed for the door.

Lucy looked at the phone to Bridgette and back. "Sir, I'm going with her," she said before running after Bridgette.

CHAPTER 30

Dom eased down the hall with his Glock in his right hand. Deke was in a mirrored position right behind him watching to ensure that no one came up from behind them.

"You feeling any better," Deke asked in a voice no higher than a whisper.

"Nope. In fact I'd say it's getting worse. We need to find a way to call it off."

"Can't. Manning's in charge. He's waited too long to have a chance like this, so there's no way he's going to want to postpone this. He thinks this is the way to get himself promoted."

"If we're not careful, it's going to get us all killed."

Dom looked down the hall. He could see the other team of Manning and Thomas creeping in from the other side. They were at the door, and Manning had the key card in his hand, ready to swipe it through the reader.

His hand shook, Dom wasn't sure if it was from excitement or nerves. Manning dropped his hand and looked to his feet. Nerves,

Dom thought.

Dan squatted down looked at something, tapped Thomas' arm and pointed to something on the floor.

Booby trap, Dom thought. His fears were spot on. Dan quietly walked over to him.

"Found a line attached to the doorframe. I'm going to call for a flexible camera and perhaps the bomb squad."

"Good idea," Dom said and then relayed the information to Deke.

Dan was back a minute later, "Phones still aren't working. I sent one of the plain clothes guys down to make the request. It's going to put us back about fifteen minutes."

Dom nodded. "That's all right by me. I'd rather wait a while than get blown to kingdom come by some twerp's jury rigged bomb."

Dan's estimate was off. It took twenty-five before the team showed up. The bomb squad guy, dressed in his protective suit, reminded Dom of the Michellin Man, but he could respect what the suit did for the wearer.

Dan walked over a few minutes later. "We're clear. They can see some movement, but they've got the lights off as well, so it's a bit hard. Still got two heat sources. Ready to do this?"

"Let's do it," Thomas said, going back to the door. "You want high or low?" he asked Dan.

"I'll take low," Dan decided, and unknowingly saved his life.

Thomas kicked the door open and swept into the room with his Glock held in front of him.

A single shot rang out, and Thomas fell backwards.

Manning still low, rolled to the side and opened fire. Between the noise and the muzzle flashes, everything seemed to strobe. He could see the moving shapes, not human, but roughly the right shape. But they didn't go down when he shot them. They kept moving. Every couple of seconds, one of the shapes would fire a shot at him, hitting close enough that he was feeling trapped.

The windows shattered, and suddenly the air was full of gunfire.

Dom and Deke were trying to get to Dan, but every time they moved by the door, bullets ricocheted off of the metal frame.

On their third attempt, they managed to pull Thomas' body out of the door.

"We need help, man," Deke said. "I don't know what they've got in there, but this is getting out of hand."

Dom peered inside the door, and could just barely make out the two shapes that were closing in on Manning. "We've got to do something. Whatever those things are, they're herding Dan into the corner. They get him there, he's dead."

"You got any ideas?" Deke asked.

"No. I was hoping that you had some, seeing as you spend most of your time in the lab. I figured you'd have some McGyver skills stashed away somewhere."

"Sorry. No dice," Deke said risking a glance inside. "If we're going to do something, we'd better do it soon. He's got about five feet before he's done for."

Dom thought of Bridgette, and fervently hoped that he'd get a chance to apologize for his next course of action. He holstered his gun, crouched by the door and yelled. "Dan! I'm coming in. Don't shoot me!"

He bolted from the floor, launched himself at the two human-like shapes and tackled them. He landed on the two shapes hard enough that he thought he heard his wrist snap. But nothing under him moved.

"They're some kind of hard plastic. Some kind of robot."

He heard Deke running in behind him and pulling Dan up.

They'd almost made it to the door when the sound of a machine gun ripped through the air.

Bridgette rode in silence while Lucy navigated the streets of Baltimore doing close to seventy with the lights of the SUV flashing. Her mind wandered bouncing between thinking of Dom and praying that he was alive and okay to wondering how much she was going to lose tonight.

"We're almost there," Lucy said in a voice that was very close to sounding calm.

Bridgette looked at her friend, saw the determined look on her face, and knew that Lucy was a much better actress than she was. "Do you have a plan, or are you just going to wing it?" Lucy asked.

"From what I got out of the message, they, Wilson and Martin, were going to be holed up on the fourth floor of the building right across the street from the hotel. I don't have any idea on what kind of weapons they're going to have. I guess we'll just have to make it up as we go along."

"Listen, I've got a spare pistol on my ankle. When we get there, you're taking that. We can try to get to the room they're in and get the drop on them from there.

Bridgette looked over. "I can't take the gun, Lucy!"

"I'm not going in there with you being unarmed. That's suicide, Bridge."

"I'm risking enough as it is coming here. But I believe that this mission can rightly be justified and I'm hoping the courts will see it that way in a little while. But I'm not going to jeopardize anything by breaking another point of my release. Besides, I am armed. My brain is firing on all cylinders right now. I'll find something else to use as a weapon."

"Look, check the glove box. There's a list there that tells what we've got in these vehicles. Maybe there's something there that will suit us both," Lucy said squealing the tires around a turn.

In their fourth floor sniper's nest, Samantha Wilson was laughing like a loon, Terry thought. He could laugh at the chaos that his creations had caused. They'd killed the first cop through the door, and had kept the other one down until somebody had somehow disabled them.

He wondered if he qualified for his mark now, thinking of the blood drop tattoo that would go on the end of the S of his gang tat. You only got the mark if you'd killed somebody, and while he technically wasn't in the room when the first cop bought it, he'd designed the mechanism and was operating it. For that matter, he pulled the trigger on the joystick control here that fired the shot.

His attention went back to Sam who was rocking and rolling with the little Uzi submachine gun she'd picked up. It looked like fun, but he didn't think he'd like the feel of the actual recoil.

He looked out the window and saw the line of police cars that were now forming and watched as a group of three tried to make their way to the front door of the building.

"We've got a couple of people who think they're going to get in through the front door," he said loudly so Sam could hear him.

She stopped firing and looked at him. "Where? I'll give them a little reception," she said patting the Uzi.

Terry shook his head. "Don't worry about it. They're heading for the front door. I'm sure they'll get a bang out of the little surprise I left there for them," he said with a grin as he pressed a small button.

An explosion rocked the building. "See? I told you they'd have a blast," he said with a laugh.

Sam smiled widely. "I like you, Terry. At first I thought you'd be a stuck up geek, who was afraid to get his hands dirty. You do the job well, just in a different way. That's good." She looked through the spotting glass she had set up. "Ah, I see our friends across the way are trying to make it back to the door. Why don't you give them something that keeps them where we want them?"

"With pleasure," Terry said walking to another controller and pressing a button.

A muffled whoosh sounded and smoke began to pour out of the windows of the hotel.

Lucy and Bridgette had arrived just in time to witness three men be blown to pieces when they went to the front door of the building.

"You having any second thoughts there, Bridgette?" Lucy asked.

Bridgette was pawing through several non-lethal weapons that were loaded in the SUV. "Too many to count, but I can't stop to think about them right now." She glanced upwards to the window. "It seems that the automatic gun fire has quieted down. But I'm pretty sure that they haven't bugged out yet."

"So what's your plan, Bridge? I'm betting that all of the doors are hooked to explosives."

"I'm thinking up." She pointed to the top of the buildings. "If we go in the building next to the one they're in, come out on the fifth floor fire escape it leads to the roof of the building they're in. We can take the fire escape down one floor and try to get into one of the windows on the back side."

Lucy just stared at her. "You're serious, aren't you? You're really going to go through with this?"

Bridgette looked at her friend. "Lucy, I can't explain what being involved with this group has meant to me over the past few months. But right now, they've got the man I love either trapped or injured in a burning building. Every time someone tries to get near enough to get help into that building, they're taking shots at them. Somebody has to take Martin and Wilson out.

"Dom would do this for me. I-I realized how much he loves me, and I know that he'd risk everything for me, so I'm going to do the same. Because I love him more than life itself."

Lucy looked at her for a long moment, and then smiled. "Boy I like you. Let's go do some breaking and entering."

They made their way around to the back of the buildings to where a small alley ran giving access to the rear entrances. Since the building directly next to the four-story nest was an office building, getting in was easy. An elevator ride to the fifth floor, and they were looking out the window at the fire escape and the roof below.

"Ready?" Lucy asked.

"Let's go," Bridgette said raising the window and crawling out on to the small steel rungs and climbed down to the neighboring roof. On the roof, she walked as quietly as she could, over to the wrought iron ladder that lead to the ground.

Carefully she climbed down, her heart beating like it was playing a Sousa march. She stopped at the window on the fourth floor. Slowly she pushed the pane up, and was surprised when it moved.

Once the opening was big enough, she crawled through, and waited for Lucy.

The sound of gunfire was loud, and came from the front right of the building. They made their way towards the sound moving as quietly as they could, thanking providence for the carpeting on the floors that muffled their footsteps.

They crept up to the only door on the floor that was open. It was ajar only an inch, but it helped to identify which room they needed to get into, Bridgette thought. And, as a nice bonus, they weren't going to have to break the door down.

Lucy waved her hand and mouthed, "Ideas?"

Bridgette signaled with one finger, before reaching into her pocket. She pulled out a flare, and mouthed, "Smoke. Should blind them"

Lucy nodded, and then added, "Once it goes in, hit the floor. They'll probably shoot the door and the walls."

They stopped just outside the door, both crouching down. Lucy had her gun in her hand ready for action, while Bridgette extended the baton she'd carried along with the flare. Lucy counted three, before Bridgette pulled the cord and lobbed the flare into the room and pulled the door shut.

As predicted, the door and the walls splintered with the repeated hits of automatic weapons fire. But, more important to Bridgette was the choking sounds that were coming from the office.

"We've got to get out of here," Sam said. "Let's go, and watch where the hell you're going. They got in here somehow, and we don't know where they are."

Terry coughed out a response just before the door opened.

Noxious purple smoke billowed out into the hall above where Bridgette and Lucy lay prone on either side of the door.

As the first pair of legs came out, Bridgette swung the baton and was pleased with the satisfying crack of bone and then Terrance Martin was lying on the ground next to her.

His eyes bulged when he recognized her, went to scream a warning to Sam, but didn't make it before Bridgette's baton broke his nose, and knocked him out.

"Terry, what the—whoa" she managed as she tripped over the now still form of Terry. The Uzi went skittering out of her hand when she hit the floor.

Lucy pounced on her back, ramming her knee into the base of Sam's spine and wrestling the flailing woman's hands into cuffs.

With both assailants secured, she glanced over at Bridgette, smiled and shook her head.

Bridgette sat in the E.R. waiting room with Lucy on one side and a state trooper on the other. They'd been extremely nice after she'd helped Lucy bring Martin and Wilson down. The troopers had agreed to let her come to the hospital to see Dom while they waited for word from the judge on how to proceed with her.

She tried not to worry about what was going to happen to her life after tonight. Right now all that mattered was Dom. He'd suffered smoke inhalation and some burns and had shattered his wrist, but nothing seemed life threatening.

It was good to know that Deke and Dan were going to pull through okay as well, Bridgette thought. Brian had been running between floors, checking on the prisoners. Sam Wilson had already been transported to lockup, and Terry Martin was going to be staying at the hospital a few extra days. It seemed that she had done a better job than she had realized when she bashed him with the baton, and had broken his jaw as well as his nose and leg.

"From what Deke said, you've almost got to give Martin a little credit for the creativity. Using the mannequins wrapped in chemical heat packs attached to the top of remote controlled cars and then running a wire so that we'd hear what they were saying out of a speaker in that room? That's pretty far fetched stuff," Brian said when he pulled a seat around to sit in front of Bridgette.

"I'll give him the credit for creativity, but I draw the line there. What he did killed one agent and wounded three others. I only hope that after they put him in that concrete box, they lose the key," Bridgette said.

"That's pretty serious, coming from you," Brian said with a smile. "But, seeing how you stood up here, I think maybe I'll have to see if I can help that key go missing."

Her head jerked around when the door to the room opened, and her heart fell when she watched the director and Judge Forsyth walk in.

"Oh, boy, this isn't going to be pretty," she whispered to Lucy who simply held her hand.

"Miss Mahoney? Why don't we go over here and sit for a few minutes," Judge Forsyth said.

Bridgette took a deep breath and went to meet her fate. Taking the chair next the judge she looked at her feet. "I'm sorry, your Honor. I realize that what I did was against the regulations that you set when you granted me this release into the work program. I-I was afraid for the lives of people that I work, I meant worked, with. As well as for the man that I love." A single tear slid down her cheek.

"Miss Mahoney, why did you say that you worked with them? The director has spent the last hour and a half on the drive up all but singing your virtues." She paused, and when Bridgette looked up, she continued. "Yes, you deliberately broke the conditions of your release. But it was the right thing to do. If I understand the entire situation correctly, you risked your life to aid Agent Daniels in the apprehension of two wanted cop killers. And by testimony of Agent Daniels and others that were there, you refused to take a firearm to defend yourself. That's above and beyond the call of duty. I find your actions to be honorable and will dismiss any charges that arise from this issue. I would like to see you in court next week, however for a different matter."

Bridgette's face fell. "May I ask what I did?"

The judge surprised her and laughed loudly. "You did everything that you were asked, and you did it under the most horrendous circumstances. I've already cleared it with the attorneys and the Director. As of next Tuesday, you will be on a special probation. The director has been so impressed that he has requested that you be allowed to undergo the appropriate training, and I have approved. And once you've completed that, you will be moved into a permanent position with the Bureau with full benefits."

Bridgette couldn't contain the tears. "Thank you. Oh, thank you so much."

"You've been an inspiration to us all to do what's right."

When the judge left, Bridgette went back to sit next to Lucy.

Lucy took her hand and smiled. "That's wonderful the way things worked out, don't you think, Bridge?"

"Yeah. I can't believe it. And, if I'm right, after Tuesday, I'll be able to have an almost normal life. I'll be able—"

"Is there a Bridgette Mahoney here?" a nurse asked.

When Bridgette motioned, the nurse waved her over. "Please come with me, Mr. Franchini would like to see you now."

Dom's arms were both bandaged due to the burns, and his right arm was currently in a splint, but otherwise he felt physically fine. Emotionally, he was a wreck. He'd heard that Bridgette had broken her release agreement to come and help him. Bridgette who had nearly begged him not to go, had risked everything to try and save him.

When the door opened and he saw her, he broke down.

She rushed to him, "Where does it hurt? Do you want me to get the nurse?"

He only reached out and pulled her close and sobbed.

"I'm sorry," he choked out moments later. "I'm sorry for what I forced you to do."

She ran her hand over his cheek, "Dom, it's okay. Really. I talked to the Judge, and she agrees with what I did. I do have to go to court next Tuesday, but it will be okay. I promise."

"I'll be there with you. I'll stand for you, and I won't let them take you away. You're the most wonderful woman in the world, Bridgette. I can't imagine my life without you. I need you more than I can say."

She placed her finger over his lips. "It'll be okay. The hearing on Tuesday is to finalize my release from house arrest." She smiled, leaned in and kissed him.

"You, Dominic Franchini are the sweetest, most dedicated man, I've ever had the pleasure to know. And I knew, that if the table were turned tonight, you would have done everything for me. And it was with those thoughts, that I came here."

"You saved me," Dom choked. "You risked everything to save me. I'm not sure that I'm worthy enough to ask you for this, but I'm going to. Will you do me the greatest honor, and be my wife? Share my life and build a family with me?"

She laughed, leaned down to kiss him once more. "We saved each other, Dom. And you are more than worthy enough for me. So, I'd be thrilled to marry you. So, are you ready to go home?"

"I can't wait to go home with you," he said pulling her in for one more kiss.

KEEP READING FOR A PEEK AT SILVER LININGS

AUTHOR OF THE *SLEEPY HOLLOW HIGH* SERIES

CHRISTINE CHIANTI

SILVER LININGS

A CARSON CAPER ROMANTIC SUSPENSE

ONE

"Morning, Lieutenant," I said to my supervisor, Aaron Walker, as I walked into the squad room at Police Headquarters.

"Detective." He studied my face for a moment. "Monica, you know that you've got to start taking better care of yourself. It doesn't look like you slept much again."

I sighed. "I know, Lieutenant. I've been trying to get things back under control, but the situation last night just brought everything to the forefront. Again."

"It's been almost a year since Bill was killed. You need to let him go."

"I know. I'm seeing the department counselor, but when I'm on the scene where an officer has been shot, I just can't control the memory."

He placed a hand on my shoulder gingerly and gave it a soft squeeze. "Try."

I turned and looked at the room. Fourteen desks covered the shared space. Most of the occupants had brought in small knickknacks to personalize their space. Only two desks sat void of personal clutter.

I'd cleared Bill's desk out the week after a hyped-up crack addict had gunned him down.

His death had hit me harder than anything I'd known to date. He'd been my mentor, my trainer and my friend. I'd been invited to share holidays with him and his wife, Judy, more times than I could remember. All of that was stripped away by some twenty-three year old punk who'd been too concerned about where his next hit was coming from.

I dropped my purse on the second clear desk and settled into my corner to attack the paperwork I so hated.

"Dietz!" I heard a voice yell an hour later, and turned to see Commander Willoby standing in the middle of the room.

Eric Willoby was a good boss. He'd been on the force for nearly thirty years, and the gray was starting to show in his thick black hair. He had broad shoulders and at six-eight, was commanding even when standing still. His skin was a pale white, but his eyes of piercing blue, screamed cop.

"Yes, Sir," I said timidly, wondering what I had done that would bring him down to find me.

He motioned me to follow him as he led me toward someone standing by the door. A woman of about twenty-five, dressed in a sweater and skirt and hands folded, stood there. A large leather purse was slung over her right shoulder.

"Detective, I'd like you to meet the department's newest detective, Jackie Gannon." He motioned to the woman standing there, "Detective Gannon, this is Detective Monica Dietz, your new partner. My head snapped to glare at him, "My what?" I managed to splutter out.

His eyes twinkled as the edges of his mouth curved up into something between a smile and a grin. "I knew you'd be excited.

Detective Gannon was just promoted and transferred to this division, and since you need a partner, the two of you will be working together. Good day, ladies," he said as he strolled down the hall whistling a tune that sounded familiar, but I couldn't place it.

"Guess he caught you by surprise, huh?" my new partner remarked.

When my eyes focused on the woman I looked intently at her. My first reaction was that she was exactly my polar opposite. She was about six inches shorter than my height of five-ten. She had the body of a model, and a face that was sure to cause speech impediments. When this was combined with her pin straight hair, and with the way she filled out the sweater combo, I would guess she was going to be spending quite a bit of time fending the single men in our squad off. I would have given up right there, but I saw something else.

I recognized the look in her eyes. I had seen it in my bathroom mirror for the past eight years.

I huffed out a breath, "Yeah, he did. I should have expected it, but he got the drop on me with the idea of a partner. Welcome aboard, Gannon." I held out my hand.

She smiled, shook my hand, "Please, call me Jackie."

"Well, come on in and meet the rest of the team," I said as I led her back into the room.

"Who we got here, Dietz?" Matt Jenkins called out.

"The loud mouth over there with the broad shoulders and crew cut is Matt Jenkins. He's mostly harmless, and he keeps assuring everyone that he's had all his shots. When push comes to shove, he's a great one to have in your corner. Next to him is his partner, Ted Anderson. They spend most of their day working with the schools and juvenile.

"Over here," I said pointing to the other side of the room, "we have Sylvia Crowne and her partner, Bill Kenner. They tend to do quite a bit with the narcotics teams. Across the side of the room, we've got Mark Sibly, Nate Martin, Adam Westly, Todd Cunnigham, Dave Lerch, Ken Fricano and Kerri Marsbury. Keri is usually partnered up with the Lieutenant. The others tend to pair up in odd ways, but they stick to most of the everyday stuff."

"And you handle what?" Gannon asked.

"I keep seeing dead people," I deadpanned. "Actually, I'm more of a troubleshooter. I've got a knack for dealing with the minutia that tends to be overlooked. Because of that, I get the cases that require it, high profile cases like homicide and kidnapping. Thankfully, we don't usually have too many of those here in Blackberry Creek. We'll jump in and do whatever needs to be done, but if we end up with one of those cases, most likely, the captain will pull us off whatever we were working on to take the high profile one."

I led her back to our little corner, "This will be your's" the words caught in my throat.

Jackie looked at me, and I could see the sympathy in her eyes. "The Commander told me that your last partner was killed in the line. I'm very sorry."

I nodded, "I keep thinking that I'm past it, but every once in a while it comes up and sucker punches you. The case that I was working for the last four days blew up last night. It ended with the suspects having a shoot out with police. Both perps were killed, but more worrisome are the three officers they shot and the two civilians who were run over when the perps tried to flee the scene of their latest robbery." I didn't have to tell her that it brought everything that had happened with Bill back to the surface again."

"What are we working on now?" she asked.

I slid the paper work over to her, took my own seat, and proceeded to fill her in.

It was getting close to lunchtime, and the paperwork was completed. "Thanks for the help, Jackie," I said as I stood to stretch. "I'll drop this on the Lieutenant's desk, then we can¾" the phone on my desk cut me off.

"Dietz," I answered.

"You and your partner are to report to my office immediately. We've got a heck of a case to break your new partner in on."

"We're on the way, Sir," I said as I hung up the phone. "Let's go, Jackie. Time to go see the boss." I checked to ensure that my badge was on my waistband and my weapon was still in the holster on my hip, and then tossed a light jacket over my shoulders. I headed over to the Lieutenant's desk to drop off the paperwork and turned and waited for my partner.

"Do I take it we're going on one of those high profile cases?" she asked with trepidation.

"If I was a gambler, I'd say that the odds are pretty good, but until we know, we don't worry about it."

We walked to the captain's office in relative silence, the only noise being the constant clack of Jackie's high heels. I wondered how she would fare if we had to chase anyone down today. All I could do was hope that we wouldn't need to test that theory.

I knocked on Commander Willoby's door, and was greeted with a terse "Come".

"You sent for us, Commander?"

He looked up from his desk, motioned to the two seats across from his desk. "We've got a bit of situation. Looks like a robbery gone bad. About fifteen minutes ago, Cathy's Collectibles was attacked. That's the best word that I can use to describe it.

"The shop owner from across the street called it in and reported that it sounded like a war zone. The nine-one-one dispatcher said she could hear what sounded like automatic weapon fire. Uniforms arrived at the scene within three minutes. They found the carnage. At the present, we've got one confirmed dead, one in the hospital and one who is still unaccounted for."

"Sir, what exactly is Cathy's Collectibles? And who is the missing person?" Jackie asked timidly.

She was going to have to toughen up, but helping her through that process was going to be my job.

The Commander looked at her briefly before he continued. "From what I've been told, the store was a high end antique and specialty shop. People paid big bucks for the merchandise. As for who the missing person is, we don't have an identification."

"How do you know that they're missing then?" Jackie asked.

The Captain looked at her for a moment. "The eyewitness, a neighbor from across the street, said she saw a woman whom she thought to be the owner go in to open the store this morning. The car that was pointed out as the owner's is still there, but there is no sign of her. Three men were seen to have gone in. There are conflicting reports about what they had when they came out. Reports say that two men carried a large bag together while the third man continued to fire into the building. The responding officers have the information on the vehicle."

"Thanks, Captain," I said. "We've got it from here. Let's roll, Gannon."

"One more thing, Detective. Keep me in the loop on this. I want reports daily."

I turned back to him, "Yes, Sir."

Cathy's Collectibles sat in the middle of a block of small shops on Main Street. The plate glass windows were now scattered with the debris from the gunfire. I pulled the departmental Dodge Challenger over behind a black-and-white that had its lights going.

"What did they teach you about investigations, Jackie?" I asked as I pulled the crime scene kit out of the trunk.

"Well up until the promotion became official three hours ago, I'd been a uniformed officer. Basically I just secured the scene."

We started walking toward shop, "Okay, lesson one. Listen to the evidence." She turned her head to look at me, and I could see the question she wanted to ask. "I know it can't say a verbal word, but it is your best resource. As long as the scene has been properly secured, the evidence will tell you the story. It won't lie or change its story. It is the one thing that we can depend on.

"Lesson two, we look at the whole thing first. Document where everything is, get as many photos as we can and identify everything that we can. This is all done before we go and talk to any of the witnesses. Questions?"

"I don't think so, Monica. I'm just really, um, you know, nervous right now."

I stopped a few feet short of the doorway. "Are you afraid that you wont be able to hold through this?" I asked sternly.

"No, it's not that. I've seen dead bodies before. It's just that I'm starting to understand how important what we're about to do is, and I'm worried about making a mistake."

"Buck up, Jackie. We all make mistakes. It's how we learn. The trick is to work together so that we can back each other up. Keep each other from making those mistakes. We'll talk about every step that we're going to take and we'll do it together."

She smiled, "Okay. Thanks."

"All right then, let's do this."

We ducked under the crime scene tape, and I flashed my badge at the officer who started over. "Detective Dietz," I said and he waved us on. "Good grief," I muttered as I rounded the edge of the doorway.

Every window in the building appeared to have been blown out and glass sparkled in the sun covering the hardwood floor. What I guessed to be the main counter was only defined by the steel framing, it's glass sides and top decimated. The wall nearest the entry way looked like a colander. "There has to be at least fifty bullet holes in this little area alone," I stated.

"What were they after with that kind of fire power?" Jackie asked.

"I don't know. But obviously there was something here that was of major importance to somebody and they weren't worried about people noticing that they were here."

I leaned in and traced one of the bullet holes with my finger. "Doesn't look too big."

"That'd be a good thing, right?" Jackie asked.

"Depends on what else we find. Either way, it should help us narrow down what kind of weapon or weapons were used here."

As we came around the main counter, I noticed that there was a small room off to the right. I could see three officers standing just inside the door. "What've we got?" I asked as I approached the door.

One of the officers turned and when he saw me, his eyes lit up. "Dietz, how you doing?"

"That you Lockhorn?" I asked with a grin of my own. "They letting you out to play a little now?"

"I'm not a rookie any more, Monica. In fact, I'm sitting for my sergeant's exam in a bit over a week."

"Good luck, Mike." I waved Jackie over. "Jackie, this is Officer Mike Lockhorn. I had the dubious pleasure of training him when he was a rookie. That was just before I upgraded to detective. Mike, this is Jackie Gannon. My new partner."

They shook hands briefly, and then Mike's smile faded. "It's bad, real bad, Monica. Coroner is coming for the guy over in the corner. Room's been disturbed by rescue personnel as they were working to save the other vic. Don't know what they were looking for, but, man, they blasted everything."

"Well, let's take a look. Did you get an ID on the deceased?"

"I fished out his wallet," Mike said as he pointed to a clear plastic evidence bag that was set on the floor a few feet from the body. "Contained a Massachusetts Drivers license in the name of Toby Williams, age fifty-two. He shows an address over on Weston Woods. Not sure if he was an employee of the shop or a customer."

Jackie peered over at the body again, "Whichever, he was in the wrong place today."

"Mike, what else do we have on the other two victims?"

"EMS took one, a young guy probably in his twenties, maybe early thirties, to the hospital. Nobody's said anything to us. I know that an officer was going in to stand guard. As far as the woman who is missing? Best guess there is that that is the proprietor, Catherine Evans, age is listed on DMV records as thirty-five. She actually lived upstairs."

"Okay. Thanks, Mike." I turned my attention to the body on the floor. "What can you tell me, Toby?" I whispered as I made my way towards the body.

I stepped over the broken pottery that lay on the floor and knelt by the body. Pulling out the small digital recorder that I habitually carried, I flicked it on. "Deceased is a male, mixed-raced identified as Toby Williams. The body is lying with the head pointing north-east and on the left side. Visual inspection shows seven bullet entrance wounds on the back, three exit wounds on the chest." I paused the recorder, "What were you trying to protect that got you shot in the back, Toby?"

"Monica?" Jackie asked softly. "How do you know that the wounds on the back are entrance wounds as opposed to exit wounds?"

"Look at the sizes. See how these on the back are relatively small and circular? This indicates that the projectile was spinning along its axis when it went in. In the front, notice how irregular the holes are shaped? That tells us that the shot hit something inside and began to flip around."

I took a cursory glance around the room. "Did anybody find a safe or an alarm button back here?" I asked the officers who were still standing guard.

Mike looked over, "Honestly, I never even looked, Monica. Do you want us to do a quick search?"

I thought about this for a brief second. "Yeah. Be careful of the evidence, but do a quick sweep. Williams took it in the back for a reason, and we need to know what that reason was."

By the time we left the shop, it was after six, and we still hadn't figured out what the perpetrators were after. "So much for lunch", I said to Jackie. I noticed that she was starting to limp a bit. "You okay there, Gannon?"

She grimaced at me, "I didn't exactly think that they were going to be throwing me out into the field right away. I thought that I'd get a day playing desk-jockey before this happened. I ended up wearing the wrong shoes."

I chuckled. "You've just figured out lesson three there, Jackie. Dress comfortably, because there is no telling what's going to happen."

"I'll be ready tomorrow," she said as we climbed back into the car. "What happens next, anyway?"

I pulled out into traffic, and aimed the car towards the police station. "Well, the FBI is treating this as a kidnapping. We're playing nice with them, and they're going to let us work the homicide end of things, so we'll start by meeting with the witnesses, and going over their statements. From there, we'll check on the progress of the Medical Examiner, and see what he can tell us. At some point, we're going to need to run by the lab and get briefed on what we've found. Somewhere in this mess is the answer to what happened here."

As I watched her drive away, I turned my own car towards home, dinner and Sam, and thought about what I had told Jackie. Somewhere in this mess was the answer. But where?

ABOUT CHRISTINE CHIANTI...

Christine Chianti is the pen name used by a multipublished author when writing fiction. As Christine Chianti, she is the author of more than twenty titles ranging from short stories to novels. Currently she is splitting her time writing between the Carson Caper series and the Organized Crime Taskforce series.

Christine is a member of Romance Writers of America and is at home in Western New York.

For more on Christine please visit her at www.christinechianti.com and sign up for her Member's Only section for behind the scenes details of her works in progress.

To find out more about her available work, please visit the publisher at www.goldenlarkpublishing.com

CONNECTING WITH CHRISTINE CHIANTI....

www.christinechianti.com
www.twitter.com/cchianti
www.facebook.com/christinechianti

Join Christine's Members Only Group now and get a free digital copy of one of her selected books! For more details, go to: www.christinechianti.com.